FALL of RADIANCE

RANGER'S OATH

ALSO IN SERIES

FALL OF RADIANCE

RANGER'S OATH

BLAKE ARTHUR PEEL

RANGER'S OATH
Published by Vault
In association with Aethon Books

Copyright © 2026 Blake Arthur Peel

ISBN 978-1-63849-323-5 (hardcover)

First AETHON: Vault Edition: Spring 2026

Printed in the United States of America.
1st Printing.

Aethon Books
www.aethonbooks.com

Vault Storyworks
www.vaultstoryworks.com

Cover art, book design, and title type design by Adam Cahoon.
Print formatting by Kevin G. Summers, Adam Cahoon, and Rikki Midnight.

AETHON: Vault books are published by Vault Storyworks LLC in association with Aethon Books LLC. "Aethon", the Aethon Logo, "Vault", the Vault logo, and the "AETHON: Vault" logos are copyright and trademark Aethon Books, LLC and Vault Storyworks LLC.

*"For Kimberly, thanks for supporting my dreams,
no matter how far-fetched."*

FALL OF RADIANCE

RANGER'S OATH

TARSYNIUM

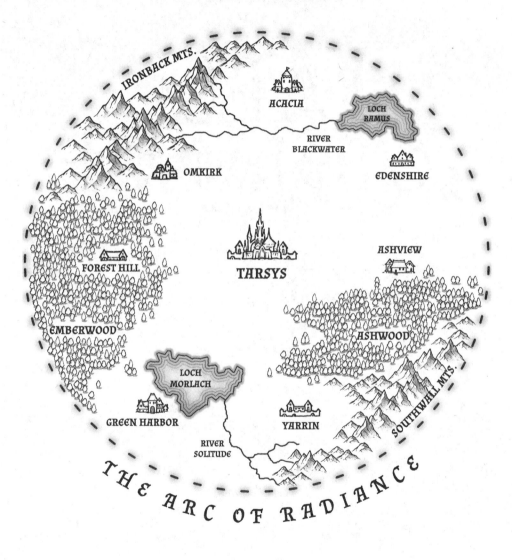

CHAPTER 1
OWYN

The curved yew creaks as I pull on my bowstring. The feathers of the arrow brush my cheek as I stare down the shaft at my prey.

A stag, standing twenty paces away in a clearing, dips its antlered head into the grass and begins severing stalks with its teeth. For a moment, I marvel at its muscled frame, the way it remains alert even while grazing in the forest.

And yet, I think, watching the deer with one eye closed, *it is not even aware that it's about to die.*

I exhale softly and let the arrow loose, the bowstring launching it forward with a snap. At the last second, the stag takes a step forward, and the arrow embeds itself deep into the animal's flank. It jerks with the force of the impact and immediately bolts, running away with the reckless gait of a wounded animal.

"You missed the heart," Elias murmurs from his spot in the bushes next to me. The observation, delivered so candidly, makes my own heart sink.

"It moved," I mutter in reply, knowing it's a lame excuse for a ranger's apprentice. I lower the bow and turn to look at my master. "What do we do now?"

Elias frowns as if the answer is obvious. "We follow it."

He stands up from the ferns and shoulders his bow. His gray-green mottled cloak allows his broad frame to blend in perfectly with the foliage around him.

I shoulder my own bow and follow Elias out of our hiding place, trying hard to mimic his every movement. My master has been a woodsman since before I was even born, and his skills are the stuff of legend. As his apprentice, I strive to learn everything I can from him.

We make our way to the spot where I shot the stag, and sure enough, we find a trail of blood leading us deeper into the forest. Wordlessly, we backtrack to our horses and begin our pursuit through the shady trees of the Emberwood.

I can't believe I missed, I think glumly to myself as I gaze at the quiet woods around me.

The golden light of the sun filters through the branches above and casts everything in a warm, emerald glow. My eyes find it difficult to follow the blood trail; however, Elias knows the woods the way a hawk knows the sky. For him, tracking game is as natural as breathing.

Moving at a steady pace, we weave our way around trees and wade effortlessly through the light undergrowth. As we ride, I hold the reins of our pack mule, the placid beast plodding easily beside me.

Before long, Elias guides us to the stag. We find it in an open clearing, quivering in a growing pool of blood.

I dismount, eyeing the stag uneasily as we approach. Despite my training, I cannot help but feel sorry for the animal. It makes no move to flee from our presence as we draw near. Its hind legs have given out, and it lifts its head pitifully to regard us, mewling in pain.

It knows that it is dying.

Elias reaches to his belt and pulls out his knife, a long-bladed, slightly curved weapon, which he hands to me. "Here," he says gruffly. "It's time to put it out of its misery. A clean cut across the jugular should do the trick."

I take the knife in my numb fingers and stare at it. The cold steel glints imperiously in the sunlight. "You want me to kill it with this?"

Elias nods grimly. "You failed to kill it with your arrow. Now you must finish the job with the blade." He walks over to the stag and crouches, pointing to a spot on its neck. "Start here and guide the knife down. This will sever the main artery and kill it quickly. A good, clean death."

He moves out of the way as I approach, watching me with an appraising eye. I barely register his gaze. My eyes are focused on the stag lying in front of me, noticing the way it strains to keep its head up, its breaths coming in labored, huffing gasps.

I've trapped animals before, even shot them with my bow, but I've never had to kill them with the blade. It seems barbaric, something a butcher would do, not a ranger.

Kneeling down, I quickly locate the spot Elias indicated. The knife feels as heavy as an anvil in my hand. Raising the unforgiving steel to its neck, my eyes flicker down and meet the stag's. They are deep pools of black fear. The animal knows what I am about to do. My stomach twists as the knife quivers in my hand.

I suddenly feel very ill.

"I don't think I can do this, master," I say shakily as I sit back, feeling a profound sense of shame at my admission. "I'm sorry."

"You must," Elias says, cool and unmoving. "It is part of being a ranger. There will be times you will find an animal in the wilderness that needs to be put down. Better to kill it quickly rather than allow it to suffer. It would be a crime to let it go on living like this."

I take a breath and look back at the stag. This time, I am careful to avoid looking into its eyes. Leaning forward, I place my hand under its neck and grab a fistful of skin. I raise the knife. Squeezing my eyes shut, I plunge the blade deep into the stag's flesh and begin to cut downwards, gritting my teeth in disgust.

The hide is much tougher than I anticipated, and I can feel the knife catching on rubbery tendons as I saw through it. Its body goes rigid, and I feel it start to shudder, warm, wet blood spilling over my hands.

After one final spasm, it lies perfectly still.

Grunting, I open my eyes and stand up on wobbly legs, looking from the stag's lifeless body to my own bloodstained hands. They appear garishly red in the afternoon sun.

"Take this," Elias says, handing me a clean rag. "For the blood."

I do my best to wipe off my hands and clean the knife before giving it back to my master. The rag removes most of the blood, but my fingernails and the cracks in my skin are still stained a deep red.

Elias takes the knife back but does not return it to his belt. "You did well today, Owyn," he says, putting a hand on my shoulder. "It is one thing to shoot an arrow from a distance, but something else entirely to take a life when you are close enough to look it in the eyes. Remember this feeling. Killing only gets easier the more you do it."

I nod but do not reply. I still feel a little queasy.

Squatting down, Elias wastes no time in opening the stag's belly and pulling out its entrails, placing them in a neat pile in the dirt. The squelching sound makes my skin crawl, but I force myself to watch him finish the task. I never know when I may be expected to do this myself.

When it is all done, Elias calls me over. "Help me get the carcass up on the mule," he says, stepping around the corpse and grabbing it by its hind legs. "It's time we start heading back to town."

Together, we hoist the dead animal up onto the placid gray mule and strap it down with leather ties so it remains secure during the ride back. Despite my disgust, I am surprised at how light the body is without any of its guts. And yet, a slight pang of guilt still grips me as I see its proud head lolling like a rag doll.

Once we finish, we mount our horses and begin riding due east for Forest Hill, a journey that will likely take us a full day to complete. This will mean spending one more night beneath the trees of the Emberwood.

As we ride, my eyes keep catching glimpses of the stag bouncing limply at my side. I avert my gaze and look out at the forest around me.

The Emberwood is the largest forest in Tarsynium, growing along the western border of the Arc of Radiance. It is known for its beauty and diverse plant and animal life. For the last few months, it has been my refuge, my home.

When I started this apprenticeship with Elias, I knew nothing of forestry. I was just an orphan who needed a purpose in life, searching for a place to belong. Now, under his constant instruction on the harsh realities of nature, I am learning everything involved in tracking, hunting, and wilderness survival. Today was my first time butchering an animal up close. My stomach churns at the thought as I am reminded of the dried blood caked beneath my fingernails.

But most important of all, I think to myself, reassuringly, *I am training to be a fighter.* Aside from being expert woodsmen, rangers are skilled warriors. They are the protectors of the kingdom's borders and have been for a thousand years.

Or so the legends say.

As we continue our ride, I lose myself in my memories, idly watching the oak and ash trees as they pass by. I think of when I took the ranger's oath and everything in my life that has brought me to this point. My thoughts carry me back to my childhood in Edenshire, and the idyllic summers I had spent there, playing with the other children and pretending that we were gallant knights.

Consequently, those thoughts eventually bring me back to my mother's death, so I quickly shift my mind to other things. It pains me to think of her, but I have found that the longer I've lived here in the Emberwood, the more I feel a kinship with the rangers. They are my family, now. And the wilderness is where I belong.

I continue to study the forested land surrounding me. Every so often, I catch a glimpse to my left of the Ironback Mountains rising up in the distance. At the base of the mountains, the lowland trees give way to the mighty pines of the north, the landscape becoming more rugged and varied. I have never been to the mountains, but I have heard that they are as dangerous as they are beautiful, replete with savage beasts and rebel fighters.

I am shaken from these thoughts as Elias abruptly pulls his horse to a stop, raising his fist as a signal for me to do the same. I pull on the reins, bringing my horse to a halt and the mule as well.

"What's going on?" I ask.

Elias does not reply. He merely dismounts and walks into a clearing that lies just ahead.

Frowning, I hop out of my saddle and jog to his side. *Why have we stopped?* I wonder silently. *We can't actually be making camp now. Usually, Elias wants to get as much riding out of the way as possible before the sun goes down.*

I open my mouth to voice my question, but the words die on my tongue when I see what has caught Elias' attention.

The clearing in front of us is littered with lifeless bodies.

I realize, in half-relief and half-horror, that the bloody limbs strewn about are not human but animals. Though it is only a herd of deer, it is still a grisly sight to behold. The clearing, probably no more than twenty paces across, is akin to the floor of a slaughterhouse. A dozen or so carcasses lie scattered about, but it is hard to tell since most of them have been shredded to pieces, gore staining the grass everywhere.

Judging by the smell, they have been out in the sun for more than a few days.

"What happened here?" I ask, my voice barely above a whisper.

"I'm not sure," Elias replies, sounding genuinely disturbed. For the first time since I've known him, he looks shaken. He continues to study the scene in front of us, unease painted plainly on his weathered face. "A predator of some kind would be my guess," he says after a moment. "Perhaps there is a rabid wolf about."

I suppress a shiver. "I've never seen a wolf do anything like this."

We move into the clearing to get a closer look at the carnage. The smell is almost unbearable. I choose to breathe through my mouth, but even then, I can barely tolerate it. The rot in the air is so thick I can almost taste it. It takes everything in me to keep from covering my face with my sleeve to block out the stench. The urge to retch almost overwhelms me.

It appears as if an entire *army* of wolves attacked this herd of deer, only these wolves had no interest in food but simply tearing the animals apart. We walk past the stinking corpses, and I can't help but wonder if the stag I killed had been a part of this group. Maybe some of these deer were even his family.

That thought sickens me further.

"I need to mark this spot on the map," Elias says after a few minutes. "The other rangers should be informed about events like these. If there is a rabid animal roaming these woods, we'll need to be extra careful."

I watch him go back to the horses as I stay where I am to continue surveying the clearing. Once Elias is gone, however, I quickly cover my mouth and nose with the edge of my cloak.

I notice that some of the deer have long claw marks raking their skin. I crouch down to inspect a particularly ravaged body.

These gashes are far too deep to be from common wolves or cougars. And why has most of the meat been left behind to rot?

Looking around, I realize that there are also no carrion eaters feasting or even flies buzzing around my head.

Where are the buzzards? Where are the crows and the maggots?

Suddenly, I get the feeling I am being watched, an uneasy sensation that prickles my skin and makes me forget about the horrid stench of the corpses.

I turn and look around, scanning for any signs of life.

Nothing.

A branch rustles off to my left, and I spin, trying to locate the source of the disturbance. Again, I see nothing.

But a few seconds later, something emerges from the shadows.

It is a hulking creature resembling a great wolf, only it is unlike any wolf I have ever seen. The figure is as black as midnight with thick, matted fur covering its body from head to tail. Despite its size, it moves through the undergrowth with an easy grace, reminding me of a prowling mountain lion. Great scythe-like claws adorn its feet, and a whip-like tail trails behind it, dark and sinewy. Its long, toothy snout lifts up and sniffs the air, revealing a glowing red eye on the side of its monstrous head, and I feel my heart begin to thunder loudly in my chest.

I remember the stories people would whisper when I was a child, tales of monsters that could devour whole villages and fight with the strength of a hundred men. The red eyes of R'Laar are all too common in campfire tales.

Only, this is not a campfire tale.

My breath catches in my throat as I realize exactly what this creature is.

A demon.

I take a step back and wince as a twig snaps under my foot. Instantly, the demon turns its gaze on me, its eyes like two burning coals smoldering in its skull.

I immediately feel the hairs on the back of my neck rise.

Pulse pounding, I take a step behind me and nearly trip over the rotting corpse of a deer. I barely manage to catch myself before I start to run, pumping my legs as fast as I can toward Elias and the horses.

"What's wrong?" my master asks urgently, his eyes darting up from the map he is holding.

"A demon," I breathe, all pretenses of bravery gone. "Over there, in the trees." I turn and point, but when I look at the spot where the monster had been, there is nothing there.

It has completely vanished.

CHAPTER 2
ZARA

A smoldering ball of magefyre hurtles toward me.

My body reacts by instinct, diving out of the way as it whizzes past my head. I conjure a shield of radiant magic as I fall to block any residual heat that could burn me. My shield clings tightly to my body like a second skin.

I land hard, but in an instant, I am back on my feet, gripping my talisman and pulling in source energy to cast another spell. My opponent, surrounded by a radiant shield of his own, looks at me warily, both of his hands shimmering with flickering blue magefyre.

"*Fas morag ti ma'tel*," I intone, channeling the source energy into a tight sphere in my fist. My skin tingles from the power, sending a shock up my arm, but it does not burn me.

Magic cannot harm the person channeling it.

I extend my arm forward, palm facing out, and release the source energy, shooting a radiant missile of magefyre at my opponent. He raises his hands as if to block, his own magefyre dissipating as the beam punches through his shield like an arrow ripping through paper. It strikes him square in the chest and sends him tumbling backwards. He lands in a heap on the grass.

"Match!" The arbiter shouts, raising a red flag that matches the color of the band on my arm. I hear clapping from the mages surrounding us.

Somebody runs over and helps my opponent to his feet. There is a smoking hole in his tunic, but he bears no serious wounds. I had purposely used just enough source energy to punch through his shield, but not enough to permanently harm him. Such an oversight would get me expelled from the Academy.

He looks over at me with thinly veiled hatred, then winces as his companion laces an arm around his shoulder and escorts him off the practice field.

That's right, I think to myself triumphantly. *You've just been bested by a girl.*

I let out a long breath as the clapping dies down, my ears still ringing from the exertion. Channeling can take a heavy physical toll, and at the moment, I am going through the effects of using too much magic. My body feels drained and weak, and my head is beginning to throb. Though the fatigue is decidedly unpleasant, it is nothing a little food and rest won't fix.

"Well done, Initiate Dennel!" Evoker Laramie exclaims, rushing over to my side. He grins widely at me, his white beard extending down his chest to where it is tucked firmly into his belt. "You're officially ranked number one in your class!"

I give the withered old mage a lopsided smile. In truth, I presently feel more exhausted than proud. "It was nothing," I say casually as I allow the source energy to seep out of my body. The sensation causes me to shiver. "I was at least hoping for a bit of a challenge today." I let go of my talisman, a small azure crystal on a silver chain, and place it back around my neck.

Laramie chuckles. "Oh, my dear, you remind me of myself when I was your age, so full of life and light. And a healthy dose of ambition, I might add," he says with a wink. "I wonder if the duties of an initiate still suit you. Are you ready, perhaps, to move on to bigger and better things?"

My eyes widen at the elder mage's implication, and this only causes him to chuckle more.

"Of course," he says, "such matters are not for me to decide. Even though you *are* one of my brightest pupils, mages can only be raised by the Circle."

I wipe a sheen of sweat from my forehead with the cuff of my shirt sleeve. "You are too kind, Magus."

He nods as his expression becomes more serious. "I must admit, I did not come here to merely enjoy the spectacle of two apprentices bludgeoning each other with magic. I come bearing a message. Arch-Magister Elva Tyrande requests your presence at the Pillar of Radiance as soon as possible. But she gave no indication as to why."

"Arch-Magister Tyrande?" I ask, astonished. "She wants to meet with *me?*"

"Indeed," Laramie says, stroking his beard. "And knowing her reputation, I do not think it would be in your best interests to keep her waiting." He rests a wrinkled hand on my shoulder. "I had a special feeling when you first came to the Conclave. And now, it seems there are significant people who have begun to notice you. If you continue in this manner, I have no doubt that you'll soon be raised to a full mage."

This time, my smile is indisputable, despite the sudden queasy feeling in my stomach. "Thank you, Magus," I manage. "I'll go straightaway."

He nods and totters off, leaving me alone in the center of the practice field.

I look around, and for the most part, the crowd of mages has dispersed, wandering off to watch the other magical duels currently being moderated. I decide not to waste any time. The Pillar of Radiance is a good distance from the Academy, and I don't have the money to pay for a carriage.

Taking a deep breath, I start walking briskly toward the center of the city.

Why does Arch-Magister Tyrande want to meet with me? She reports directly to the High Magus herself, and I am just an apprentice! I hope my after-hours research at the library hasn't gotten me into some sort of trouble.

My thoughts are a whirlwind, and it doesn't help that I am left feeling drained from my bout on the practice field. Hopefully, the Arch-Magister will not mind my disheveled appearance.

I make my way to the marble stairs leading up to the streets, taking the steps two at a time as I try to groom myself on the go. I wipe the last of the sweat from my face and pull the loose strands of my hair back into some semblance of a ponytail. I only wish I had enough time to go back to my dormitory and change into my more formal robes. Right now, I am wearing my long-sleeved training tunic and trousers—hardly the most flattering of outfits.

It'll have to do, I think resolutely as I step out onto the street.

My eyes can't help but gaze up in wonder at the high, glistening towers of Tarsys. Like giant spikes of burnished silver, they rise up into the heavens, making the city itself look like a jagged mountain peak covered in bright snow. It could not be more different from the tiny fishing village where I had been raised. Even after living here for five years, I still marvel at its vast architecture.

Five years... has it really been that long?

It is hard to imagine that I am no longer the scared thirteen-year-old girl who came to the City of Mages seeking to study magic.

The people out on the street are as diverse as they are numerous, walking and conversing animatedly with one another and wearing clothing that ranges from neat and humble to outlandish and gaudy. The wide boulevards in this district of Tarsys are clean and well-kept; King Aethelgar will not settle for anything less in his kingdom's capital.

I take it all in with a sweeping glance. This is the beating heart of our civilization, the epicenter of Tarsynium. Living here makes me feel like I am a part of something truly magnificent.

As I pass a row of food carts, my nose is assaulted by an array of different smells. Roasted meats, candied nuts, and succulent pies fill my nostrils with their aromas and make my mouth water. I am reminded of just how famished my magical sparring has left me, but I press onward, knowing how important it is not to delay.

Fighting against my gnawing hunger, I take a turn onto the Street of Light, walking toward the ring of towers that makes up the Conclave. There, standing taller than all of the others, is the central spire, the greatest wonder man has ever built. Even now, I see it looming in front of me, a gleaming edifice that puts all other structures in the world to shame.

Like an enormous obelisk forged from ivory and gold, the Pillar of Radiance ascends from the earth and seems to touch the sky. This tower, the focal point of magical society, is the source of power fueling the Arc of Radiance which protects humanity from the blighted lands beyond Tarsynium. Day and night, it endlessly shoots radiant energy into the air, creating a magical dome encapsulating the whole of the kingdom.

I stumble on a cobblestone as I gaze upward, but fortunately, I remain upright. Flushing, I stride past a pair of armored guards who are smirking at me beneath the visors of their helmets.

Approaching the gates of the Conclave, I pull in a smidge of energy and quickly produce a flash of magefyre. This spurt of blue light acts like a sign, showing the gatekeepers that I am an initiate.

They nod and open the iron gates, allowing me to walk through without slowing my pace.

The inner courtyard at the base of the tower is beautifully manicured like the rest of the city, with blooming gardens and babbling fountains that add to the Conclave's grandeur. The front doors, colossal slabs of intricately carved wood, stand open to allow streams of mages to flow in and out, welcoming all students of the magical arts to its hallowed halls.

My bedraggled appearance draws more than a few stares from passersby, but I ignore them, holding my head high while focusing on my destination.

The atrium of the tower is a great domed chamber with a series of fluted columns rising from the white marbled floor to the high vaulted ceiling. There are hundreds of them, all painted with different symbols and colors. Each varies widely in circumference, some as wide as ten people standing shoulder to shoulder, while others are the width of only a single individual.

These ingenious mechanisms of transportation, or *lifts* as the mages often call them, give quick access to nearly every single level of the tower.

Quickly locating a wide one with golden symbols painted on the side, I make my way over to its base.

As I approach, a gentleman standing beside it looks me over with a bored expression. He holds a slate in his hands, elaborate blue mage robes covering his heavyset body. "Name?" He asks in an equally uninterested tone.

"Initiate Zara Dennel," I reply as authoritatively as I can muster. "I was told that Arch-Magister Tyrande wanted to see me." I straighten my tunic and try my best to act confident.

He glances down at his slate and nods, turning and pressing his hand against the wall of the column. Light blooms around his fingertips, and a doorway opens up in the stone directly in front of me. "Mind your feet," he says. "The Arch-Magister is on the one hundred and eleventh floor with the rest of the Circle."

"Thank you," I say primly as I step inside.

He merely blinks at me as the door slides shut, leaving me alone in the cylindrical tube. I stand there for a moment, anxiously waiting in the darkness. Promptly, shimmering blue light blossoms beneath my feet, forming a platform that fills the bottom of the chamber. My stomach drops, signaling that I have begun to ascend up into the tower. There are no windows in the lift, so it is impossible to tell how fast I am going, but it is not long before the door opens up again, depositing me on the floor of my destination.

I step out and look around, finding myself in the foyer of an immaculate office wing.

"Initiate Dennel?" I hear my name coming from a delicate, sing-song voice. Turning to my left, I see a blonde woman sitting behind a desk in between two exotic-looking potted plants.

"Yes," I confirm, stepping up to the desk.

The woman, no doubt the secretary, is stunningly gorgeous with her perfect skin and delicate nose. She stares at me with striking green eyes and a bright smile, revealing a mouth of straight, white teeth. "Arch-Magister Tyrande is expecting you," she says. Her smile falters somewhat when she notices my appearance. "Should I let her know that you have arrived?"

Light, I think to myself, suddenly very self-conscious about what I am wearing. *I really wish I would have brought a change of clothes to the training grounds.*

I brush a strand of hair out of my face and tuck it behind my ear, smiling apologetically at her. "That would be wonderful. Thank you."

She nods and stands up, then disappears down the hall, skirts swishing.

Twin radiant lamps rest inside sconces on the wall, their glass frames filled with glowing sapphires that spill blue light into the foyer. They are an extravagant display of artifice but are ultimately unnecessary as the wide windows on the far side of the room offer more than enough natural light to fill the area.

I stand beside an uncomfortable-looking decorative couch as I wait for the secretary to return, feeling terribly out of place in this impeccable environment. When she does, she smiles at me again and gestures for me to follow her. "Thank you for waiting. The Arch-Magister will see you now."

She leads me down the hall to a door and knocks twice, eliciting a terse, "Enter," from the other side. She pushes the door open for me, and I step inside.

Arch-Magister Elva Tyrande sits behind a polished wooden desk in a room as sterile as the foyer outside. From the wall-length curved glass window behind her, I can see a spectacular view of the Tarsys skyline, but I find my eyes drawn away from the cityscape and instead toward her.

The Arch-Magister is a thin woman with hawkish features and frosty blue eyes, her short dark hair perfectly coiffed in the latest fashion. Sitting with flawless posture in her high-backed chair, she looks up from a stack of papers and fixes me with an appraising stare.

"Initiate Dennel, I presume? Please, girl, come in and sit," she says, eyeing the chairs in front of her desk. "That will be all, Lana."

The secretary gives me an encouraging smile before closing the door. I nervously move forward and sit in one of the offered chairs. Involuntarily, I shiver and hope that the Arch-Magister doesn't notice. The room feels a great deal colder than the hall outside.

"It truly is an honor to meet you, Magus. I've always admired your achievements and your leadership of the Circle." I wince at how shrill and timid my voice sounds.

"Yes, yes. Thank you, child. It is nice to meet you as well." Her reply is both dismissive and curt, her expression cool and unyielding. She sets down her pen and leans back, proceeding to look me up and down the way a cat would eye a mouse. "I wanted to meet you first-hand to see if the rumors were true."

"Rumors, Magus?"

"Rumors," she repeats, pursing her lips together thoughtfully.

I try not to squirm under her gaze as she looks me over, but eventually, her lips curl up in a small smile that does not reach her eyes. "Several of the professors at the Academy have informed me that you are at top of your class, excelling in spellcraft, theory, and artifice. Is this true?"

I nod, but it still feels like I am being crushed under her commanding gaze.

"That is good. The Academy only accepts the best applicants in Tarsynium and to distinguish yourself from those as well is quite an achievement."

"Thank you, Magus."

"Call me Elva, dear. And I shall call you Zara. Is that acceptable?"

"Of course, Mag—Elva," I reply, though I try not to let my confusion show. *Is that why she invited me here, to praise me for my academic achievements?*

"You are probably wondering why I called you here," she says, as if reading my thoughts. She stands up from her desk and turns to look out the window. Against the light of the sun, her narrow frame looks like a mere shadow.

I nod, even though her back is to me. "Yes, Elva," I respond awkwardly a second later. "The thought did cross my mind."

"I have just received word from one of our field agents that there has been some sort of disturbance on the borders of the kingdom, in a region known as the Emberwood. I have been tasked by the Circle and the High Magus to take a team of mages out there in order to investigate." She turns her head and fixes me with an enquiring look. "Would you be willing to accompany me?"

My eyes quickly widen in surprise and I am unable to keep the shock from showing on my face. "*Me?* Go with *you?*"

"Yes," she replies coolly, turning back to look out over the city. "It is common for mages to choose wards to accompany them on important missions. It is seen as a way to prepare young initiates for full magehood within the Conclave. As the top candidate at the Academy, I can frankly think of no better choice to become my ward." She pauses for a moment and returns to her chair, turning her icy blue eyes back to me. "I won't lie to you—there is a chance that a considerable amount of danger will await us on this journey. The Circle only involves itself in the most critical of operations. However, I can assure you that this is a once in a lifetime opportunity to learn from some of the greatest mages in the kingdom. The knowledge you acquire with me will benefit you for the rest of your career. That being said, do you accept my offer, Initiate Dennel?"

Despite the nervous lump in my stomach, I act on impulse and immediately reply, "Yes."

Her mouth turns up in that same, knowing smile, as if she is amused by something in her own head. "Excellent," she says, picking up her pen and returning to the papers in front of her. "We are leaving tonight. Pack whatever you feel is necessary for the journey and report back to the Pillar no less than an hour before sunset. You are dismissed."

Feeling a strange mixture of fear and excitement, I nod as I exit her office and begin making the trip to my dormitory.

Light almighty, I think as I quickly walk back to the lifts. *What have I just agreed to?*

As soon as I am outside, I sprint frantically across the city, running faster than I ever have before. My heart is pounding in my chest as I reach the Academy, and several of the students give me strange looks as I race by.

I fly up the stairs to the dormitory wing, then hurry down the hall until I reach my room. Closing the door behind me, I lean against its solid wooden frame, finally taking a moment to catch my breath.

Now that I am alone, everything comes crashing down on me.

The Arch-Magister, Elva Tyrande, notorious in the Conclave for her iron will and exceptional skill with magic, just asked me *to be her ward. She wants* me *to accompany her on a secret mission, and we leave at sundown.*

By the grace of the Light, how is this even possible?

For the last five years, my studies have been everything to me. I have labored and pushed with everything I have to become the best initiate possible. It wasn't easy. I climbed to the top of my class by putting in long hours of practice and study, setting myself apart from my peers with my high marks and sheer determination. My own professors tell me that my future at the Conclave looks bright, but I *never* thought I would get the attention of the *Circle of Magisters.*

Is leaving the city worth putting my studies on hold? Am I ready to prove myself to the Circle, or will I only end up making a fool out of myself?

I blow out a breath and go to my bed, but hesitate to sit down, a new thought coming to me.

Perhaps I am looking at this all wrong, I think to myself. Any other student would be ecstatic to have the opportunity to work with a Magister, especially Arch-Magister Tyrande. This could help catapult my career at the Conclave to heights I never dreamed possible. She did say that this is a once in a lifetime opportunity.

I frown, my stomach twisting itself into knots. *Then why do I still feel so uneasy about the whole thing?*

Shaking my head to clear away the doubts, I reach for my trunk and begin packing, shoving clothes and necessities into it without a second thought. The Arch-Magister did not give me much time to prepare myself for the journey, and at this rate, I will not have a chance to say goodbye to any of my friends at the Academy.

Not that I have many friends, I think regrettably.

Striving for perfection tends to make others jealous of your success, and over the years, I have not done particularly well at balancing my studies with my social life. While the other initiates involved themselves in extracurricular activities and interacted with one another in their free time, I found myself alone more often than not, reading books and practicing spellcasting as much as I could. The extra hours substantially improved my magecraft, but it did little to aid my ability to socialize with others. The only person who will likely miss me while I am away is Evoker Laramie, but he is my professor, not my peer.

There's no point in dwelling on the past, I tell myself firmly, bundling up a pair of stockings. *The only thing that matters is my future as a mage and my service to the Conclave and Tarsynium. Though, it would be nice to become the youngest mage in Conclave history.*

I throw in a few extra robes before making my way to my nightstand, where I quickly inventory the various lotions and powders resting haphazardly on its surface. When I glance at my reflection in the mirror, I stop short, taking stock of how I look.

My brown eyes look weary, gazing back at me from darkened circles due to lack of sleep. I rarely wear any makeup, and today is no exception. My pale skin is as plain as milk, and my lips are drawn in a thin line beneath my nose. To top it all off, my straight brown hair is pulled back into a sloppy ponytail, loose strands poking out every which way and framing my face like an unfinished painting.

No wonder my appearance had given the Arch-Magister's secretary pause—I look absolutely *dreadful*.

Shaking my head, I look away from my reflection and begin picking up the items I deem necessary to take: a tin of tooth powder, a toothbrush, a hairbrush, and a bar of lye soap. I hesitate for a second before I decide to also bring my small pouch of makeup. I place them all into a satchel, which I deposit into my trunk with the rest of my things. Looking at the size of it, I realize that I am going to need to commission one or two of the servants to help me carry it back to the Pillar of Radiance.

Glancing out my window at the sun, I grimace. *I'll need to hurry if I am going to make it in time.*

Shedding my training tunic and trousers, I hastily splash some water on my face and do my best to wash away the sweat from my body. The water is cold but refreshing, invigorating me after the long day of training. Shivering, I pat myself dry with a towel and grab a clean pair of initiate robes hanging in my armoire. The clothing is a dull gray color, like slate or granite, with golden thread woven in at the cuffs and hem. Even though all of the initiates at the Academy wear similar robes, I still feel disdain for their drab color and appearance. Every day I dream of one day wearing the azure robes of a full mage, with silky fabric the color of magefyre. It is a symbol of a mage's station, a testament to the power and skills they possess.

As my fresh clothing settles on my skin, I begin to breathe a little easier. The weight of my responsibilities grounds me and forces me to remember my training. I close my eyes and run through a mental list of all the things I may need on my trip. *Robes, night clothes, soap, and grooming items...*

I can't help but feel like I am missing something. Then I notice my shelf stacked with copious amounts of books.

Stepping over to the far wall, I begin scanning the spines of my collection, looking for anything that may be of use to me while traveling with the Arch-Magister. There are texts on spellcraft and artifice, treatises on talisman crafting, and essays on source energy. Of course, they all look fascinating, but I know that I cannot take every single one with me.

I carefully pull out a tome titled *Radiant Magic in Combat* and another one simply called *Radiant Shields*. There is no telling what sort of things I may encounter on this journey, and the Arch-Magister herself informed me that there could be danger.

After a few more seconds of searching, I turn my head and notice the book lying open on my desk.

Setting the other two in my trunk, I walk over to it and curiously lean forward to inspect its pages. The yellowed parchment is covered with archaic script and faded illustrations of fierce-looking monsters. It is an antiquated volume, one I had checked out from the library at the Academy.

Well, I think, smiling ruefully as I mentally correct myself. *I didn't exactly check it out.*

The section of the library I had found this particular book is off-limits to initiates. I had rather clumsily batted my eyelashes at a doltish steward to convince him to borrow it for me and was more than a little surprised when my ploy actually worked.

The tome is an ancient account of demonology, one of the oldest in the kingdom. I have always been interested in the study of demons, though I am not quite sure why the subject strikes my fancy. Perhaps it is the mystery that piques my interest, or maybe it is the fact that none of my professors can answer my seemingly endless questions about ancient creatures. Demonology is widely regarded by the Conclave as a pseudoscience, a relic of a time long gone. Mages have always been discouraged from dedicating themselves to their study, though in truth, I never understood why.

Beyond the magical walls of the Arc of Radiance lives a race of beings who ravaged our ancient homeland, and who, by all accounts, came from another plane of existence entirely. They are an enigma, completely alien to anything I have ever known, which is probably why I have taken to researching them in my spare time, attempting to unravel the secrets that the years have long since eroded away.

Picking up the book, I mark my place before carefully closing its leather cover. Wherever we are going, I am likely going to need something enjoyable to read while we are traveling.

Nobody from the library is going to miss it while I am gone, right?

I gently slide it in between some clothes before closing the trunk. Looking back out the window, I remember that sundown is fast approaching.

Steeling myself, I step out of my bedroom to grab a quick supper before leaving the Academy for good. There is no telling when I will return.

CHAPTER 3
OWYN

Elias raises a skeptical eyebrow as he looks at my terrified face. "You saw a *demon?*" He sets his map aside and places a hand on his belt knife, squinting at the spot I had indicated. "I don't see anything."

Again, I scan the tree line, but the shadowy monstrosity is still nowhere to be seen. "It was just over there," I insist, "looking at me from the trees. It had glowing red eyes, just like in the stories, and it was *gigantic*—bigger than any beast I've ever seen!"

Without another word, my master unslings his bow and nocks an arrow. He walks across the clearing and begins inspecting the trees on the other side. The man reminds me of a bloodhound, a master tracker in his element. As I stand there watching him anxiously, I cannot help but envy his ability to remain calm as he scrutinizes every detail of his surroundings.

To my dismay, Elias eventually looks back at me and shakes his head.

"There are no footprints and no tracks anywhere to be found," he says, relaxing now that the supposed threat is gone. "A beast of that size would have left broken branches and crushed plants in its wake. I see no evidence that anything was here."

My heart sinks. I feel like a complete fool. "There was something there," I mumble lamely, looking away to avoid his stern gaze.

After a moment, Elias clears his throat. "I do not doubt that you think you saw something," he says, gesturing at the rotting carcasses around us. "Sometimes our eyes can betray us; especially, when we find things like this. Perhaps it was a trick of the light playing on the shadows of the trees."

"Perhaps," I reply, trying hard not to sound disappointed.

Elias gives the tree line one final look before shouldering his bow once again. "The Arc prevents demons from entering the kingdom. It has for a thousand years. Nobody in living memory has seen one. If you did see something, my guess would be that it was the predator that attacked these deer. There could be a chance that it is still lurking about."

I nod, but in my mind's eye I can still see those ruby eyes staring at me from the darkness. They had given me the distinct impression that the creature hated me, that it wanted to do me harm.

Shaking my head, I suggest moving on to hide my embarrassment. "Let's get back to the horses," I say, feigning nonchalance. "We can still ride for the few hours of daylight that are left."

Elias eyes me for a moment before nodding in agreement.

Together, we pick our way through the field of bodies and quickly mount our horses, riding away from the clearing and back toward Forest Hill.

We ride for the rest of the day without incident, traveling through the rough terrain on our way to the largest settlement in the Emberwood. As the hours grow late, the sun casts long shadows through the trees, and I have a difficult time thinking about anything else besides the dead deer and the creature I could almost bet had been silently watching me.

It must have been a demon, right? The stories all speak of their glowing red eyes.

But Elias is right. The mages had created the Arc a thousand years ago when the R'Laar threatened to consume them all. No demons have been able to threaten Tarsynium since that time. Yet, I find it strange that I saw a red-eyed monster at the same time we stumbled upon the herd of slaughtered deer. *Could it really have just been my imagination?*

The sun eventually sinks below the horizon, and Elias has us tether our horses beside a small, babbling stream. Even for rangers, it is dangerous to be riding at night. We begin setting up camp as we have done countless times before, gathering wood, lighting a fire, and clearing a space for our bedrolls. They are menial tasks, but I find comfort in them as I lose myself in the work.

Once we complete our chores, we eat our supper in silence. I tear off a bite of crusty bread and wash it down with the tea brewed over our fire.

Elias remains alert while we rest, his longbow and belt knife never far from his reach.

Finally, after I finish my food, I find the courage to break the silence. "Elias, why were the rangers founded?"

He frowns into his cup of tea. "You remember the ranger's oath," he replies softly. " *'Our solemn duty is to protect the borders of the realms of men from those enemies who would seek our destruction.'*" He quotes the line perfectly.

"Yes, but what enemies are we defending against?"

Elias looks up and gives me a flat look. "This is about the incident in the clearing today, isn't it?"

I nod.

Sighing, he sets down his cup and leans forward, stoking the coals with a stick. "We are the *'watchers in the woods,'* Owyn. We watch for beasts, bandits, and anything else that could threaten the peace of Tarsynium. Our job is to eliminate the enemies of the crown."

I take another sip of my tea. "Are demons included in that list?"

Elias grunts. "Yes, I suppose they are."

I try to choose my next words carefully. "What I saw out there... it was unlike any animal I have ever seen before. It was real, master. I swear it was. The shadows gathered thickly around it, and those eyes... they glowed red with a light of their own."

Elias does not reply immediately, and I start to feel uncomfortable in the silence that ensues.

"It is true," he says finally with his typical gruffness. "Our order was originally created to watch for demons. After the Doom, our sole purpose was to ensure that the Arc of Radiance kept the last of our people safe. But that was a long time ago. Most in the kingdom don't even believe they exist anymore. Hells, aside from the red eyes, we've forgotten what the demons even look like."

"We have the stories," I counter, but I know that it is a lame response.

"Yes, but that's exactly my point," Elias insists. "We only have stories to go by. Owyn, the Arc is a shield of pure magic surrounding the kingdom. It has stood for a thousand years, and not once has anything made it through. In my many years as a ranger, I must have walked the edge of that shield five hundred times. You know what I saw on the other side? Nothing. Just desert and wasteland as far as the eye could see. I have never seen a living creature beyond the Arc, demon or otherwise."

I look down and begin staring into the flames, crestfallen.

"I understand that what you saw may seem real to you, lad," he says, his voice softening somewhat. "Light knows, I've seen my share of mysteries since I became a ranger. But the demons left our world alone long ago when they realized they couldn't destroy Tarsynium. I suggest you try and forget about it and focus on what's real, like finding the animal that killed those deer."

I nod again, but my eyes are still on the fire. I watch as the flames lick the charred wood, popping and crackling and throwing sparks in the air.

Eventually, we decide to retire to bed. I volunteer for the first watch, knowing that sleep is going to be hard to come by tonight.

Elias concedes and climbs into his bedroll fully clothed, his long knife laying in the dirt beside his head.

Turning my back on the fire, my eyes begin to adjust to the darkness. I stare out at the forest, letting my mind wander as time slips by. I mindlessly start fingering the blade of my hatchet as I go over the words of the ranger's oath in my head.

> *I swear by my life and my hope for salvation that I will abide by the oath of the rangers until my dying breath.*
>
> *Our solemn duty is to protect the borders of the realms of men from those enemies who would seek our destruction. The wilderness shall be our homestead, the sun and stars our only hearth. We will sacrifice everything, even our very lives, for the defense of the kingdom, unto the death of those who would do us harm.*
>
> *We are the watchers in the woods, the arrows in the darkness.*
>
> *None shall pass by while we stand guard.*

Every young man and woman who joins the rangers must take the oath before they are given their bow and cloak. For me, that was one year ago, after I had come to the Grand Lodge and trained following the death of my mother.

I used to dream of walking in my father's footsteps, though I barely knew him. He died when I was only three, but my mother had told me that he was one of the greatest rangers of his generation. The hatchet I now carry with me had been his weapon of choice, and it was the only heirloom I took with me when I left my village of Edenshire. It is a simple weapon of polished oak and quality steel. Leather binds the handle, giving it a sure grip. And windblown leaves are embossed on its head, carved into the metal itself. Holding it always makes me think of him, even though my mind has long forgotten his face.

Idly, I begin to wonder what he would have done if he had seen a demon.

A branch snaps distantly in the woods, and I look up in alarm, putting a hand on the handle of my hatchet. After a few moments, I relax but pull my cloak more tightly around me.

All this thinking about demons is making me jumpy.

Time passes slowly while I stand watch. I add wood to the fire when it is needed and try to stay alert for the possibility of an attack. The minutes bleed into hours, and the hours crawl by even slower. Finally, it comes time for me to swap places with Elias.

His eyes snap open as I approach him. He immediately sits up as if he had never been asleep at all.

"Nothing to report," I say quietly, my voice raspy from hours of disuse.

"Good," he says, standing up and slipping his knife into its sheath on his belt. "Get some rest. We ride at first light."

I nod and let out a jaw-popping yawn as I make my way to my bedroll, not even bothering to shed my cloak before climbing beneath the covers.

Despite my tiredness, I have a difficult time falling asleep. Every time I close my eyelids, I find two hateful red eyes waiting for me in the darkness. It takes time, but ultimately, I drift off, slipping into a restless sleep.

Monsters with blade-like claws plague my dreams, chasing me through the forest before eventually running me down. They tear me apart like the deer in the meadow, ripping my limbs away and slicing open my flesh. Whenever I die, the nightmare starts over again, filling me with a subconscious terror that causes me to thrash and mumble.

I jolt awake when Elias shakes me, and I am jarred by the image of him outlined before me in the purple hues of the morning light.

"It's time to wake up," he says, standing and wrapping himself in his cloak. "Help me break down camp. Today, we eat breakfast in the saddle."

I groan but force myself out of my warm bedroll. My nightmares have made me more tired than I was the night before.

With numb fingers, I put away my things and saddle the horses. Elias douses the coals with his water skin, and they hiss and sizzle, sending up clouds of gray ash in the chill morning air. Before long, we are riding away from our campsite with little indication left that we had been there at all.

My eyes burn as I eat breakfast astride my mare, watching as the low light of dawn gradually brightens to the golden brilliance of day. It is considerably warmer with the sun up, and I resist the urge to shed the heavy cloak from my shoulders.

The nearer we get to Forest Hill, the thinner the forest becomes. Before long, the untamed wilderness grows more populated; farmhouses dot the land, sending up columns of white smoke from their chimneys. Our narrow game trail eventually becomes a gravel highway, and soon we begin to see other travelers on the road. All of them, from the weathered ranchers to the wide-eyed children, gaze up at us in awe, bowing their heads and greeting us with respect. For centuries, the rangers have protected their lands, and it has bred an admiration for them that is rivaled only by the mages of Tarsys.

We stop near a cluster of houses and sell the dead stag to a local butcher. He takes it gratefully into his shop with the help of his sons. Elias hands me my share of the earnings, and again we are off, riding toward the large hillock that gives Forest Hill its name.

Though not considered a city by anybody's definition, Forest Hill is a fairly large town and by far the largest settlement in the Emberwood. Families, farmers, and tradesmen of every sort live peacefully on the hill, bringing some semblance of civilization to this frontier province. We ride past them all like lions among sheep, our weapons rattling with every clopping step.

About halfway up the hill is the town's inn, a quaint, nameless building that has been our home in Forest Hill for the past few months. As we arrive at the stables, a gangly man with a sorely receding hairline stops us. I recognize him as the governor's steward.

"Hail, rangers," the man calls out, raising a hand.

Elias and I pull our horses to a stop.

"Greetings," Elias says, his gruff voice sounding less cordial than he probably intended.

Turning, the steward speaks directly to my master. "You are needed at the top of the hill."

"We are just returning from a hunt and seek rest from our travels."

"I'm afraid that your rest, though no doubt deserved, will have to wait," the steward says dryly, stepping forward and handing Elias a folded letter. "Your presence has been requested by Governor Prior. He awaits you at his manor to discuss a matter of some importance. The governor *insisted* that he did not want to be kept waiting."

Nodding at each of us in turn, he hurries off without another word.

Frowning, Elias breaks the seal and reads the letter, scanning its contents. After a few seconds he looks up at me abruptly, his frown deepening.

"There has been an attack," he says, pocketing the piece of paper. "An entire village has been destroyed."

My face reflects my shock as I hear my master saying my name as if from far away.

"Owyn!" he calls to me again sharply. "Let's go!"

Snapping out of my daze, I kick my heels into my horse's flanks and push her to a near gallop as Elias and I begin to race up the hill.

In all my time as an apprentice, I've never heard of an attack happening in the Emberwood. I try to keep pace with Elias, my thoughts a jumble. *And I've never heard of an entire village being destroyed. Such things simply do not happen.*

This has to be some kind of mistake.

Ahead, I can see Governor Prior's manor house resting at the top of Forest Hill. It is a gaudy villa that looks out over the town and the surrounding forest. I've only been there a handful of times, usually for Elias to deliver his reports to the Governor and his advisors.

Most of the Emberwood and the snow-covered Ironbacks to the north are visible as we reach the crest of the hill. On a clear day like today, I can even see the great spire of Tarsys spewing its light and magic into the sky. Under different circumstances, it is truly a wonder to behold.

Again, my thoughts turn to the events at hand. *A village is attacked at the same time we find those mutilated deer in the woods? That's too much of a coincidence for it to not be connected.*

My stomach abruptly growls, but I ignore the hunger, my growing sense of dread overpowering my need for food. Pushing away all other thoughts, I ride hard until we make it to the end of the road, pulling up in front of the manor house with a cloud of dust following in our wake.

As we rein in our horses, a stable boy runs out to greet us. We dismount and hand him our reins, including those of the pack mule, and stride up to the front door. It is a finely carved piece of oak with a singular frosted glass window.

"I know that I usually meet with the governor alone," Elias says in a low voice as we climb the steps, "but today, I want you in there beside me. Your perspective could help us figure out what is going on here, and I can't afford to leave you in the dark." He pauses just before knocking, then gives me a strangely hesitant look.

"But there'll be no mention of the... *incident*," he continues, saying the last word with special emphasis. "No need to make him worry needlessly."

I nod but inwardly cringe.

Grunting in satisfaction, Elias hammers on the door three times with his fist. I half expect there to be dents in the wood because of how forcefully he hits it.

A plump woman in an apron answers and gives us a warm smile. "Ranger Keen," she says, looking at Elias as she opens the door wide for us to enter. "Governor Prior will be with you shortly. Please wait for him in the study and make yourselves at home."

As we enter the house, I feel even more out of place than usual. The governor is quite the wealthy man, and it shows in his lavishly decorated home. The furniture is made from the finest wood and leather money can buy. All manner of decorations, including paintings, tapestries, and vases, are on display, most likely brought here from craftsmen in Tarsys. The governor's manor stands out like an ornate sore thumb amongst the rustic homes that are common in Forest Hill, giving it the distinct impression of superiority.

By contrast, Elias and I are unkempt, covered in a gritty layer of road dust, and have the foul smell of many unwashed days spent out in the wilderness.

I feel that if I were to touch anything, I'd ruin it.

The plump woman leads us to a large study and closes the door behind her, leaving us alone.

I look around, taking stock of the room around me. A roaring fireplace crackles on one end, filling the area with warmth, while a closed balcony sits on the other side. Rows of bookshelves line two of the walls, holding more books than I have ever seen in my life. A desk sits in front of the balcony, facing a pair of plush sofas in the middle of the floor, and a cabinet full of bottles of liquor is set up between a pair of the bookshelves.

Everything looks expensive and spotlessly clean.

"Don't touch anything," Elias says, taking a seat across from the door. "The things in this room are worth more than you'll make in a lifetime."

"I won't," I reply, walking over to examine one of the bookshelves from a distance. It is lined with dozens of leather-bound tomes, some of which are thicker than the haft of my axe. *They're so thick they could probably last the whole night as firewood,* I think derisively.

I have never found reading to be particularly enjoyable. In my experience, folks who read are usually those trying to take advantage of you, like noblemen or mages.

I slowly wander around the room, looking at various odds and ends, before finally ending up at the governor's desk. A curled map has been spread out across it, weighed down by a couple carved, stone paper weights. It is a detailed rendering of the Emberwood, marking every single settlement and farming community within its borders.

These are all under the governor's rule, I realize, bending over to get a closer look.

If there really had been some sort of attack on one of these villages, then the governor would likely want it sorted out right away. The king will not be pleased when he learns that something terrible has happened to the people under his watch.

Or our watch, I suppose.

Just then, the door opens up and a fat man bedecked in rich clothing enters the room.

Governor Prior.

Elias stands, and I take a step away from his desk, trying to look innocent.

"Governor," Elias says as he puts a hand on his belt knife and bows slightly. I do the same with my father's hatchet.

"Yes, yes," Prior says, waving his hands as if to wave away any formalities. "Thank you for coming on such short notice. I understand that you have just returned from a hunt." He walks over to his desk and sits down heavily, pulling out a handkerchief to wipe the sweat away from his upper lip.

"Such is our duty, my lord," Elias states, also making his way to the desk. I find it amazing that even while wearing boots, he still manages to move silently on the hardwood floor.

The governor lets out a sigh and looks from Elias to me, then back to Elias. "You know that I would not ask to meet unless it was absolutely necessary. I'm afraid that something terrible has happened in the Emberwood."

"Your note mentioned that there has been some sort of attack," Elias says. "Tell me everything."

Prior glances at me nervously, but my master gives him a look that seems to say, 'you can trust him.'

The governor heaves another sigh. "I'm afraid that one of the villages under my stewardship was indeed attacked only a few days ago."

"Which village?" Elias asks, his face a stony mask.

"A small farming community called Haven. Do you know it?"

"I've been there once or twice."

Prior leans forward and points to a spot on the map on the eastern side of the Emberwood, near the border of the Arc. "My tax collector, Jeramie, just returned yesterday from gathering taxes from the outer settlements. When he stumbled back into town, he looked haunted, white as a ghost and unable to speak in coherent sentences. Once he could to tell us what happened, he informed us that Haven had been completely destroyed. Down to the last man, woman, and child."

"Hells," I utter quietly, but neither of them looks at me. I have never been to Haven, but I have heard of it. The people there are said to be a hardy but gentle folk living on the very edge of civilization.

Why would anybody want to attack them?

I feel as if a stone has settled in the pit of my stomach.

"Did he say anything else?" Elias asks, his face still an impenetrable mask.

Prior shakes his bald head and again wipes his face with the handkerchief. "No, that is all we were able to get out of him. The physicians are looking at him now, but he does not seem to be improving. He was one of the smartest men I know, but now, his mind appears to be broken... addled."

Elias grunts. "That's not a lot to go on, my lord. I'm curious to know what *your* thoughts on the matter are." He looks directly at the stout man before him.

Folding his hands in front of him on the desk, the governor furrows his brow in consternation. "I'm going to be frank with you, Elias. It does not look good. If my man is right and the village has been destroyed, it would be the largest tragedy Tarsynium has seen in more than a century. Part of me wants to blame bandits for the attack, punishing the community for not paying them protection money or some such. But my gut... my gut tells me someone else is to blame." He leans forward conspiratorially and whispers a single word, "Nightingales."

Hearing their name fills me with a smoldering ire that threatens to erupt in the form of an angry outburst. Somehow, I manage to keep my mouth shut, though I can still feel my face growing hot.

Elias' reaction is much more composed. "The Nightingales are rebels and freedom fighters, not butchers. It is not their way. They're prone to harrying the king's supply lines, not slaughtering innocent villagers."

"That may be so," Prior says, leaning back in his chair, "but my reports from the capital seem to indicate that the Nightingales are growing bolder. If it is a war with the kingdom they want, then what better place to start than striking out against the king's loyal subjects, especially, those easiest to reach and farthest from his protection?"

"Perhaps," Elias says, though he does not appear convinced.

"Regardless," the governor continues, "we need to confirm that Haven has indeed been attacked in the manner which Jeramie described. I need additional witnesses and evidence before I can file a report to King Aethelgar."

My anger had begun to cool somewhat at Elias' words, though again I'm filled with the same sense of dread I had felt earlier.

I can tell where this is going.

"I would like you and your apprentice to travel to Haven and confirm the destruction of the village. Search for survivors and gather whatever evidence you can. If you encounter any enemies along the way, do not engage. Your job is to merely observe and report back to me. Is that understood?"

"Understood," Elias says without hesitation.

They both turn to look at me.

"Understood," I declare as I stand up straighter and try to mimic my master's professional demeanor.

"Excellent," Prior says, lifting his immense frame out of his cushy leather chair. "I will see that the both of you are compensated generously for your efforts. But please, bear in mind that time is of the essence. I ask that you make haste and return as quickly as you can."

He opens his office door and bids us farewell. We walk through the manor to see ourselves out. As we step into the light of the noonday sun, a refreshingly cool breeze ruffles my tangled hair.

Elias looks at me as we mount our horses, his ordinarily hard eyes softening with concern.

"Are you all right?" He asks, patting his gelding on the neck.

I nod assuredly, but within I am a whirling storm.

He looks out over the sprawling forest around us and says with a sincere voice, "Despite what the governor says, I do not think that the Nightingales are involved."

Elias can always see right through me. I hate that my emotions are so easy to read. I open my mouth to reply, but cannot find the words to speak.

An awkward moment passes before Elias clears his throat. "First the deer in that clearing and now Haven. Perhaps the two incidents are connected. Perhaps not. Whatever the case may be, it is our duty to discover the truth and make sure that another massacre does not occur."

Despite my best efforts, an image flashes before my eyes. Red eyes in the darkness and claws like scythe blades.

The demon.

I push the thought away and give Elias a grim smile. "Then let's have another hunt."

With that, we spur our horses down the hill, delving once again into the wild, untamed frontier that is the Emberwood.

CHAPTER 4
ZARA

The carriage bounces noisily on the dirt road, painfully jostling my limbs as I sit inside the cab. I try to steady myself, gripping the armrest and bracing my back to the seat, but it still feels like my teeth are rattling around in my head.

Could this ride get any bumpier? I think to myself, trying unsuccessfully to get comfortable in my seat.

I hold no particularly pleasant memories of the few times I have ridden in a horse-drawn carriage. And this time is no exception, sitting in this wooden box that is more akin to a coffin. I clench my jaw as the axle grinds beneath the floorboards, straining my ears.

Still, I think, wincing at an especially violent bump. *I suppose it is better than riding on horseback.*

My only experience with horses was when I was a little girl, and it involved a particularly angry pony that bit my hand. Ever since then, I have tried to avoid contact with the beasts. All things considered, this carriage ride is still preferable to wrangling an unpredictable animal.

I try to keep this thought in mind, ignoring my aching backside as I once again shift in my seat. Glancing out the window, I let out a yawn.

From the time Arch-Magister Tyrande had asked me to be her ward on this mission, it was a mad rush to gather my things and prepare myself for the journey. I made it to the Pillar of Radiance with my trunk in tow, just as they were preparing to leave. Elva had sternly given me a lecture I'd been expecting, about how important it is to be on time. But my nervous excitement far overshadowed her reproof as I stepped into my carriage and watched the city lights fade into the distance.

Sleep somehow still managed to elude me, even though I had been completely drained from my magical sparring the day before. Perhaps it was the nerves or my uncomfortable sleeping arrangements, but I was only able to drift off once briefly into a short, restless slumber.

At least there is plenty of food, I think, stifling another yawn.

I reach over to the platter on the seat next to me and pick up a sweet roll, taking a decidedly unladylike bite. As I eat, I begin flipping through pages of the book on my lap, its parchment ancient and smelling mildly of dust. In the filtered light of the sun, I idly skim the archaic text on demonology.

Tuning out the noise around me, I finally settle on a chapter titled "Understanding the R'Laar," and attempt to let its words take my mind off my present circumstances.

> *The cause of Byhalya's Doom was, of course, the demonic horde that came to our world from the plane colloquially known as the Eleven Hells. It is interesting to note that the demon army refers to itself as the R'Laar, which roughly translates to "world eaters" or "eaters of worlds."*
>
> *These "world eaters" are a loose-knit organization of beings that differ widely in appearance. They consist of many different species of varying levels of ability and intelligence, and are led by a cadre of high demons known as "princes." Nevertheless, they are united by a single purpose—the will to dominate all life.*

I take another bite of my sticky pastry and turn the page.

> *Though no historical record exists, legends state that eleven demonic princes led the initial invasion of Byhalya. Under their leadership, the R'Laar conquered much of the civilized world, destroying the greater part of humanity and enslaving the rest.*
>
> *Asmodeus, the Prince of Darkness, was said to be the one who led the attack against Tarsynium in the latter days of the Doom, culminating in the infamous Last Battle. In that heroic final stand, Luca Dhar and the Legion of Light fought against overwhelming odds, giving the Conclave the time that it needed to create the Arc of Radiance, thus saving the war-weary kingdom from destruction.*
>
> *May their sacrifice never be forgotten, and may the Light forever bless their souls.*

Yes, yes, we all know about the Legion of Light, I think, eagerly turning another page. *I want to know more about the demons.*

POSSIBLE MOTIVATIONS OF THE R'LAAR

> *Many postulate that the R'Laar required vast resources in order to keep their infernal armada fully functioning. In fact, the historical consensus states that their primary purpose in coming to our world was to devour its resources, similar to the way a swarm of locusts devours crops.*

It is the belief of this magisterium that ours was not the first world to fall prey to this demonic foe, nor will it be the last. The R'Laar will continue its destructive quest until every world that the Light created is consumed by their unquenchable lust for power.

I quickly turn another page, forgetting about my sweet roll and instead, devouring the words written there. I can barely feel the jostle of the carriage as the book draws me in.

Even after old Byhalya was destroyed by the demonic invasion, we know precious little about the R'Laar and the inner workings of their society. We have a rough understanding of the different demonic species within the horde, but as for their culture, if one exists, we remain in the dark.

One thing, however, is certain: our ability to protect Tarsynium with radiant magic continues to be a thorn in the side of the R'Laar. Historical and religious texts make this abundantly clear. A civilization that exists solely to conquer worlds cannot be content allowing survivors to linger on. If time has taught us anything, it is that the R'Laar are a patient lot. They will bide their time and wait for the day that a weakness in our defense is exposed.

They will not rest until the last kingdom of man is finally crushed. We must remain ever-vigilant, lest we fall like the people of old Byhalya.

I stare at the page for a long moment, reading and rereading the last two sentences.

Light. Could they still be out there, waiting to destroy us all?

Living beneath the protective veil of the Arc, it is easy to forget that just beyond the radiant shield lies a shattered wasteland potentially filled with bloodthirsty monsters.

The mere thought of it sends a shiver up my spine.

Unexpectedly, a high-pitched screeching fills my ears as the carriage comes to an abrupt stop, and I can hear muffled voices speaking outside the cab. For a moment, I wrestle with myself on whether or not I should go and see what is happening. *Would it be presumptuous of an initiate to leave her carriage?*

After a minute, my curiosity gets the better of me, and I decide to investigate. I snap the book closed and sit up, sliding my feet back into my soft slippers on the floor. Though they are comfortable, I know they will offer little protection out on the rough road. Setting the book on the bench beside me, I cover it with a pillow, then push open the side door and poke my head outside.

At first, I am momentarily blinded by the sun reflecting off the rolling green fields surrounding us, but my eyes quickly adjust as I take in the brilliance of the Heartlands. We are in the middle of nowhere, with not a town or village in sight. The land itself is vibrant and beautiful, reminding me of an uneven canvas covered in emerald-colored paint.

The air is warm and fresh, and I take in a deep breath through my nostrils, filling my lungs with the scents of nature. The outdoors is a refreshing change to being cooped up in the musty carriage for hours.

Craning my neck, I look to see what has caused our caravan to stop, but from this angle I am unable to see around the other carriages.

"I must advise you to stay inside, young lady," my driver says from atop his perch. "The mages will take care of the problem, and we will be on our way in short order."

My first reaction is to listen to him, to duck back into the carriage and wait for the disturbance to pass, but I force myself to stand my ground. *You're not just an initiate anymore*, I remind myself. *You're ward to one of the most powerful women in the kingdom. Act like it.* Raising my chin, I look him dead in the eye as I determinedly step out onto the hard-packed dirt road.

"I appreciate your concern," I reply, my voice cool and authoritative like Elva's. "But I am *not* a young lady. I am ward to the Arch-Magister—a mage in training."

The driver opens his mouth to respond, but I quickly turn away from him and make my way to the front of the caravan, ignoring his sputtered protests that I should remain behind.

Several curious mages look out from their carriages as they try to catch a glimpse at what is causing our delay. I stride past them, gathering more than a few strange glances, my attention drawn to the two armored soldiers standing at the front, warily facing down a small army of thugs.

They surround the head of the caravan, their ragtag group blocking the road and carrying mismatched weapons ranging from clubs to dull-looking swords. Their clothes are worn and dirty, but what they lack in appearance, they more than make up for in sheer number.

Light almighty, I think, stopping dead in my tracks. *There must be a hundred of them!*

One of the thugs steps forward menacingly, and I watch in fear as the two guardsmen draw their swords.

"What is the meaning of this delay?" I hear Elva's voice from somewhere behind me, and I turn to see her approaching the gathered host with two mages flanking her on either side.

The brigand who had stepped forward, a man with a snarled beard, hefts his sword threateningly and lifts his voice for all to hear.

"Beggin' your pardon, dear lady," the man booms with an astonishingly deep voice. "But this highway is a toll road. Passing through this area ain't free."

The guards glance at one another, their armor clinking as they shift nervously.

"A toll road?" Elva scoffs, lifting her chin in the air and looking down her nose at the big man. "Ridiculous. This is the king's road, and I know of no tax for traveling on his lands."

The bearded man grins, revealing a mouth full of rotten teeth. "This here is *our* land, dear lady. And the king is a long ways away."

My palms start to feel moist. I have heard tales of roving bands of thieves beyond the walls of Tarsys, preying on unsuspecting travelers and robbing them blind. According to the stories, those who were only robbed were considered the lucky ones.

These bandits do not look to be the merciful type.

The cutthroats surrounding their leader chuckle, and I can see that there are an equal number of vile women amongst the men.

"Highwaymen, then," Elva states, not losing her confidence one whit in the face of the man's brashness. "Thieves come to rob us of all our possessions. Is that it?"

The bearded man nods. "'Fraid so," he rumbles, slapping the flat of his blade down on his open palm. "You see, out here we are far away from your little king and feeding so many mouths ain't easy. Now, if you'd please give us a look at your goods, we can get through this without any blood."

One of the guards steps forward menacingly, his sword held out in front of him. "What are your orders, Magus? Should we dispatch these knaves?"

The thugs begin laughing again, openly mocking the guard's bravery.

Elva raises her hands and steps forward, putting herself between the highwaymen and the guards. "I'm afraid the answer will have to be no," she says, addressing the bearded man. Despite her diminutive size, she does a considerable job facing down the entire gang. I catch a glimpse of the silvery chain of her talisman hanging from her fist, the magical crystal hidden from the view of the highwaymen.

The man frowns, looking genuinely disappointed. "I'm always amazed when people choose to die over their possessions." He shrugs and raises his sword as if to cleave the top of Elva's skull.

My skin tingles as I sense her pull in source energy, though I can barely hear the words of her incantation. Suddenly, her hands are alight with magefyre, and the bearded man becomes engulfed in flickering blue flames.

He is instantly blasted backwards, sword dropping harmlessly from his hand as he begins screaming in pain. His fellow ruffians all cower back in fear, watching with horrified faces as he frantically tries to put out the fire by slapping at his body.

Elva sprays him again with magefyre, causing his shrieks to grow louder and more severe as the flames intensify brightly around him. He falls to his knees, then collapses in a heap on the ground, his skin sizzling and popping like raw chicken that has been dropped onto the coals of a furnace.

My nostrils fill with the stench of burnt flesh, and I gag, quickly covering my mouth with the sleeve of my robe. I realize that I am just as horrified as the thieves who all stare at the scorched body in shock.

I have never watched anyone die before.

Looming over the man's crackling corpse, Elva stands tall, looking out at the host gathered in front of her with dispassionate coldness. "I am Arch-Magister Elva Tyrande of the Conclave of Mages. Either depart from these lands and never harass travelers on this road again or suffer the same fate as your leader. The choice is yours."

For a moment, everyone is silent, the only sound being the crackle of the burning man's skin, and then the mob begins to break apart. Some of the thugs back away slowly, expressions of hatred painted plainly on their faces. Others throw down their weapons and run, disappearing into the fields as fast as their feet can carry them.

It is not long before the way ahead is clear. Elva turns back around to address the caravan in the same calculated manner she had the highwaymen. "The threat is gone," she declares coolly, walking away from the body as if walking away from a bug she had just squashed. "Let us continue. We still have a long way to go before we reach Forest Hill."

She disappears inside of her carriage and closes the door shut behind her.

Staring on in stunned disbelief, I catch another whiff of burnt flesh, and my stomach lurches. I'm not sure if my revulsion is from the stench or the fact that I just watched a respected mage burn a man to death.

Probably a bit of both, I think in disgust as I move to cover my nose again.

The two guards sheathe their swords and begin the revolting task of pulling the bandit's charred remains from off the road. The magefyre has all but evaporated, leaving behind a smoking husk of blackened skin and bone.

I avert my eyes and begin to numbly make my way back to my carriage.

How easily she killed that man, I think to myself, seeing the gruesome scene play out in my head again. A chilling thought crosses my mind. *Would she hesitate to do the same to me if I ever cross her?*

In my stunned and delirious state, I can see that several of the other mages look as pale and uneasy as I do, though nobody dares say anything. Aside from the High Magus herself, Elva is one of the most powerful and well-connected mages in Tarsynium. Speaking ill of her would no doubt cause many problems to any member of the Conclave.

I honestly don't know what to make of any of it. I shake my head and blink back sudden tears. Overwhelmed at this unexpected turn of events, I now fear what my future holds.

The driver clears his throat as I reach my carriage. I look up at him defensively, expecting some sort of lecture, but I find only sorrow in his eyes. Though he does not say anything, I can practically feel him uttering the words, "I told you so, little mage."

Shaking with uncertainty, I climb into the coach and pull the door shut. The horses begin pulling us away, and as I gaze back out at the green expanse of hills outside my window, a single thought echoes inside of my head.

I think I might have made a mistake in coming here.

CHAPTER 5
OWYN

A dense layer of fog blankets the Emberwood, an icy mist blotting out the sun and making it difficult to see. Everything, including sound, seems dampened by the heavy air. I find myself glancing uneasily at every passing shadow as I attempt to figure out our location. For the first time in months, I feel completely and utterly lost.

Elias adeptly guides his horse through the ferns carpeting the forest floor, leading us onward despite the low visibility of the foggy morning.

How in the Eleven Hells does he know where we are going? We've been traveling like this for hours! Frustrated at my inability to navigate the woods, I dig my heels into my horse's flank and urge her to follow him as I try to keep up.

After our meeting with Governor Prior, we had left Forest Hill in such a hurry that we had not even stopped to resupply before heading back into the woods. Under normal circumstances, I would not mind the abrupt change in plans. However, our packs have grown perilously light, our only supplies being hardtack and heavily-salted strips of meat, and I find it difficult to think beyond my empty belly. *It would have at least been nice to get some fresh bread and cheese at the inn*, I think glumly to myself. *Dried venison gets old after a while.*

I grimace as I try to stretch in the saddle, my back aching from having spent yet another night on the hard ground. Somewhere in the back of my mind, a voice tells me to have a better attitude about all of this, but I choose to ignore it. Rangers rarely get days off, and when what little respite we can manage is taken away, it tends to thoroughly annoy me.

"This fog is getting thicker the farther we go," I call out to Elias, holding the reins in my gloved hand. It is late summer, but without the sun, it feels cold beneath the canopy of trees.

Elias does not reply. He rides straight-backed ahead of me, his eyes on the foliage around us.

I wait for a few moments before I call out again. "I know that this is probably a stupid question, but do you know where we're going?" As soon as the inquiry leaves my mouth, I immediately regret it.

Elias stops his horse, and I pull up beside him. He stares at me for a moment, his face a tolerant mask. He only replies with a simple, "Yes."

I wait for him to continue, but quickly realize that no explanation is forthcoming. *Sometimes I wonder if living in the wild for so long has dulled his ability to hold a conversation.* Against my better judgement, I decide to follow up my question with yet another one. "How can you tell?"

Elias frowns, looking at me as if I am a complete idiot, before he somewhat softens his expression. He points at some of the flora in front of us. "Ridgeback ferns," he says simply, as if that should explain everything. Upon seeing my still-perplexed look, he continues. "They only grow in the eastern hinterlands of the Emberwood. Look at the fronds, the way they curl inward. They are different from the ones that grow near Forest Hill." He points ahead of us. "The ground is sloping upward ever so slightly, which indicates we are entering a region known as the Ridgeway. The hills all converge on a valley with a stream cutting through it. *That* is where Haven is located. If we continue in this direction and follow the Ridgeway, it should be relatively easy for us to locate the village."

I nod my head, trying not to look overly surprised. It is one of the longest explanations I have ever managed to get out of him, and now he made it all sound so simple. *Perhaps I should pay more attention the next time he drones on about the local plant life,* I think to myself, attempting to maintain a neutral expression.

"There is more to becoming a ranger than learning how to fight and hunt," he says sternly, motioning at the path ahead. "Shall we continue?"

I nod, and we both nudge our horses forward, continuing our long expedition through the forest.

As we ride, I begin to notice the slight incline to the ground, realizing that we are indeed climbing higher in elevation. The Emberwood is in a giant basin that encompasses the eastern reach of Tarsynium. The far edges of that basin border the Arc of Radiance, where few people dare to venture.

I have only seen the Arc a handful of times in my life. My recollection is a sheer wall of energy rising from the earth and into the heavens, disappearing among the clouds where I know it curves inward toward the great tower in Tarsys. It was truly a marvel to behold, and yet I still understand very little about it, except that it is all that separates us from what lies beyond the veil. Many in the kingdom avoid settling close to the Arc for superstitious reasons, believing it unlucky to be so close to the edge of the world. Perhaps they think that demons will cast spells on them or murder them in the dead of the night while they sleep.

This dark thought instantly brings up unbidden memories of red eyes in the shadows, of claws like scythe blades, and teeth like knives. Fear begins to seize my heart in a vice-like grip, its fingers squeezing me tightly and threatening to smother me with despair.

I shake my head and recite the ranger's oath under my breath. Its mantra is a source of strength to me, reminding me of my father. He was a *real* ranger, who would not have been afraid of encountering some creature in the woods.

We travel for another hour, riding our horses in a switchback pattern as the incline becomes steeper. Unsurprisingly, Elias declares that we will eat lunch in the saddle, and I struggle to swallow my complaints as I chew on my salted jerky.

The fog does not abate the further we go. In fact, it appears to gather more thickly, swirling around our horses' legs like misty spirits rising from the earth.

My master suddenly stops our ascent and raises his fist into the air, signaling for me to halt as well. A moment later, he looks back at me, concern plainly written upon his face.

"Smoke," he says, dropping his voice low.

Frowning, I lift my nose and sniff. I can smell it, too, a faint whiff of char in the stale air.

Elias points up the hill, a little to the right of our current trajectory. "It's coming from up there. We're not far now." He unslings his bow and kicks his horse, his pace more careful than before.

My ranger senses are not nearly as keen as Elias', but I am able to discern that what we smell is not simple wood smoke. It is an acrid stench of tar and burnt leather mixed with the scent of scorched timber.

It is the smell of burning buildings.

We creep forward, and I deftly pull out my hatchet, scanning the woods around us and looking for any signs of an ambush. The entire world seems deathly quiet, as if the forest itself is holding its breath.

As we crest the top of the hill, the slope tapering off, we find ourselves in somewhat of a clearing. The trees are thinner here, and every so often, I see an old stump, indicating that some of these trees had been cut down for lumber.

Our horses carry us deeper into the clearing, and as the fog begins to thin, our worst fears are revealed.

A village has clearly been ravaged.

Elias gestures to me, and we dismount, readying our weapons and crouching down to observe the scene in front of us. My master nocks an arrow and looks around for a moment, searching for any signs of life.

There is no movement among the blackened buildings.

"It looks deserted," Elias notes, his voice barely above a whisper.

I try to sound hopeful. "Maybe the villagers were able to escape?"

Without taking his eyes off the buildings, Elias mutters, "Maybe," though he does not sound convinced.

We wait a few more minutes, then wordlessly begin making our way forward, moving stealthily through the tall, unkempt grass and toward the empty village of Haven.

As we approach, the smell of smoke becomes even stronger, stinging my nostrils and filling my lungs with its stench. I tightly grip the handle of my hatchet as I try to suppress the overwhelming sense of dread that settles in my stomach.

There could be Nightingales waiting for us in there. Or maybe something worse.

I swallow my fears and force my feet to continue moving, careful to mind my surroundings and remain alert and ready to fight.

The buildings look to be in even worse shape as we draw near. Their walls are gouged and scored by flames, ceilings have collapsed in smoldering, ash-covered heaps. They remind me of black skeletons standing motionless in the mist, mere shadows of their former selves.

We do not see any movement as we slink between the ruined farmhouses, and we hear nothing other than the sounds of our own footsteps. Most disconcerting of all, however, is that we do not find a single body.

It's as if the people simply vanished as their village burned to the ground, I think, trying to make sense of the emptiness around us.

We pause in the middle of the gravel road. Elias looks at me and indicates with hand signals that he wants us to split up. My heart clenches, but I agree. He goes one way, and I go the other, combing quietly through the village and searching for anything of note.

I turn a corner and approach what looks to have been the village inn. Its singed door hangs open by only one hinge, and I peek inside to see if there are any survivors.

Nothing. There is no one, living or dead.

The inside of the building is dark with soot, and a pile of rubble sits in the middle of the common room, still smoldering with faintly glowing embers. Judging by the massive hole in the roof, I figure that if there were any survivors, this would be a poor place to hide out. The whole structure seems to be on the verge of collapse.

I step back outside, taking a deep breath of fresh air through my mouth.

It doesn't make any sense, I think to myself, frowning in bewilderment as I survey the wreckage before me. *Where could they have gone? Did they somehow manage to escape whoever burned this place down?*

"Owyn!"

I jump, the sound so sudden in the stillness of the abandoned village. I can practically *hear* my heart thundering within my chest. It takes me a second to realize that it is my master's voice, calling from somewhere nearby.

He sounds urgent.

Standing up, I begin jogging in the direction of his voice, my eyes darting around in search of danger.

"Owyn!" he shouts again, his gruff voice coming from the center of town.

I begin to sprint, my quiver bouncing noisily on my back. I pass building after broken building, all of them looking like desiccated husks, until I finally reach Elias, who is standing with his back to me in the middle of an open field.

As I approach, the fog begins to part, carried away on a light breeze, and it reveals what has stopped him in his tracks.

An elder tree, ancient and gnarled, rises up from the mist like a dark sentinel standing guard over the destroyed village. It is taller than any tree I have ever seen, its roots spreading out into the field like bony fingers clawing at the grass. There are large objects hanging from the thick, twisted branches.

My mouth goes dry as I realize what they are.

Bodies.

"The villagers did not escape," Elias says grimly, gesturing with his bow at the tree before us. "They've been here all along."

Dozens of corpses hang from the massive tree. Strung up by their necks, they sway gently in the breeze. Men, women, and even children gaze sightlessly out at the village, their expressions ghastly in death. Even from this distance, I can see that the bodies are starting to bloat and decompose, making the elder tree look like something straight out of a vicious nightmare.

As I stare out at the scene in mute horror, the wind suddenly changes direction and causes me to deeply inhale the scent of rotting flesh.

My stomach lurches, and I turn away, retching my meager lunch into the grass. I continue to gag long after my stomach is emptied, the smell stuck in my nostrils. It permeates my entire body and worms its way into my clothes and skin, making my eyes water.

When I can finally stand, shivering and pale, I turn back to face the horrible sight before us. Elias is still looking at the tree with his jaw set, a touch of fury in his gray eyes.

"We need to cut them down," he growls, shouldering his bow as he unsheathes his belt knife.

The thought of touching the rotten bodies makes me want to vomit again, but I do not argue. These people were under Elias' protection, and somebody came here and murdered them all.

There will be no convincing him otherwise.

"Go and get the spades from my horse," he commands, walking determinedly toward the elder tree. "We are going to give these people a proper burial."

Making my way back through the ghostly village, I approach the horses and retrieve the miniature spades from Elias' saddlebags. Usually, we use these tools for digging trenches in camp. Today, we will be using them to dig graves.

I return to find that Elias has climbed up into the tree and is already in the process of cutting down the villagers, slicing the ropes and lowering them to the ground one at a time. Steeling myself, I plunge the spades into the soil and go to help him. Catching the bodies as he eases them down to me, I lay them gently on the grass.

It is a long and grisly process, one that I will likely never forget. Their flesh is pale and blotchy, their bodies bloated with fluids, and I have to stop three times so that I can turn away and retch into the grass. Though I want nothing more than to jump into a stream and scrub my skin raw, I continue working, trying hard to keep my emotions in check.

After what feels like a lifetime, we finally finish cutting down all the bodies and observe the grim sight before us.

Seeing so many people butchered and laid out like cattle makes my skin crawl. One little girl, who looks like she is no more than nine years old, looks both innocent and frightful lying on the ground. Her frame is so dainty and frail, the way all of the village girls back at Forest Hill are, and yet her neck is bent at an odd angle as the maggots have begun to nest in her mouth and eyes.

I begin to quietly weep, tears falling freely down my cheeks. For the first time, I am not ashamed to show my weakness in front of Elias.

And for the first time, he does not seem to mind.

Elias shows emotion much differently than I do. He handles the process of moving the bodies with cold professionalism, his face a careful mask of detachment. However, when I look in his eyes, I can see a storm. It rages beneath the surface, violent and intense, and I realize that my master is more furious than I have ever seen him before.

Whoever is responsible for this massacre is going to pay for it dearly.

Once the corpses are all clear from the tree, we begin to dig, silently shoveling a mass grave in the middle of the field. The soil is soft and easy to turn, but it is not long before we are both sweating again from the exertion.

As I dig, the same thought keeps running through my head. *Who or what in the Eleven Hells could have done such a terrible thing? Surely the beast I saw a few days ago cannot be to blame. This was the work of a mob, not the attack of some mindless monster.*

For a moment, I think that this must be the work of the Nightingales, the so-called freedom fighters who make their home in the mountains, but I quickly discount the thought. Elias is right. No matter how much I hate them, this sort of thing is too extreme, even for them.

This is nothing short of cold-hearted butchery.

The fog makes it difficult to see the sun, but I estimate that it is about midday by the time we finish digging the mass grave. I take a step back and gaze into the gaping pit in the center of the village green. Even with all of our efforts, it is a pretty shallow thing, a poor resting place for these unfortunate villagers.

Wiping a bead of sweat from my forehead, I turn and look to my master for further direction.

He gestures mutely to the line of bodies, and we begin to pick them up one by one and gently lower them into the pit. We handle the ordeal with reverence. Neither one of us speaks until each villager is laid to rest at the bottom of the grave, their eyes staring blindly to heaven.

Taking up our shovels, we begin the long process of filling in the expansive grave. My hands scream in protest from the blisters that have formed, but I ignore them. It would be obscene for me to complain about my pain while standing over the remains of an entire village.

After countless shovelfuls of dirt, the pit is finally filled in, covering the pale, lifeless faces and thankfully, the smell with a layer of freshly turned earth.

We wearily return to our horses, sweaty and filthy, and pack away the spades in Elias' saddlebags. Mounting up, we turn our backs on the gravesite and ride away from Haven, our hearts heavy in our chests.

The fog continues late into the evening, even as we stop to set up camp. The woods feel much more foreboding than they ever have before, a hiding place for untold dangers.

We tether our horses where they can drink from a shallow brook, then light a small fire to ward away the evening chill. Sitting on a rock, I warm my hands by the flickering flames, hoping I will wake from this nightmare. I shake my head to clear it, but my mind is plagued with images of the burnt farmhouses and the tree full of dead villagers.

Finally, Elias breaks the silence with his typical gruffness. "Come morning, we will need to ride with all haste for Forest

Hill. The governor needs to be notified of our discovery as soon as possible."

"If we push ourselves, we should be able to arrive before nightfall," I remark off-handedly.

He nods, and silence follows, surrounding us with only the sound of the babbling brook and the crackling fire.

After a few minutes, I look back up at Elias and speak. "What *was* that back there, master? I've never heard of such a thing happening before." I shudder as memories of the little girl with the broken neck come unbidden to my mind. "It was more than an attack. It was as if whoever did this was trying to send a message."

Elias is silent for a moment before uttering his reply. "I cannot say for sure," he says, pulling his cloak more tightly around him. "There were no notable tracks, no signs of a struggle, and the bodies did not bear any obvious wounds. It's as if they went to be hung willing without putting up any fight."

"Why would they do that?" I ask quietly.

"I'm not sure," he replies, his eyes reflecting the light of the fire. After a few heartbeats, he looks up at me. "I want you to know that I still do not think that the Nightingales were involved."

I nod, though his mention of them still stirs up involuntary anger within me.

"They rarely travel in the sort of numbers that would be required to wipe out an entire village," he continues, ignoring my discomfort, "and I do not think they would be motivated by killing farmers. Most of the Nightingales *are* farmers."

"I came to a similar conclusion," I admit resentfully.

Elias fixes me with an intense look. "Nothing about this makes sense. Whoever—or whatever—attacked Haven threatens the entire Emberwood, maybe even all of Tarsynium. They need to be hunted down and brought to justice at once. We should turn in early tonight. Tomorrow we will leave before dawn and ride hard for Forest Hill."

Elias takes the first watch so I can sleep, but despite my physical and emotional exhaustion, I find it difficult to drift off. Every time I close my eyes, I see that accursed tree and feel the sightless eyes of the little girl *watching* me. When I do finally manage to fall asleep, my mind is riddled with nightmares.

I'm relieved to be pulled from my dark dreams when Elias wakes me for my shift.

The second half of the night passes slowly, and I find myself mindlessly sharpening my hatchet with a whetstone. My thoughts are just as dark as my dreams, drifting from demons to rebels to the dead villagers.

I wonder what it is we are up against, and how in the Light we are going to fight it.

An hour before dawn, I wake Elias up, and we begin preparations to depart. By the time we start riding, there is just enough light for us to see as we make our way into the woods.

Guided by Elias' uncanny ability to find clear paths through the dark forest, we push our horses to the limit, heading back to Forest Hill as fast as we can. We eat our meals on the go and only stop when one of us needs to relieve ourselves.

For anybody else, it would have been a perilous journey, but we are rangers. The wilderness is our home. And this is our life.

We still have an hour or two left before sunset by the time we make it back to the outskirts of Emberwood's capital. Everything appears as it had when we left it, a town untouched by the nightmare we just lived through. Our horses are lathered from the journey, but we push them onward, making our way to the top of the hill where the governor's mansion is perched.

Upon our arrival, we quickly tie off the horses' reins to the hitching post and rush up to the front entryway.

The door opens before we have a chance to knock, revealing a very flustered-looking Governor Prior standing in the portal. The hall behind him is bustling with activity. He dabs his forehead with a handkerchief as he regards us with anxious eyes.

"You've returned," he states breathlessly.

"Yes," Elias replies frankly, wasting no time. "The reports are true. Haven has been attacked, and everyone in the village has been killed. Owyn and I buried the ones we managed to find, but we were unable to discover who was behind it."

Prior swears under his breath. "I feared as much," he says as he folds his handkerchief and puts it in his pocket. "However, we now have bigger problems to deal with. I've just been informed that a delegation of mages is on its way here from Tarsys. They will be arriving first thing in the morning."

Elias and I look at each other, both of us equally surprised by the revelation.

"Mages?" I ask before I can stop myself.

At the same time, Elias growls, "What do they want?"

Prior shakes his head. "I don't know, but whatever it is, it has come down from the Circle itself." He compulsively pulls out his handkerchief again and wipes off his face. "Light, help us all."

CHAPTER 6
ZARA

It is mid-morning by the time we reach Forest Hill.

Another sleepless night in the carriage has left me feeling tired, but my exhaustion is overshadowed by the sense of excitement I feel traveling through the overgrown Emberwood.

I barely give my aching back a second thought as I gaze with wonder out the window at the passing trees. The landscape of the Emberwood is vastly different from that of city life in Tarsys. No textbook or essay could have captured the lush beauty springing up around me.

Even so, a part of me still dreads getting out of the carriage and having to face Elva.

The incident with the bandits has caused me to view the Arch-Magister in a new light, a much more intimidated one than before. Since then, whenever Elva has attempted to tutor me, I cannot help but inwardly cringe, remembering the horror of watching that man get burnt alive.

At the beginning of the trip, I could hardly wait to learn at the feet of the Arch-Magister, to glean everything I could from such a legendary mage. Now I worry about what might happen if I were to end up on her bad side, but I must not show Elva that weakness; especially, after everything she has done to bring me here. The fear that clutches my heart and makes my stomach turn when she is instructing me, leaves me homesick for my dormitory and my classes.

Fortunately, my anxious feeling departs as I watch the hill that has given the town its name come into view. Forest Hill is like a small mountain covered in buildings and trees, an idyllic blend of nature and civilization. Smoke curls from the many chimneys like wisps of cotton, and vegetation sprouts from every nook and cranny, giving the place a wild, overgrown look.

It is beautiful, a town from out of a fairy tale. Seeing it makes me forget all about my current worries.

Wanting to get some fresh air, I decide to exit the bumpy carriage and walk alongside the horses, taking in all of the sights and sounds like a flower absorbing the sunlight. The driver gives me a displeased glance, but I ignore him and look out at the woods around me. I've never been to this part of the country, but I have heard stories about its vast frontier.

There are more trees around than I have ever seen in my life, making me, a city dweller, feel more than a bit claustrophobic. That being said, I cannot deny the natural charm of the land surrounding me. Everything, from the leafy boughs overhead to the gnarled roots and spongy moss underfoot, seems to be alive, filling me with a sense of untamed grandeur unseen in the crowded streets of Tarsys.

And Light, who knew that the world could be so green?

As we enter the town proper, I begin to catch glimpses of the locals going about their daily lives. The people seem to be a reflection of the wilderness in which they live, their demeanor reserved and quaint. Their clothing is modest, homespun cotton worn in fashions that haven't been seen in the Heartlands for decades. The men are bearded, the women wear bonnets, and all of them regard the black lacquered carriages with narrow-eyed suspicion.

These are simple folk, farmers and lumber harvesters, and they live in simple dwellings of mud brick and raw timber. They are far removed from the affairs of mages and bureaucrats, carving out their existence on the very fringe of society.

This is a completely different world, I think to myself in amazement as I walk by them. *I wonder if they have ever seen a mage before.*

The road leads us past the townsfolk toiling in their fields and over an arching wooden bridge, where it eventually slopes upward to snake around the more densely populated hillside. I glance at a group of barefoot children who look up at us with wonder. They whisper excitedly to each other, pointing at the carriages as they pass.

Regarding the children casually, I touch the crystal talisman around my neck and pull in a touch of source energy, then use my other hand to throw a burst of blue flames into the sky.

The children jump in surprise, huge grins splitting their adorable little faces. They immediately begin cheering and exclaiming, elated by my simple display of magic.

I smile back, unable to maintain a serious, professional expression. Children have always been a soft spot for me. Waving goodbye, I continue my long march up the hill, the carriages rolling relentlessly onward.

After being cooped up in that tiny box, the uphill climb is a welcome change, and it feels good to stretch my legs. The warmth of the sunlight on my skin reminds me of my summer days spent as a child on the shores of Loch Morloch, dipping my toes in the icy cold water.

Eventually, the caravan pulls to a stop in front of a beautiful manor at the top of the hill, the first modern-looking building I have seen since arriving in the Emberwood. A delegation of people stands with respectful attention as they wait outside, wearing what I assume is their finest apparel.

Breathing heavily from my climb, I step up to where the other mages are disembarking. I brush the loose strands of hair out of my face, trying to look presentable.

It is windy up here on the hilltop, all the surrounding trees having been cut down, and as my fellow mages exit their carriages, I can see their robes whipping around them. Despite the late summer weather, the wind is actually quite chilly up here.

We all gather around Arch-Magister Tyrande; eleven mages and a few armored soldiers form a semicircle and do our best to appear impressive. This was one of the things Elva had emphasized before we arrived. First impressions can mean everything when it comes to matters of diplomacy.

A rotund man with a bald head comes forward. Dressed in lavish clothing that does not match his surroundings, he wears an ornately embroidered coat that bulges around his midsection, threatening to pop the hand-carved ivory buttons running down its front.

That must be the governor, I think to myself, observing from my place at Elva's side.

"Arch-Magister," he says over the wind, bowing his shining head in deference. "Welcome to Forest Hill." Judging by his accent, it seems that he is from Tarsys. His silky voice actually sounds cultured and refined. "We are so very grateful that you have chosen to visit our home."

Elva looks at him imperiously and extends her hand, which he proceeds to kiss reverently.

Lifting his head up to regard her, he shuffles back to a respectful distance before continuing. "I am Governor Timothy Prior, Lord Regent of the province of Emberwood. These," he says, gesturing to the people gathered behind him, "are my closest associates and colleagues. We would like to formally invite you and your fellow mages to sample our hospitality. Our home and hearth are yours."

Elva gazes at the group and nods. "Thank you, Governor Prior," she states with courtly elegance. "We accept your invitation wholeheartedly. This is a beautiful part of the kingdom, and we are honored by your generosity."

Governor Prior bobs his head, beaming.

There is an awkward silence, which Elva breaks by clearing her throat. "Shall we go inside to discuss the purpose of our coming here?"

"Yes, yes, of course," Governor Prior says, his face reddening. Turning, he gestures at the group, and they spring into action, opening the front door and approaching the drivers to help move our things into the house.

As I follow the mages in, I steal several glances at the governor's people, trying to glean as much information about them as I can from their appearances. There are a few servants among them, and they are the ones doing most of the heavy lifting, with a few advisor-looking people thrown in the mix. Two individuals stand out from the rest, though. They watch us from the side without moving to help us in any way.

The first one is tall and broad shouldered with a square jaw and salt and pepper hair that has been cropped short. Stubble covers his weathered features in a way that makes him look rugged and coarse, like an uncut stone.

The second one is a little shorter and much younger than the first, with a tousled mess of brown hair atop his head. He looks as if he is trying a little too hard to mirror the man standing next to him but isn't doing a very good job of it. He is lean and long-limbed with a sturdy jaw and dark, forest green eyes. I would go so far as to say that he looks handsome, in a quaint, boyish sort of way, if he didn't look so dour.

Both of them are armed with a bow and a quiver of arrows and an assortment of weapons on their belts. What catches my attention, however, are the gray-green cloaks hanging from their shoulders, which seem to blend in with the woods below.

Those must be rangers, I think, tearing my eyes away from them as I enter the house. *They look much more... human than the stories always made them seem.*

Everyone knows that rangers are an important part of the kingdom, but they are rarely seen in civilized society. The King of Tarsynium pays them to live in the wilderness, guarding the Arc and the countryside from any influences that would threaten the peace. Mages have always had a healthy distrust of rangers, considering them to be dangerous warriors who adhere to no laws but their own.

They look like normal men to me. Hardly the stuff of legends.

My thoughts are interrupted by a kindly old woman who directs me to a side wing of the mansion. She says that this is where the other mages and I will be sleeping, and we should settle in before supper is served.

So far, the mages have barely acknowledge my existence. While they do not treat me coldly, they do not give me the same respect they would give to a full mage. I am little more than a child to them, an initiate come along to observe the mission rather than participate in it. It comes as no surprise when I am given the smallest of the bedrooms, which really is little more than an oversized closet. In truth, I do not really mind. Any initiate at the Academy would be envious of my position, traveling across the country with some of the brightest minds the Conclave has to offer.

I make my way to my new bedroom just as a pair of servants are bringing in my things. Thanking them for their help, I begin to unpack, taking out my books and sorting through my clothes.

A few minutes in, I hear a knock at my door, and I look up to see that it is the Arch-Magister. She regards me with a hint of curiosity on her otherwise impassive face.

"How are you feeling?" she asks, stepping inside and clasping her hands behind her.

I stand up and try to block her view of my undergarments sitting in a pile on my bed. "Excellent, Arch-Magister," I answer, plastering on a big smile. "The trip was very comfortable, thank you."

"We've been over this before, child," she says sternly. "You may call me Elva."

"Forgive me, Elva," I reply, faltering only a little. "Is there anything I can do for you?"

Her eyebrows knit together as she stands there, studying me like I am some sort of puzzle to be solved. "You are probably wondering about the true nature of our mission. You should know that I have kept you in the dark for a reason."

I give her a curious look.

"I wanted to see if you possessed the virtue of patience," she says, continuing. "It is something that many initiates your age lack tremendously. I am pleased to inform you that you have passed my little test. We've been away from the city for three days and not once have you questioned or inquired any further into the details of why we have come here. Most impressive."

I shrug my shoulders. "I didn't think that it was my place to ask."

She smiles only briefly. "You're right, of course. It is not an initiate's place to question a member of the Circle, only to follow. Over the last few days, you've proven yourself capable of following orders. This is good, considering the delicate nature of our mission." She hesitates before going on, her expression uncertain for a split second before hardening into resolve. "I believe that I can trust you, my dear. How would you like to accompany me to a private meeting with the governor?"

My eyebrows shoot up in surprise, but I quickly reply, "I would be honored, Elva."

"Excellent," she responds curtly. "We are going to discuss recent events with him and the two rangers who are stationed in this backwater town. The rangers are an outdated organization, relics of an age when men still had reason to fear the world beyond the Arc. However, I have been told that they have become embroiled in the troubles we are here to investigate. No matter how backwards these woodsmen may appear, they are not without cunning. Stay alert and let *me* do all the talking. Understood?"

I nod.

"Good," she replies. "Let us depart." Turning on her heel, she strides out of the room without another word.

Being a reclusive bunch, I never imagined that I would have a chance to meet a ranger, much less sit in the same room and have a formal meeting with them. Are they the uncultured bush people that most mages think they are, or are they truly the legendary fighters from the stories? I suppose that only time will tell.

I take a deep breath before following her out into the hall. *This trip is becoming more interesting by the minute.* I shut my door and hurry to catch up with the Arch-Magister.

Time to prove yourself, Zara, I think, subconsciously touching the talisman hanging from my neck. *Don't mess this up.*

CHAPTER 7
OWYN

Elias and I wait with Governor Prior in his study, idling away the minutes before the mages come to meet with us. The governor paces anxiously between the window and his desk, muttering to himself and dabbing his forehead with his handkerchief every few seconds. *He looks even more nervous than usual,* I observe from my place on the far side of the room.

My master stands as still as a statue beside the governor's desk, his furrowed brow indicating that he is deep in thought.

Trying to cure my own uneasiness as we wait, I turn back to stare at the books lining the many shelves on the wall. *What does somebody do with this many books? Surely, he doesn't have the time to actually* read *them all.* The very thought of so much studying makes my head throb.

I look up sharply as someone raps on the door, and a servant holds it open to allow two mage women to step inside. The first one is older, probably middle-aged, and I recognize her as the sour-faced leader who met us outside of the manor. The second appears to be close to my age, pretty, with chestnut hair and soft brown eyes. She wears gray robes, not blue, and stands with perfect posture, her every movement practiced and poised.

Probably some spoiled rich girl, I think, watching her from across the room. *She's so fair, I doubt she's ever seen the sun. Light, this is probably the first time she's even left the city.*

My first reaction as the mages enter the study is to keep guarded. I draw my lips in a tight line as I study them. From all that I know about mages, they will use whatever means necessary to get what they want. They are tricksters, untrustworthy, and masters of manipulation.

Elias continues to look the way he always does, stoic and unbending.

The governor smiles timidly at the newcomers.

"Please," he says, simpering. He gestures for them to sit with an emphatic wave of his meaty hands. "Make yourselves at home. My servants are standing by to supply you with anything that you should desire."

They sit down on the cushy sofa near the hearth. Elias remains standing, so I decide to do the same. An uncomfortable silence ensues, and Prior shoots us a reproachful look.

"Arch-Magister Tyrande," he begins after a moment, practically groveling, "to what do we owe the pleasure of your company?"

The older mage, the one he referred to as the Arch-Magister, wastes no time in diving right into the discussion.

"Governor Prior," she says tersely, "the Conclave has received reports that there has been a disturbance in your province. Would you care to elaborate?"

The governor looks stricken. "A... disturbance, Magus? Well, yes, of course. One of our villages was attacked. But we only learned about it a couple of days ago. Truly, I was going to notify the capital as soon as we were able to gather a little more information—"

"Be at ease, governor," the Arch-Magister interrupts him coolly. "This is not a condemnation. I was merely trying to understand how much you know about the situation."

"Ah, yes of course." He relaxes a little bit, but still seems to be on edge. He produces his handkerchief again from out of his pocket and begins wiping his upper lip, a habit that has become somewhat amusing to me.

"One of my tax collectors returned from his rounds early. He was in shock and babbling that the village of Haven had been severely attacked. But his mind is now addled. That was pretty much the only information we were able to gather from him."

It's a wonder I'm not addled, I think to myself, *having seen what I saw.*

Not wanting to dwell too long on that thought, I find myself glancing again at the younger mage, observing how her slender body sits primly next to her much less attractive superior. She catches me looking at her, brown eyes making contact with mine, and I quickly look away, my cheeks flushing with heat.

"Have any attempts been made to look into the incident further?" Elva leans forward, her eyes intent on the sweaty governor.

Prior nods. "Yes, Magus. I sent the ranger, Elias, and his apprentice, Owyn, to investigate the situation. They only just returned to Forest Hill last night." He gestures over at us, all too eager to turn the mage's attention away from himself.

The Arch-Magister turns and regards Elias with the same intensity she had with the governor. She doesn't even bother to look at me. "Were you able to learn anything, ranger?"

Elias seems completely unfazed by her presence. "Yes, Magus. When we arrived at Haven, the village had been completely destroyed, its citizens murdered in brutal fashion. We managed to bury the dead before returning to deliver our report."

The younger mage can't hide her shock and brings her hand up to cover her mouth.

The Arch-Magister, however, does not seem surprised at all. Instead, she looks like she is mulling over my master's words, weighing their sincerity. Eventually, she stands up from her seat and turns to once more regard the governor.

"Then it is as we feared," she says ominously. "The first blow has been struck. The Nightingales have attacked the sovereign nation of Tarsynium in cold blood."

My expression twists into one of incredulity, and I am not the only one. Everyone in the room, with the exception of Elias, looks at the Arch-Magister as if she just proclaimed something completely ludicrous. If this attack *was* from the Nightingales, then that would mean all-out war. And there hasn't been a real war in Tarsyinium in centuries.

But the elder woman is not finished. She fixes both of us with a cold stare and continues, "You two will submit yourselves to a panel of mages for questioning. If there is even a hint that you have been collaborating with the enemy, then I will not hesitate to sentence both of you to exile."

What in the Eleven Hells? My jaw goes slack as I stare at her in shock. *We were out there at the governor's request! We have an alibi!* Bad blood has always existed between the rangers and the mages, but to threaten us with exile is more than severe... it's bloody *psychotic*.

Prior lets out a horrified gasp. "Exile, Magus? Doesn't that seem a bit... extreme?"

The Arch-Magister shakes her head. "The most secure measures are often considered extreme, governor. Especially, when it comes to traitors. If there is even a small chance that these rangers are involved, we must do what is necessary to protect the realm."

Elias takes a step forward, his broad frame appearing to loom over the mage woman even from the other side of the room. "My apprentice and I are *servants* of the realm," he says in a dangerously low voice. "We have pledged our entire lives to protecting Tarsynium from its enemies. We are not traitors."

"This is not a condemnation," she replies coolly, reiterating what she had told the governor. "We simply need to ensure that there are no connections between you and the rebel insurgents. If it is as you say, and both of you are innocent, then you have nothing to fear. I can assure you that my colleagues and I are honest upholders of justice. We speak with the authority of the Circle."

The thought of sitting before a panel of mages makes my skin crawl, even though she claims there is nothing to fear. *I would rather die than find myself working with the Nightingales, but how can I prove that to her?* Looking up, I make eye contact with the Arch-Magister. Her icy expression sends a shiver down my spine.

After a moment, Elias gives her a curt nod. "Fine," he growls, though he does not break away his intense stare. "We will submit ourselves to your interrogation."

"Excellent," she says evenly, as though she expected nothing less. She then turns her gaze back to the governor. "My ward and I will gather the other mages and reconvene shortly. Where, might I ask, would be the best place for us to go?"

Prior clears his throat. "The basement will probably do just fine, Magus. I'll have some of my house servants go down at once to clear a space for you."

The basement? More like the jail where the governor keeps his delinquents, I think bitterly.

She gives him a slight nod of the head and clasps her hands behind her. I watch as the young brown-haired mage stands and follows suit. "Thank you, governor. Rangers, I shall send for you when we are prepared to commence the hearing. Good day."

They stride out of the room without another word.

As soon as the door closes, I turn to Elias. "Master, you cannot seriously be considering submitting yourself to their questions. Mages cannot be trusted!"

"I will do what I have to do," Elias replies sternly. "And you will, too."

I try to rein in my emotions, but my words come spilling out in a frustrated jumble. "Me? Why? How can you...? We've done nothing wrong!"

He folds his arms in front of him and looks at me disapprovingly. "Because our fight is not with the mages. They are our allies, no matter how uncomfortable that makes us. Our duty is to the people of the kingdom. We must do everything we can to get to the bottom of whatever is going on, even if that means sitting before all those mages and answering their foolish questions."

I fight back the desire to curse in frustration.

Governor Prior grunts as he pushes himself up from his desk, breaking the silence that follows. "Well... I'd better see about preparing the basement. It won't do to keep the Arch-Magister waiting." He looks at us apologetically, but shrugs, knowing there is nothing he can do.

We follow him out of the room and make our way outside to see to the horses. There is no telling how long this will take, and our animals will need to be fed and watered. Right now, even for all the traveling we have done, I wish that I could climb back into the saddle and ride far away from here.

The thought of facing monsters in the woods sounds a thousand times more appealing than facing down the mages of the Conclave.

CHAPTER 8
ZARA

At the direction of the Arch-Magister, I make my way with the other ten mages to the basement of Governor Prior's mansion. They quietly whisper amongst themselves about the information just given to them from Elva, discussing the rangers and the events that transpired at the border village of Haven.

I pause for a moment before I reach the stairs to the basement and gaze out a small window at the beauty of Forest Hill.

Should I have agreed to come out here on this journey? I think to myself, not for the first time. *It's as if I'm caught up in something much bigger than myself—bigger than any initiate from the Academy.*

Forcing down my anxiety, I follow the blue-robed mages downstairs, already feeling like I am one too many steps behind them.

First, I find out that the Nightingale rebels have declared all-out war on the crown, destroying an entire village. Then I learn that two of the kingdom's rangers might be involved. The thought makes me shake my head in wonder. *How in the Light did I get wrapped up in all of this?*

As I descend into the wide chamber below the manor, everything starts to feel surreal. A vain hope remains that I will wake up in my dormitory, only worrying about being late for class, and all of this will have been nothing more than a strange dream.

Yet, as I step into the basement, I realize that this is all too real. My choices have led me here, and now I am being forced to live out those consequences, good or bad.

Oil lamps have been lit in sconces on the lower level, casting the stone walls in a flickering dim light. The stone floor is bare and dirty, and all along the walls are nondescript crates and sacks which are no doubt used for storage. In the furthest corner stand two iron wrought cells with thick bars and heavy chain locks.

I hope they don't have to use those, I think to myself nervously.

Servants have set up chairs in a wide semicircle in the middle of the room, all facing a lonely bench resting against one of the walls. We each take our seats and wait for Elva to arrive. Some of the mages talk with each other in hushed tones, but I sit quietly at the end, wringing my hands in my lap.

When the Arch-Magister finally enters the room, she takes her place in the middle of the semicircle, beckoning for the servants to bring in the ranger named Elias.

I watch as the powerfully-built man comes down the stairs, his eyes hard and his head held high. He is wearing his ranger cloak, but I notice that he no longer carries any weapons with him. Elva must have had them confiscated before his questioning.

Light, I think to myself as he sits down across from us. *He looks just as dangerous, even without that big knife of his.*

When he is seated, Elva stands and begins directing the meeting.

"Elias Keen," she declares authoritatively. "You have been brought before this body to testify of your investigation into the massacre at Haven. Is there anything you would like to say before we begin?"

Elias looks as if he is carved out of stone. "No," he replies evenly.

She sits. "My fellow mages," she says, looking down the line of chairs on either side of her. "You have all been informed about the circumstances surrounding this meeting. You may now ask your questions at will."

A heavyset mage by the name of Willus stands up, fixing the ranger with a watery-eyed stare. "Ranger Keen," he asks in a resonant voice, "would you recount what happened when you found the village of Haven two days past?"

Eyes straight ahead, Elias replies tersely, "It was as we had indicated to the Arch-Magister."

After it becomes apparent that no further explanation is forthcoming, Willus lets out a grunt. "Indulge us with the details, if you please."

"The village was sacked," Elias responds, biting off his words curtly. It is obvious that he resents the fact that he is being forced to sit here. "Everyone was killed. My apprentice and I found their bodies hanging from a nearby elder tree."

The entire village? Slaughtered? Hung? The details of the event are even worse than I had imagined. Suddenly, I start to feel very ill.

Willus, however, looks skeptical. "*All* of the villagers, Ranger Keen? Hung from a single tree?"

Elias returns the mage's skepticism with a look of pure iron. "Yes. We found no other inhabitants, dead or alive, around the village," he replies gruffly.

Another mage, a mousy woman named Torrie, speaks up. "Evoker Willus, an elder tree can grow to be three to four times larger than the common oak. If it was a small village, then such an occurrence is plausible."

This seems to placate Willus somewhat. But he is not done asking questions. Turning back to Elias, he continues. "And what, might I ask, did you and your apprentice do after you found the dead villagers?"

"We buried them," Elias replies coldly. "In the middle of the village green. Then we returned as quickly as we could to report our findings to the governor."

Willus nods and sits, and an elderly mage named Jarrius stands.

"Ranger Keen," he asks, "would you please share with us any evidence you were able to uncover at the scene of the crime?"

"Aside from the ruined buildings, there was not much evidence to be found," the ranger answers. "The bodies we buried from the tree did not have any visible wounds on them. I'm not sure why they did not put up a fight, but if there were additional victims, they must have been carried off. As of yet, I do not know who was behind the attack."

"I think the answer is patently obvious," Elva declares. "The attack was perpetrated by none other than the Nightingales." Many of the mages nod in agreement.

"I do not believe that is true," Elias responds. I am amazed at how blunt this man is while facing down an entire room of mages. Most people would break under such pressure.

There are more than a few mutters at the ranger's comment.

"And what makes you think the Nightingales are *not* involved?" Elva asks, raising one of her eyebrows. "I find it peculiar that you would be so eager to defend them."

"I am not defending them," Elias replies simply. "I am only stating the facts as I understand them. The Nightingales have always been content to raid granaries owned by the king or to rob tax collectors. They've never been in the business of executing entire communities of innocent people. Their war is with the king, not with his subjects."

I watch as Elva leans forward, regarding Elias like he is some sort of anomaly. "Curious," she says after a moment, before settling back in her chair. "I would think that a ranger would have more cause than anyone to hate the Nightingales. Aren't they the primary enemies of the Grand Lodge?"

"They are."

"Then why are you so eager to defend them?"

Elias chuckles humorlessly. "I am not defending them, Magus. I am merely stating the facts," he repeats himself as if the Arch-Magister had not heard him the first time. "Though the Nightingales are enemies of the crown, I refuse to use them as a scapegoat. Someone *did* murder those villagers. If we blame the wrong people merely because it is convenient, then the guilty parties will walk free. My oath as a ranger demands *true* justice."

Dead silence follows his bold statement, and for an instant, my jaw drops. The other mages shift uncomfortably as they all give Elva sidelong glances.

She draws her lips in a tight line of disapproval, her eyes seeming to bore into him. "Elias Keen, are you prepared to swear before this magical tribunal that you are in no way involved with the Nightingales or their attack on the village of Haven?"

"I swear," he says, without breaking eye contact.

"Very well." She stands up again and casts her eyes around the room. "All those who believe the ranger, Elias Keen, to be innocent in collaborating with the Nightingale rebels, please raise your right hand."

I raise my hand, along with most of the other mages in the circle, although not including the Arch-Magister.

After a quick count, Elva nods. "The majority stands with the accused. Ranger Keen, you are free to go. But know that we will be keeping an eye on you."

Without saying another word, Elias stands and exits the chamber, moving with an easy grace that reminds me of a cat. I can barely hear his footsteps as he strides past me.

A wiry servant girl pokes her head in the room, and Elva tells her to bring in the ranger's apprentice, Owyn.

We wait for a few minutes before the younger ranger enters the room and sits down on the bench. He seems like he is trying to be brave, but it is a poor front. He is clearly nervous.

Owyn glances around the room, looking like a cornered animal, but he sets his jaw and stares right at Elva, his expression stern. His eyes catch my attention, and I find myself studying them from across the room. They seem to belie his age, with hard lines at the corners that should not belong to one so young. There is intelligence there, but also sadness.

Those eyes have a dark, almost haunted look to them. I find myself wondering what things he has seen.

"Owyn Lund," Elva says, the quiet conversations in the room quickly dying down. "You have been brought before this body to testify of what you saw in Haven. Is there anything you would like to say before we begin?"

He shakes his head. "No, Magus." There is no defiance in his tone, only thinly veiled timidity.

Elva opens the inquiry as she had before, inviting her fellow mages to ask their questions.

Jarrius, who was interrupted before, stands again and begins speaking. "Apprentice Lund, in your own words what transpired in the village of Haven?"

Owyn takes a deep breath. "We had just returned from a hunting trip when Governor Prior told us about the attack at Haven. He wanted us to go investigate there as soon as possible so he could know exactly what was going on. My master and I left immediately, barely stopping to rest, but when we arrived..." his voice trails off as if reliving a traumatic memory. After a brief hesitation, he continues. "It was all gone."

He visibly shudders, then takes another breath, regaining his composure.

"It looked like Haven had been hit by an army. We found the villagers... even the children, hanging dead from the village's elder tree. It was as if they had been hung there specifically to be found."

Jarrius, unperturbed by Owyn's story, continues with his questioning. "And what did you and your master do next, Ranger Lund?"

"We buried them," he says, voice barely above a whisper.

It is clear that recounting this tale is dredging up some painful memories for him. As I sit here, I cannot help but feel sorry for him.

Next, a plain woman stands. I cannot remember her name.

"You are very young, Apprentice Lund, but that still does not put you above suspicion. To the best of your knowledge, have you or your master ever conspired with the rebels who call themselves the Nightingales?"

Owyn's eyes widen in shock. "No, Magus. Never. I swear it!"

"This is a safe place, child," she says, pressing the point. "You may speak out against Ranger Keen without any repercussions if he is in any way involved."

It could be my imagination, but for a split second, I think I see a flash of anger in his eyes.

"No," he says firmly. "Elias is a great man who follows his duties above all else. There is no way that he is involved in any of this."

The plain woman sits down as Elva speaks up. "Bold words coming from one so young." She sounds vaguely impressed. "However, I would like to echo my associate's words. This is a safe environment. You may speak freely here. Other than what you have already told us about the village of Haven, did anything else out of the ordinary transpire in the last few days that you would like for us to know?"

I watch as Owyn seems to wrestle with something, an internal struggle about whether or not he should share what's troubling him. I assume that Elva can sense it as well.

"I swear as the Arch-Magister of the Circle," she presses gently, "that your words will have no consequences in this room." I can tell that she is trying to sound soothing, but it comes off as patronizing.

Owyn clears his throat. "You promise not to tell my master?"

Elva nods. "I promise."

"Alright," he says, resigned. "I... may have seen something in the woods while my master and I were out hunting. Before we went to Haven."

Collectively the mages lean forward, hanging on every word as he speaks.

He continues. "I had just felled a stag with my bow, when we were making our way back to Forest Hill. We stumbled upon something in the woods, a clearing full of deer. Only, the deer had all been killed. Torn apart. A meadow full of body parts that had been left out to rot in the sun."

I lean forward as well, suddenly very intrigued by the young man's story.

"There were no carrion eaters in the clearing, and we could not locate any visible tracks or signs of struggle. Elias thought that it must have been a rabid animal. Maybe a wolf or a cougar. He left to go mark the spot on his map, and that's when I saw it. Something lurking in the trees."

"What did you see?" Willus asks, stroking his beard thoughtfully.

"A demon," he says after a brief hesitation, and I can feel my blood run cold.

For a moment, everyone falls completely silent, as if unsure they heard him correctly. Then, the room bursts into laughter, the mages chuckling loudly at the apprentice's claim. Owyn cringes visibly, his eyes dropping to the floor as his cheeks begin to flush. The only two mages not laughing are myself and Arch-Magister Tyrande, whose expression has grown hard as stone.

"Can you describe this creature?" she asks over the sound of her colleagues' laughter, her eyes narrowing.

Owyn's flush deepens to crimson. "It was large and moved on all fours like a bear, only it was not a bear. It moved like a mountain lion and had a head like a great wolf. It had huge claws and glowing red eyes, and its fur was as black as pitch." He seems ashamed for having even brought it up. "I know it sounds crazy, but I've seen every predator in the Emberwood, and this thing did not look like any of them."

The laughter dies down as Elva stands, her face as serious as I have ever seen it. She silences the last of the snickering with a cutting motion of her hand. "All those who believe the ranger,

Owyn Lund, to be innocent in collaborating with the Nightingale rebels, please raise your right hand."

Everyone raises their hands.

"You are free to go, Apprentice Lund," Elva says, lowering her arm. "But a word of caution for you. Claiming that you have seen a demon in Tarsynium is a serious offense. If any citizens were to believe your story, it could cause a panic that could severely weaken the kingdom and give the rebels an opportunity to seize power. I admonish you to never bring this up again, to anyone. Your ability to speak freely ends when you leave this room. Is that understood?"

Owyn nods, looking even more crestfallen than before.

"Excellent," Elva says. "You are dismissed."

CHAPTER 9
OWYN

As I step out of the interrogation room, I feel like a complete fool. *Why in the Eleven Hells did I bring up the demon? I should never have even mentioned that part. Light, I'm such an idiot.*

I pass several servants on my way up the stairs, and I rush by them, intent on getting out of there as fast as possible. When I step out into the main hall, though, I find Elias waiting for me with my weapons in-hand. He gives me my bow and quiver, then hands over my hatchet.

The grip feels good in my palm as I accept it, the grain of the wood familiar to my fingers. I quickly slide the shaft into my belt loop and pointedly avoid making eye contact with him.

"How did it go?" he asks quietly after a moment.

"Aside from me making a fool of myself, I'd say it went well," I reply, glancing up and forcing a smile.

He nods. "Mages can have that effect on people. Especially ones like the Arch-Magister. The more you deal with them, the less that will happen as you grow used to their methods."

We leave the governor's manor without so much as a word to anyone else, making our way down the steps and toward our stabled horses.

"I brought up the demon during their interrogation," I find myself quick to admit as I lead my horse out by the reins.

He regards me silently for a moment, then asks, "How did that go?"

I sigh. "About as well as you might expect. They laughed at me and told me to never speak about it again."

Elias grunts. "That sounds about right."

We mount up and begin riding down the hill. The cool wind feels good on my still-flushed face. After our debacle with the mages, I am glad to be getting far away from the governor's stuffy manor.

It is not long before we reach the town's inn. The sights and smells are as familiar to me as coming home. As we approach the wooden two-story building, my nostrils fill with the scent of cooking meat, which causes my mouth to water.

We tether the horses in a stall and make sure that they have plenty of feed and water before making our way to the front door.

I pause, however, before going up the steps.

"What's wrong?" Elias asks, turning to look inquiringly at me.

"There's still some daylight left," I reply after a brief hesitation. My stomach rumbles, but I ignore it. "I think I'm going to take some time and train for a bit. I'll come back later for supper."

Elias eyes me for a moment before finally nodding and heading inside alone. Warmth and the sounds of laughter pour out as he opens the door, but instead of following him, I make my way around to the back of the inn where a private yard has been carved into the hillside. It is well-manicured and covered in thick, green grass, complete with a wooden practice dummy and several bales of hay with canvas targets. Many of the local hunters use this area to practice with the bow, but lately Elias and I have used it for combat training.

I set down my pack and walk over to the practice dummy. It is a replica of a man holding a mock sword and shield. Blowing out a breath, I assume a fighting position, widening my stance and balancing on the balls of my feet. Next, I pull out my hatchet and begin hacking away at the dummy, practicing different techniques with heavy strokes.

Thunk.

The blade sinks into the wood with a dull thud.

Thunk.

I pull it out and attack again in quick succession.

Thunk. Thunk.

It feels good to vent my frustrations on the practice dummy. The exertion works my muscles and helps me to relieve the irritation that has been building up inside.

Curse those arrogant mages, I think, continuing to train with my hatchet. *Are they so confident in their magic that they can't entertain the possibility of a demon getting through the Arc?*

Thunk.

I know what I saw. That creature was real... no matter what anyone else says.

Thunk.

As I hack at the dummy, my thoughts turn to the mangled deer, and then to the slaughtered villagers: men, women, and children, hanging like rag dolls from the elder tree. My heart clenches at the memory, a fierce anger bubbling up within me. I channel the anger, the fears and anxieties, and the doubts I feel into the repetitive motions of my strokes, using it as fuel for my training.

My attacks take on a new intensity. I savagely chop at the wood until my muscles burn, and my hatchet blade begins to grow dull.

Panting, I step back and examine the dummy. I realize that I have chipped and gouged it beyond recognition.

Light, I'm going to have to carve a new one pretty soon.

I hang my hatchet on my belt and go to grab my bow. Pulling an arrow from the quiver on the ground, I nock it to the string. I take a few steps back, pull, and aim down the shaft, drawing a bead on the dummy's chopped-up head.

Letting out a breath, I loose the arrow, launching it across the field in the blink of an eye. It thuds right into the middle of what's left of the wooden man's head.

The demon, the village, the mages... all of this is connected somehow. It has to be. But why is it that I am the only one willing to consider other possibilities? Elias said it himself. The Nightingales, Light curse them, are not involved. If it isn't them, then who killed those villagers?

I shoot another arrow, this time hitting the dummy directly in the heart, then I shoot a third, hitting it in the torso.

The older mage woman, the Arch-Magister, didn't laugh at me. In fact, she seemed angry when I brought up the demon. What would make her react in such a way?

Picking up another arrow, I nock it and accidentally nick myself on the knuckle with the broadhead, drawing blood. I curse and throw the arrow to the ground, rage once again welling up inside my chest.

None of this is fair! None of it! All I want to do is help, but no one will believe my story.

I discard my bow and pull out my hatchet once more, letting out a scream of frustration as I throw it at the dummy. It hits it square in the forehead, the blade biting deep into the wood. When my vision clears, I notice something strange about the last arrow I shot.

As I jog up to the dummy, my fury is replaced with amazement at what I managed to do. Apparently, I had thrown the hatchet perfectly enough to cleave the arrow in two.

Despite myself, a small self-satisfied smile crosses my face when I pull the hatchet out, and the two halves of the arrow fall lightly to the grass.

Not bad for an apprentice.

Abruptly, my stomach growls, reminding me that I am famished. Giving one final look at the mangled dummy, I bend down and pick up my gear. I unstring my bow and make my way back around to the front door of the inn, feeling slightly better than I had before. My weapons practice has done much to temper my anger, but I still find myself troubled by these recent events.

Something strange is definitely afoot, and I'm not sure Elias and I are equipped to handle it.

Pushing open the door, I enter the common room of the inn. It is a wide room filled with tables and glowing candlelight and all the sounds, smells, and sights associated with most taverns. There is a fire roaring in the hearth and someone strumming a lute in the far corner. Men play dice and drink, laughing while serving girls bring them plates of food and mugs of ale from behind the bar.

Many of them glance up at me as I step inside, but quickly return to their conversations, recognizing me as the ranger's apprentice. If any had heard me yelling outside, they give no indication of it now.

I find Elias sitting alone at a table on the far side of the room, hunched over a bowl of stew. Picking my way through the common room as I move to sit next to him, I overhear the conversations buzzing around me.

"What do you think those mages are doing sniffing around here?"

"Didn't you hear? They've come to demand more taxes for the capital."

"That's not what I heard. I heard that they're here to put down a rebellion started by the Nightingales in the north."

"Damn Nightingales. Traitors and charlatans, all of them."

Their voices fade from earshot as I approach Elias' table. I take my seat after setting my pack down on the floor. "How's the stew?" I ask, waving at a serving girl to bring me some food.

Elias grunts as he shovels a spoonful of beef into his mouth.

"It smells good," I say, leaning back in my chair. *Although,* I think wryly, *just about anything smells good after weeks of living on venison and dry bread.*

He swallows and fixes me with one of his emotionless stares. "How was training?"

I shrug. "I'll probably need to sharpen my axe tonight."

His lips quirk into a half-smile. "That sounds familiar."

Mrs. Ellis, the innkeeper's wife, comes over with a steaming bowl in one hand and a pewter mug in the other. She is a large women, nearly as round as she is tall, with an infectious smile and a messy bun of graying brown hair atop her head. "Here you are, dear," she says, placing both the bowl and the mug in front of me. "Beef stew and your favorite spiced wine, just the way you like it."

I grin at her appreciatively. "Thank you. This looks good."

"It tastes even better," she replies with a wink. "Just remember to chew your food. Enjoy." With that, she makes her way back to the kitchen, her movements surprisingly agile for one of her size.

I take a long pull on the wine, savoring the flavor before turning my attention to the stew. Elias stares at me from across the table, his eyes unreadable.

"I've been thinking," he says quietly as I plunge my spoon into the broth. "Those mages do have something of a point."

I pause before taking the first bite and give him a questioning look. "What do you mean?"

"Our oath states that our job is to protect the people of Tarsynium. Inciting irrational panic is the opposite of that. It would undoubtedly disturb the peace and give the Nightingales the upper hand in their rebellion." He says it bluntly, with all the expression of a boulder.

Immediately, my heart sinks. "You don't want me to talk about the demon anymore."

He shakes his head. "No, I don't. At least not until we have more information about what we are dealing with. I'm not saying you were in the wrong. I'm just saying that where the mages are concerned, we should tread carefully. Their authority supersedes our own in these kinds of situations, and the Arch-Magister is known for her ruthlessness. It would not be wise to make an enemy out of her."

I nod, but inside I can't help but feel dejected. *I don't understand why he won't believe what I saw in the woods. How can I prove to him that there was really something there?* I push these troublesome thoughts out of my mind. There's no point in dwelling on things outside of my control. *If nobody is going to believe me, then I will just have to find a way to prove that I'm telling the truth.*

Glancing down, I lean forward and begin digging into my stew, letting the matter drop.

CHAPTER 10
ZARA

A ball of magefyre floats in the air beside my head, smoldering with a soft blue light that casts long shadows across my room. I sit cross-legged on the lumpy bed, engrossed in my book on demonology, the day growing late outside my room's only window.

Owyn's testimony stuck with me for some reason, igniting my curiosity like a struck match. He seemed so earnest, like he genuinely believed he had seen a demon.

He had not deserved to be mocked the way he was.

I feel a twinge of remorse as I turn the page, empathizing for a moment with the haunted-looking ranger's apprentice. *I should have said something,* I think to myself glumly. *I should have stood up for him in some way.* I shake my head, trying to rid the guilt from my mind. Touching my talisman, I channel more source energy in order to make the magefyre brighter.

Intervening during the inquisition would have been very stupid. It would have turned the entire group of mages against me, and likely drawn the ire of the Arch-Magister herself, something I'm determined not to do.

You can't be raised to full mage if you go against the will of the Circle, Zara.

I turn my attention back to the archaic book sitting in front of me.

The chapter before me describes the different species of demons identified in ancient times, with detailed information about their appearances, temperament, and abilities. I am amazed by how diverse and terrifying the R'Laar horde was. The garish illustrations of demons leer up at me from the book and cause my imagination to run wild.

I scan the pages for anything matching the description Owyn had given during his questioning. The one constant amongst the demons is their fiery red eyes. Other than that, they all vary wildly in appearance. Some are gargantuan horned monsters wreathed in flame and bedecked with heavy armor. Others are spindly beasts with wings and barbed tails. Page after page depicts a different monstrosity that looks as if it had come straight out of a nightmare, but none of them match the description I am looking for.

Perhaps it was *merely his imagination,* I think, fighting back a yawn. *It must be awfully dull being a ranger, living out in the woods without anything to read.*

Just when I am about to give up and close the book, an image catches my eye and my breath sticks in my throat.

I turn the page back and see a picture of a beast that looks lupine in nature. Its fur is sleek and black, and it has the long snout of a wolf, complete with jagged and uneven teeth. The most striking feature of all, however, is the blade-like claws adorning each of its four feet. Underneath the image is written the words:

Genus: Shadowling
Species: Darkhound

My eyes glance over to the full description on the opposite page, deciphering the ancient script, I read the words aloud:

Of all the shadowlings used by the R'Laar,
the darkhound was widely believed to be among
the fiercest. The greater demons often kept them as

pets and trained them to be as vicious as possible. With keen senses and otherworldly strength, the darkhound was an apex hunter that was known to kill for sport, seeking the thrill of the hunt. Despite their great size, they could blend in incredibly well with shadows. They did not leave any footprints in their wake, which made them difficult to track, their infernal magic granting them advantages unseen in the natural world. Before the Doom, the R'Laar would often send forth their darkhounds as scouts to eliminate human sentries and make the way clear for their armies to advance unmolested.

Beneath that paragraph, there is a smaller description written in a hastily scrawled hand. I read on as a shiver runs down my spine.

Though shadowlings were considered by historians to be the lesser of the demonic races, darkhounds displayed an intelligence that set them apart from their more bestial cousins. The Light should be praised that man no longer needs fear these terrible beasts.

A knock at my door causes me to jump, and I let out a pathetic-sounding squeak. Closing the book with a snap, I shove it under my pillow and bid them to enter.

Torrie, the mousy mage who has spoken to me more than most, pokes her head into the room. "I'm sorry," she says softly. "I did not mean to frighten you, child. I just wanted to let you know that supper is being served downstairs in the kitchen."

I give her a wan smile. "Thank you, Magus. I will be down shortly."

She nods and closes the door behind her, leaving me alone once more.

Closing my eyes, I take in a deep breath and exhale through my nose. *Coming on this trip has certainly made me much jumpier.* I glance over at my pillow and cannot help but shiver again. *That creature, that darkhound, seems awfully similar to what Owyn described earlier today. Could it be that he was telling the truth?*

Troubled by the thought, I hop off my bed and make my way to the door, letting my little ball of magefyre dissipate behind me.

The wooden stairs creak beneath my footsteps as I descend to the first floor, using the smells of cooked meats and freshly-baked bread to guide me to the kitchen. When I arrive, I find that the dining room is completely full. Mages, servants, and the governor's family all gather around the tables of food, chatting and eating, reminding me of every awkward party I have ever attended in my life.

Looking down, I also realize that I have come to the gathering a little underdressed.

Everyone seems to be wearing their finest apparel, the mages in their traditional robes and the others in neatly pressed tunics and dresses. My comfortable night clothes, both shapeless and unflatteringly plain, make me feel like a fish out of water as I timidly walk into the wide room.

Luckily, nobody seems to notice my presence, and I decide to use that fact to my advantage. To the mages, I am just an initiate. To the servants and the governor's family, I am part of the magical delegation, and thus above reproach. It is a wonderfully unobtrusive position to be in, allowing me to remain in obscurity even when surrounded by so many people.

This puts my mind at ease as I approach one of the tables and pick up a plate. Nobody says a word as I fill it with chicken, potatoes, bread, and more sweets than I've ever had available to me at the Academy.

Once finished, I gaze hungrily down at the mountain of food piled on my plate and smile.

Not wanting to engage in any conversations, I quickly exit the kitchen and begin making my way back up the stairs to my room. As I walk down the hall, however, I see light shining through a door that stands ajar. Peeking inside, I catch a glimpse of Arch-Magister Tyrande sitting behind a desk, looking intently down at something.

Against my better judgment, I set my dinner down on an empty shelf and knock gently on the door frame.

"Enter," Elva answers tersely.

I slip inside and close the door behind me.

"Good evening, Elva," I say, giving her a slight curtsey.

She looks up from a sheaf of papers, eyes slightly narrowing in annoyance. "Good evening, Zara. Are you on your way to dinner?" Though her words are cordial, I can sense a layer of ice beneath them. To make matters worse, she seems to notice the clothes I am wearing, and her lips purse disapprovingly.

I try not to let my discomfort show. "I'm actually going back up to my room. But I wanted to ask you a question—if you have a moment."

Elva sighs and sets down her papers, leaning back in her chair. "Of course," she replies, her annoyance becoming even more apparent.

"Why did you tell that boy to never mention the demon he saw in the woods? I understand that we do not want to cause panic among the general population—that would be terrible—but what if he was telling the truth? What if he really *did* see a demon on this side of the Arc? Wouldn't it be wise for us to at least investigate the situation further before we pass judgment on him?"

The words, spoken slowly at first, end up coming out in a breathless rush. I wince, feeling my cheeks redden, and silently curse myself for even coming in here in the first place. *Light, I'm making it seem like I think she was wrong.*

Elva regards me in silence for an eternal minute, which causes me to squirm even more. Finally, she speaks, her voice measured but surprisingly patient.

"Your interest in this matter is surprising to me, initiate, though I suppose that it is not unwarranted. I did, after all, choose to bring you along on this mission because of your inquisitive nature. That being said, it is important for you to understand that the Arc of Radiance is the greatest magical achievement that has ever been built by mortal hands."

I give her a confused look. "Magus?"

"The Arc," she says, speaking slowly like one would speak to an ignorant child, "is perfect. There is no artifice that exists in Tarsynium today that even comes close to equaling it. Additionally, the energy output from the Heart of Light is constantly being monitored by the best and brightest mages in the Conclave. *If a demon managed to get through the Arc, we would know immediately, I assure you.*"

I can feel my cheeks begin to flush, and her expression softens somewhat. "There is still much that you do not understand about this world, Zara. And that ranger boy is no different. Imagine the horrors he has been subject to over the past few days. Isn't it more likely that the monster he claimed to see was conjured up by his own imagination?"

Then how did he manage to perfectly describe the shadowling in my book? I think to myself but do not voice my opinion. Merely nodding, I say, "Yes, Magus."

"Call me Elva, dear," she urges gently, compassion softening the hard edges of her voice. "Please, let us put this unpleasant matter behind us. You would be better served focusing your efforts elsewhere. Try learning what you can from the other mages here with us. Every single one of them is exceptionally talented and may be receptive to teaching you if you make the effort to reach out to them."

"Of course, Elva. Thank you for listening."

Placated, she leans forward and picks her papers back up. "Questions are never bad, child. Only the ones that you have to ask twice."

I say goodbye and close the door behind me, almost forgetting to pick up my plate of food before heading upstairs.

Once inside my room, I summon another globe of magefyre to give me light as I begin eating. Sitting quietly on my bed, I sort through my chaotic thoughts.

She brings up a good point. If the Heart of Light was failing, wouldn't the mages already know about it? Still, I can't help but feel like we are missing something. Owyn seems to have seen a darkhound, whether he knows it or not. Perhaps there is more to his story than he's letting on.

As I mechanically chew a slice of chicken, I resolve to speak with the ranger's apprentice as soon as an opportunity presents itself. If anyone can shed more light on this mystery, he can.

Demons and conspiracies continue to plague my mind and prevent me from enjoying the meal that earlier I had been so excited to eat.

CHAPTER 11
OWYN

Metal clashes against metal as cries of alarm from outside carry up to my room, shaking me from the depths of sleep and forcing me into sudden wakefulness.

My eyes snap open, and I sit bolt upright, bleary eyes adjusting to the torchlight filtering in through my bedroom window. Muffled shouts and curses rise from the first floor, and it looks as if dawn is still several hours away, judging by the darkness that surrounds me.

A pounding at my door shakes me from my sleepy stupor, and I half-jump, half-fall out of the bed, grabbing for my hatchet on my bedside table. I hold it warily in front of me, creeping up to the source of the disturbance.

Cautiously undoing the latch, I open the door a crack and peek out into the hall.

Elias stands in the shadowed corridor like a phantom, fully dressed in his leather armor and ranger cloak and brandishing his long belt knife. He glances at my shirtless body, then barks at me to get moving. "The inn is under attack," he bellows urgently. "Get dressed. Now!"

I spring into action, all sleepiness instantly leaving me. Rummaging through my clothes, I pull a shirt over my head and begin lacing up my boots, my fingers fumbling in the dark. As I listen to the shouting coming from outside and below, I can't help but wonder what in the Hells is going on.

Who's attacking the inn? I think to myself, as I finish tying my boots. *Are they the same people who destroyed Haven?*

Could they be coming after me?

Throwing my cloak around my shoulders, I go out into the hall and follow Elias down the stairs. In the common room, we find the innkeeper, James Ellis, standing nervously by the bar, a frying pan clutched in a meaty fist. A handful of farmers, rough men with tanned skin, are in the process of overturning tables, apparently trying to barricade the door and windows.

"What's going on?" Elias asks harshly, striding up to one of the windows and peaking outside. Over his shoulder, I can see movement on the road in front of the inn.

"I don't know, Ranger Keen," James replies, voice quavering. He looks pale and shaken, as if on the verge of fainting. "One of the lads who helps me tend the bar came in from taking a piss with an arrow stuck in his gut. He said something about strange folk before collapsing on the floor."

That's when I notice blood smeared on the floorboards near the entryway.

"Whoever they are, they're shooting at anyone who goes outside," he explains. "And now it looks like they are trying to force their way in!"

Just then, one of the glass windows shatters, and a fist-sized rock thuds noisily into the common room. A second later, a farmer cries out in pain, falling to his knees and clutching his shoulder where the feathered shaft of an arrow is sticking out.

"Stay away from the windows!" Elias orders. Sheathing his belt knife, he unslings his bow from his shoulder. "Keep focused on barricading the doors!" He turns to James and lowers his voice. "Make sure nobody gets in through the back. A keg wedged in front of the door should do the trick."

The innkeeper nods and scampers off, keeping his head down as more arrows fly in through the window.

I silently berate myself for not coming downstairs more prepared. My own bow is up in my bedroom, unstrung and useless, so I decide to make myself handy elsewhere. I help a burly man with a mustache push a table up against the front door in hopes of preventing anyone from busting their way in.

Elias moves with the speed of a viper and crouches beneath the windowsill, pulling out an arrow and nocking it in one fluid motion. He pauses for a brief moment before standing up, then quickly draws, sights, and looses, before crouching back down.

There is a sound like an arrow striking flesh—though, oddly, it is not accompanied by a cry of pain.

"Arm yourselves with anything you can find," he says to the handful of farmers hiding around the common room. "It looks like they have some sort of battering ram. Prepare for a fight."

Grumbling and cursing, the folks from Forest Hill, more accustomed to using a plow than a sword, begin searching for anything they can use as weapons. They grab cutlery from the kitchen, a broken leg from a chair, and I even see one man arm himself with a partially-broken bottle.

As they shuffle around the common room, I can hear a loud crashing sound coming from the front door. It sounds like someone is already taking the battering ram to it, hitting it hard with a steady *bang... bang... bang.*

Every so often, Elias pops up from his cover under the window and fires off an arrow, yet none of his shots elicit screams of pain.

I grip the handle of my hatchet tightly, waiting behind an upturned table not far from the door. I can see long cracks starting to form in the wood with each successive *bang.*

It will not hold for much longer.

My palms begin to sweat as butterflies dance in my stomach, my entire mouth becoming bone-dry. *This is what I have been training for*, I tell myself, even as doubts whisper in the back of my mind: *Hitting practice dummies is one thing... using my hatchet to harm another person is something else entirely. Do I have what it takes to kill?*

The farmers, five in total, begin to gather around me, their makeshift weapons held uncertainly in hand as the door begins to buckle.

Elias sets down his bow and draws his belt knife, coming to stand with the rest of us.

"Spread out when the door comes down," he growls. "I don't want any of us getting hurt by accident. Choose your target and take them down. Then move on to the next one. Don't stop until they're all dead."

Time seems to stand still for a moment as I take a deep breath to calm my nerves. To my right and left, the farmers who had just come to the inn to relax after a long day's work, look just as anxious as I do. Some of them mutter silent prayers, while others stand nervously drenched in sweat. A single thought fills me with dread.

These are no warriors. This is going to be a slaughter.

As the door bursts open, time speeds up. Splinters shower the floor, and wavering torchlight floods the common room. We hear the thundering footsteps of many men on the other side.

"Spread out!" Elias shouts, brandishing his knife. "Hold your ground! Do not let them past the threshold!"

I suck in a breath as the first of the attackers rush inside. They come one, two, then three at a time, clamoring over the broken door and scrambling toward us like a mob of blade-wielding shadows.

They all wear midnight-colored cloaks that cover armor of boiled leather and mail. Carrying swords, clubs, and axes, they charge at us with reckless abandon.

A man wielding a thick blade that looks like a meat cleaver rushes at Elias, his weapon raised high. He slashes down with a vicious chop, but Elias sidesteps him easily. As the man's attack swishes past him, he lashes out with his knife, slicing the man across the throat and sending him tumbling to the ground. He coolly moves on to his next opponent, blood dripping from his blade.

A heavy-shouldered brute wearing a leather cap runs his sword through the farmer to my right, and two of the farmers to my left gang up on a man carrying a club punctured by several nails, pushing him back on his heels.

I brace myself as one of the attackers spots me and begins running toward me, a longsword gripped in both of his hands.

Raising my hatchet in defense, I stand with my feet shoulder-width apart and wait for his attacks to come. As he draws near, I get a good look at his face, and again, time seems to stand still. He is unshaven and wild-looking with greasy tangled locks framing his face. His eyes, strangely glassy, lock onto mine as he charges. I fill with fear; those are not the eyes of a man in control.

Those are the eyes of a madman.

I duck as he takes a swing at me with his sword, the gleaming blade whistling as it passes over my head. I quickly spot an opening as his twisting motion throws him off-balance, and I instinctively move in to exploit it. Using my hatchet like a hammer, I strike him above the knee and feel the blade bite deeply into his leg.

He doesn't react to the pain; instead, he kicks at me and pushes me away. As I yank the hatchet from his flesh, I am sprayed with warm blood. For a split second, he looks down at the wound, then back up at me, his face a grim, blank mask.

The wound doesn't even seem to impede his reactions.

Lifting his sword, he comes at me again, slower this time because of his leg, swinging like a lumberjack felling a tree.

I jump backwards, the blade narrowly missing my chest. All around me there are sounds of combat and people screaming; however, I am too engrossed in my own fight to pay close attention to my allies.

The man swipes again, then tries to stab me with a clumsy thrust. I manage to bat his sword away with the flat of my hatchet before I rush in, acting on instinct. Grabbing the collar of his leather armor, I yank downward as hard as I can.

His wounded leg buckles under the pressure, and he falls down, landing hard on his knees. I raise my hatchet high for the killing blow, then bring it down in one swift chopping motion.

The last thing I notice before burying my axe in his neck are his wild, battle-crazed eyes staring up at me, reminding me of a rabid animal as it waits to be put down. Something strange swirls in those eyes, like a milky film of some kind, but I am unable to look for more than a split second. As I strike him, his eyelids flutter, and all I can see is red. His body goes rigid for an instant and then quickly becomes limp.

Grunting, I pull my father's hatchet from the man's neck, my ears ringing loudly in my skull. I feel sick, nausea twisting my stomach, and it seems like my chest has constricted, making it hard to breathe.

I have just killed somebody, I think, horrified. *His life is over because of me.* Deep down, I know that I was merely defending myself—that it was done in self-defense. But the thought of having killed a living, breathing soul still clings to my soul like hot tar. *His blood is on my hands.*

More attackers come in through the shattered doorway, and I do not have the luxury of mourning over the man I have just killed. Elias and the others are still engaged and on the verge of being overwhelmed.

I realize that I must continue on, or these townspeople will all die.

Seeing a gnarled old farmer fighting with a man with a mace, I come in from the side and hack at his exposed flank. He falters, and the farmer manages to crack him over the head with his crude table leg cudgel.

Nodding at the old man, I turn just as an attacker with two daggers tries to stab me. I let out a shout of alarm and barely manage to block his attack with the shaft of my hatchet.

He begins to press me, stabbing and slicing with such speed that I can hardly keep up. A brief look at his face shows me the same detached eyes I had seen in the man with the sword.

I dodge and weave, trying desperately to avoid being shredded by the man's wicked-looking knives. Abruptly, I slip on something wet, and one of his daggers slices me across the arm.

White hot pain lances up to my shoulder, and I gasp, throwing myself out of my attacker's reach so I can regain my balance. It feels like the cut went straight to the bone. Raising my hatchet in my other hand, I grimace and feebly wait for him to approach.

He immediately presses his advantage, coming after me with a face as blank as a sheet of parchment. He locks his blade against my hatchet and lifts his other knife for the killing blow.

This is it, I think to myself, squeezing my eyes shut. *This is how I die.*

But death doesn't come. I feel the tension on my locked weapon ease slightly, and I open one eye to investigate. The man's attention is no longer on me, instead looking down at the point of a knife sticking out of his chest, puncturing his leather armor.

His body slumps forward a second later, and I see Elias standing behind him, pulling his knife free from his back.

My master gives me a quick nod, then turns around to jump back into the fray.

I look around, feeling numb, and take in the blood-soaked carnage of the inn's common room. Four of the six farmers are down as well as about a dozen of the men in black. Their bodies litter the floor like passed out drunks, lying still as statues. Elias and the last two farmers are badly outnumbered, and still more men are pouring through the doorway, weapons in hand.

"It's impossible," I find myself muttering, my hatchet hanging loosely from my nerveless fingers. "We cannot win."

Another one of the farmers goes down, his head cleaved cleanly from forehead to chin by a battle-axe.

Elias and the last remaining farmer fall back to my position, bloodied and breathing heavily from exertion. We watch as dozens of the mad-eyed attackers move toward us, their faces empty, impassive masks.

"*We are the watchers in the woods, the arrows in the darkness,*" Elias says quietly, quoting from the ranger's oath. I join in hoarsely. "*None shall pass by while we stand guard.*" He glances at me and gives me a solemn nod, bringing his knife up to a fighting position. "*Until my dying breath.*"

I nod back, tightening my grip on my hatchet.

Just as the mob of black-cloaked warriors begins to fall upon us, a blazing beam of brilliant blue light bursts through the doorway and the broken windows, bathing us all in its glow. The advancing men all stumble and momentarily cease their attack as they look over their shoulders, trying to discern the source of the light.

Without warning, their bodies burst into flames.

One by one, the men, as if doused in oil and lit with a match, are engulfed in blue fire, their skin sizzling and popping. I watch them stand there like human torches, yet they do not react to the pain. Some try vainly to attack the light with their swords, before they are all sent sprawling back by unseen blasts of energy.

It isn't long before the unstoppable band of mysterious fighters is reduced to ash, and we are left alone, standing stunned in the back of the ruined common room.

When the light fades, it takes a moment for my eyes to adjust to the darkness.

I blink in surprise, instantly recognizing the men and women standing in the entryway of the inn. All of them wear blue robes and hold balls of magefyre in their hands.

CHAPTER 12
ZARA

Nightingales *attacked* the inn?"

Elva nods, gesturing soberly down the hill to a line of bodies laid out on the grass outside of the long wooden building. It is a grisly sight, but I force myself to look at them, to take in the scene and analyze it without emotion.

That's what it means to be a true mage.

This morning, I had awoken to a great commotion, the entire town seemingly turned on its head. The governor and his staff were frantically trying to uncover the details of what had happened at the inn last night, and the mages were doing what they could to take control of the situation and calm everyone down.

Apparently, from what I was able to glean from the bits of conversation I managed to overhear, a large group of men in black cloaks attacked the inn where the two rangers were staying, killing several patrons in the process. Luckily, a group of mages heard what was going on and managed to intervene, saving the rangers and a few others.

None of the attackers had survived.

Most of their bodies had been reduced to ash by the magefyre, but those who had fallen before the mages arrived were laid outside for proper examination.

As Elva and I walk down the hill toward the inn, she fills me in on the rest of the details.

"It is fortunate that we arrived when we did," she says as we walk. "It appears that the Emberwood has a full rebellion on its hands. Who knows what would have happened if we were not here to help them?"

I am still bewildered by the whole situation. *A rebellion? Here?* I have heard of riots sometimes breaking out in Tarsys from time to time, but they were always few and far between. *Why start a rebellion here, on the very borders of society?* This area is, after all, one of the most peaceful parts of the kingdom.

As we approach the bodies, I can feel my stomach start to writhe. Dead things always make me feel queasy, especially when real people are involved. Anatomy lessons at the Academy scarred me when I was fifteen, and the cadavers haunt my dreams even to this day.

Taking a deep breath, I set my jaw and follow Elva to the first corpse in the row, forcing a dispassionate look.

It is a bearded man with long tangled hair, lying prone on his back with his arms by his sides. There is a horrendous wound in the side of his neck, and his eyes stare sightlessly up at the morning sky.

"There," Elva says, gesturing to an insignia sewn into the fabric of his black cloak. It is the stylized depiction of a bird, its beak open and its wings spread wide in the image of flight.

A Nightingale.

"These men are scouts of the Nightingale expeditionary force," she explains, folding her arms behind her perfectly straight back. "Our reports tell us that their purpose was to come down from the mountains to scout out our defenses and establish base camps. It is still a subject of debate why they are here at all."

Grimacing, I gaze down the row of bodies. Every single one of them has the same insignia sewn onto their cloaks. "I'm curious about why they even attacked the inn," I say, looking back at the Arch-Magister. "Aren't scouts typically non-combatants? Besides,

I would think that the governor's manor would have presented a better target."

Elva gives me a curt nod. "My thoughts exactly. The circumstances of this attack are... strange, to say the least." She glances over to the inn, where people are gathered both inside and out. "My guess is that it has something to do with those rangers. They are currently the only two occupants staying at the inn."

I follow her gaze and see that the tall ranger, Elias, stands on the steps of the inn and is talking to a weeping woman with a group of forlorn-looking children. I had forgotten that the Nightingales were not the only ones who suffered casualties last night.

"I have some matters that require my attention," Elva continues, her tone sounding completely unperturbed by the death around her. "Your lessons are canceled for the morning. Take some time here. Learn what you can. If you uncover anything noteworthy, seek me out at the governor's house. We will resume your lessons this afternoon."

She departs and disappears up the road, leaving me standing alone in the middle of the field.

I shudder, turning my back on the corpses as I begin making my way toward the entrance of the inn. There are strange things happening in the Emberwood, and that ranger's apprentice seems to be at the center of it all.

Elias shakes his head sadly as the weeping woman shepherds her children away from the inn, telling them through her tears that everything is going to be all right. As I approach, he turns his slate gray eyes on me, lips drawn in a tight grimace on his scruffy face.

"Magus," he says dryly, nodding his head as I step up to the threshold.

"I am not yet a full mage," I correct gently. "I am just an initiate. My name is Zara Dennel."

He blinks but does not immediately respond, his face looking like it might have been carved from stone. After studying me for a moment, he asks, "What can I help you with, Miss Dennel?"

I clear my throat. "I was wondering if I might have a moment to speak with your apprentice, Owyn Lund? I'd like to ask him some questions about what transpired last night."

His expression darkens as he regards me, shifting slightly to stand in front of the broken door of the inn. In that moment, he reminds me of a wolf protecting its cub. "I do not think that is a good idea," he growls, further emphasizing his wolfish appearance. "The attack is still fresh in all of our minds, and the dead have yet to be buried. Surely your questions can wait until tomorrow."

"Please," I insist, gently but firmly. "I do not wish to trouble him. But I feel that the insight he can offer may prove invaluable to our investigation."

Elias simply stares at me. He does not look swayed.

"I only wish to speak with him," I press, trying not to waver before his gaze, "and I promise to be kind. Sometimes it helps to talk with somebody after a tragedy. It can aid with the coping process."

This seems to have an effect on the grizzled ranger as he appears to consider my words. Finally, he concedes with a nod, though he does not look particularly happy about it. "Five minutes," he says curtly, stepping out of the way. "But know that if you cause him any trouble, your Arch-Magister will hear about it."

"Thank you," I say, stepping past him and through the shattered door frame. As my eyes adjust to the gloom inside, I behold a truly depressing sight.

The common room has been torn to pieces, splinters of wood, broken furniture, and shards of glass are scattered everywhere. Numerous sticky puddles of blood cover the floorboards, mixed in with greasy black stains from the magefyre. In the middle of the room, I see five still forms lying on the floor, their bodies draped with white sheets.

Several people are picking through the wreckage, including the mournful innkeeper, trying to clean up after what had obviously been a terrible fight.

I spot the apprentice in the far corner of the room, sitting down on a low stool while a large woman leans over him, doing something to his arm. Carefully picking my way through the scene, I make my way over to their position.

Upon arriving, I notice that the woman is stitching up a nasty-looking gash on his left arm, threading a needle through his skin with the practiced ease of someone accustomed to needlework. What's more, I realize that he is shirtless.

I quickly look away, examining my shoes with feigned interest, but not before I notice his lean figure and muscular chest. "I'm sorry," I say, feeling the blood rush to my cheeks. "I did not mean to intrude."

"That's quite all right, dear," the woman says, pulling the string tight on the wound. This causes Owyn to grunt in pain. "We are just about done here."

I watch as she produces a tiny pair of scissors and snips the thread. "Remember to keep that cut dry and clean," she lectures sternly, washing and wiping her bloodstained hands with some water in a bowl next to her before she puts away her instruments. "We would not want it getting infected now, would we?"

"No," Owyn replies through gritted teeth. "Thank you, Mrs. Ellis."

"You're very welcome, dear." She picks up the bowl and tucks her sewing kit beneath her arm as she backs away from him, allowing him to grab his shirt off the chair. "In truth, I should be thanking you for helping fight off those horrible men. The damage can be repaired, but we would have lost so much more if you and Elias had not intervened."

With that, she gives us both a warm smile and walks away, leaving us relatively alone in the quiet corner of the common room.

Owyn puts on his shirt, wincing as he tenderly feeds his arm through the sleeve. He looks up at me with tired green eyes, his face drawn and pale. "You're one of the mages who was sitting in on my interrogation," he observes wearily.

"Yes, though I am not quite a mage yet," I reply softly, suddenly feeling very awkward. "My name is Zara Dennel."

"Hello, Zara," he says, offering me a half-smile. "I'm Owyn."

His teeth are white against his suntanned skin, and I can't help but notice the bulging muscles of his shoulders and arms. I can feel my cheeks growing even hotter. He is definitely not like the scrawny mages from the Academy. He's rugged and handsome, a young man rather than a boy.

"I... uh, have a few questions I wanted to ask you," I stammer, trying to find the right words to say. *Light, I sound like a complete idiot.*

He nods, leaning forward with an elbow resting on his knee. He looks at me, waiting expectantly.

"I was wondering about that story you told my colleagues," I say slowly, choosing my words carefully. "About the creature you saw. Do you really think it was a demon?"

Owyn blows out a breath, sounding exasperated. "Not this again," he mutters. "Listen, I don't want to talk about it, okay? Your friends made it abundantly clear that I was not in my right mind. What I saw that day was clearly a trick of the light, or just a bear or something. I was *wrong*."

I make a pacifying gesture with my hand. "No, no, you misunderstand me," I say, taking a step forward and lowering my voice. "Those mages treated you unfairly, and I'm sorry about that. But I am honestly interested in what you saw in the forest."

He narrows his eyes at me, probably considering whether or not he should believe me.

"Look," I say, feeling a little frustrated myself, "I don't know why, but my heart tells me that there is more to this story than what we are seeing on the surface. I have reason to believe that maybe you did see a demon. And if you did, I want to know exactly what it looked like so that we can have a better idea of what we are dealing with here."

His eyes widen at my little speech, before they go back to eyeing me with suspicion. "You said that you have reason to believe me. Why is that?"

I let out a small sigh. "I have this old book that I... sort of borrowed from the Academy in Tarsys. It's a book on demonology that was written just after the Doom of old Byhalya. The creature you described seems to resemble a type of demon called a darkhound."

Owyn leans forward, suddenly alert and very interested in our conversation. "A darkhound?" he repeats. "Are you sure?"

"I think so," I say uncertainly. "It had a pretty ancient drawing and short description. But that is why I would like if you could describe in detail what it looked like, so I can be sure I didn't mishear you."

"Give me a second," he says, closing his eyes and frowning. He appears to be concentrating on remembering what he saw. "It was big, and walked on all fours like a grizzly, or a cougar or something. Although its head resembled that of a great wolf. It was black, and it had really long claws that reminded me of pruning shears, or scythes. And its eyes... they glowed red like burning coals, even in the middle of the day. I could have sworn that they could see through me, like the thing was looking deep into my soul." He opens his eyes, suddenly looking very tired. "That's all I remember."

My stomach starts to feel sick again. His description matches the book perfectly. "That's... curious," I mutter, my mind starting to race.

A grim silence passes between us, the noise from the others in the common room filling the void. Then a new thought crosses my mind. I fix him with a quizzical stare.

"Was there anything unusual about what happened last night?" I ask, trying to connect all the dots. "About the attackers, I mean?"

"Unusual?" Owyn asks incredulously. "You mean, besides the fact that we were attacked by bloody *Nightingales?*"

"Yes," I reply seriously. "Is there anything that stood out to you?"

His frown returns, transforming his features into a look of concentration. "It all happened so fast," he murmurs. "One moment I was asleep in my bed, the next we were being assaulted. They broke down the door and poured in faster than we could defend ourselves. We shouldn't have stood a chance." He looks up at me, eyes bloodshot and red-rimmed. "If those mages hadn't come to save us, we would all be dead."

I decide to give him a minute. He is obviously working through something difficult inside of him. Abruptly, he perks up, as though he just remembered a new detail. "There was something," he says, rubbing his chin thoughtfully. "Something strange about the men who attacked us. They all had a glassy look in their eyes, like their pupils were covered in a film. They did not speak or shout, and they seemed completely oblivious to pain."

He shivers visibly, though by this point, I barely notice. "Was it a milky color in their eyes," I ask, unable to keep the urgency out of my voice. "The way a blind person looks?"

Owyn nods. "Yes, it was. How did you know that?"

"Mindflaying," I whisper, the pieces of the puzzle falling into place inside my mind.

"What are you talking about?" He asks, looking worried.

I look him directly in the eyes, speaking in a lowered voice, "Owyn, I believe your story. I believe everything."

His eyebrows shoot straight up. "What? Really?"

"I need you to take me to the place where you saw the demon," I say quietly, looking around to make sure that I am not being overheard. "Where all of this began. Can we leave Forest Hill tonight?"

CHAPTER 13
OWYN

The sun has already been up for two hours, yet I feel completely drained from the events of the night. By the time I make it up to my room, I crash on the bed and fall asleep with little trouble. It's the first dreamless slumber I've had in days.

The sun is already low in the afternoon sky when I awake. I rub the sleep from my eyes, feeling much better than I had earlier. The wound on my arm aches painfully, but luckily the stitches seem to be holding up well.

My tongue, however, feels as dry as cotton, and my stomach protests angrily from lack of food.

It's been almost a full day since I have last eaten.

Getting out of bed, I make my way to the washbasin and splash some water on my face, my empty stomach continuing to groan. The cool liquid feels good on my skin, and once I pat myself dry, I begin to feel a little more refreshed. I quickly put on my cloak and boots to make my way downstairs.

I pull the door open and notice a full plate of food sitting on a wooden stand in the hallway, beside a tall glass of water. Mrs. Ellis must have put it there so I could eat upon waking.

Light bless her, I think to myself, bringing the tray inside. I make a mental note to thank her the next time we talk for taking such good care of me. Sitting cross-legged on the floor, I began to shovel the bread and cheese into my mouth with vigor.

I barely even taste the food as I eat it, washing it down with the water between great chomping bites. It isn't long until even the crumbs are devoured, and I lean back against the wooden bedframe, letting out a contented sigh.

I sit alone in my room enjoying the peace, but before long, the memories of what transpired over the last few days come rushing back to me, and a heavy weight settles over my shoulders.

Too quickly, I remember that I had killed a man the night before.

Closing my eyes, I relive the terrible events of the fight. Guilt at having taken another person's life washes over me like a flood of shame. *Of course,* I think after a heart-wrenching moment, *according to Zara, those men were no longer men at all.*

My thoughts turn to the mage girl, Zara, and her wild idea to sneak away to the forest tonight and visit the spot where I had seen the demon, the demon she believes I saw.

Sitting in the inn, she had informed me that the Nightingale agents who attacked us had likely been subject to mindflaying, which she explained was a spell that demons cast on humans so they could control them. A couple of the signature side effects of mindflaying were the white film covering the victim's irises and the tendency to become oblivious to pain.

She had called these victims *mind slaves.*

The mindflaying would explain why the Nightingale scouts brazenly attacked Forest Hill, and why they seemed to fight in such an unrestrained and reckless way.

I bury my face in my hands and shake my head. *What in the Eleven Hells is this crazy girl thinking? Going out into the Emberwood when there are Nightingales or worse roaming about!*

. On the other hand, Zara *is* the only person who actually believes me.

Sighing, I push myself to my feet and test my arm by slowly rotating it like a windmill. The muscles are achy, and there is a sharp pain radiating from my wound, but I at least still have some mobility. I am going to have to be careful not to overexert myself, at least until the stitches heal.

What does she expect to find in visiting that clearing, anyway? I ask myself as I finish testing my arm. *The demon seemed to vanish after I told Elias about it. It's probably long gone by now.* I mentally correct myself. *Darkhound. She had said that it was a darkhound.*

I make my way to the window and stare through the glass at the rolling slope of the hill in front of the inn. There are still a few hours left before sundown—more than enough time to pack.

"No," I say aloud to myself, turning away and sitting down on my mattress. "Absolutely not. I have an oath to live up to, a duty to the realm. I can't just go abandoning my master to go chase shadows.*"*

But wasn't the ranger's oath about protecting the realm against such things?

The words from our pledge come echoing back to my mind:

> *Our solemn duty is to protect the borders of the realms of men from those enemies who would seek our destruction...*
>
> *We will sacrifice everything, even our very lives, for the defense of the kingdom...*

I let out a groan. Walking on hot coals sounds more appealing to me than going out and searching for demons with some pretentious mage girl from Tarsys.

And yet, in my gut, I know that it is the right thing to do.

Plus, I think to myself with the barest hint of a smile, *she isn't bad to look at. Even if she is a mage.*

Getting up from the bed, I trudge over to my pack and begin loading my things. I stuff clothing, blankets, tinder, and a whetstone into my saddlebags, along with anything else I may require for the journey.

I quickly realize that we are going to need food while we are out in the forest, and there will be little time for hunting. Somehow, I am going to have to make my way down to the kitchen and steal some provisions without anybody seeing me. Of course, I will leave Mr. and Mrs. Ellis some money to reimburse them for what I take, but the thought of sneaking away without telling anyone makes me uneasy.

Especially, when my thoughts turn to Elias.

With luck, my master will be gone long enough for me to slip away. I can't imagine that he is being idle while I rest. To be perfectly honest, my guess is that he is out scouting the woods with some of the men from town to make sure no other Nightingales are lurking about. He functions on astonishingly little sleep and can never keep still for very long.

I take a moment to restring my bow and fill my quiver to capacity with arrows. Moving to pick up my father's hatchet, I notice that it is still encrusted with blood from last night. For a moment, I stare at it leaning against the wall, before I proceed to clean it in my washbasin. Dunking it into the water, I use my fingernails to scrub the blade, the water quickly turning a deep red as the blood comes off. When it is finally clean, I dry it with a cloth and slide it into my belt, grimacing at the bloody mess it left behind.

I'll need to give Mrs. Ellis extra for cleaning this up.

With my pack full, I move to the small desk next to my bed and sit down, pulling out a blank scrap of parchment and a quill. Thinking quickly, I write a note to Elias explaining why I am leaving and asking him not to follow me. I am not a very good writer, and I know that he is not one for reading at great lengths, so I keep it short and to the point.

I hope my note will help lessen the anger and worry he will no doubt feel once he discovers that I am gone.

Taking a breath, I get up to shoulder my saddlebags and step out into the hallway, my jaw set in determination.

As I make my way over to the stairs, I try to be as stealthy as possible. Creeping slowly down the hall, I am careful to step lightly so that I avoid making the floorboards creak. I peek around the corners of every open door to ensure no one else is there. The second floor of the inn appears to be deserted, so I inch over to the staircase and begin slowly descending the steps.

When I reach the bottom, I find that the common room is empty. The glass and debris from the attack have been cleaned up, and I notice that the bodies are also gone. Most of the furniture damaged in the fight has been taken away, though several dark stains remain on the wooden floorboards. It is going to take a lot of work to sand those down and erase all trace of the blood spilled there.

Looking around to make sure that I am alone, I walk over to the kitchen to begin to search for supplies. It seems empty, so I slip behind the counter and open the pantry door. There, I find salted venison, fruits, bread, cheese, and several jars of preserves. I begin stuffing as many provisions as I can into my pack, trying to move quickly before anyone comes in and discovers what I am doing.

My heart leaps into my throat when I hear footsteps shuffling down the hall.

Cursing under my breath, I close the door and duck down to a crawlspace beside the stone furnace. It is a tight fit with my saddlebags, but I manage to squeeze in just as Mrs. Ellis walks into the kitchen, humming a tune under her breath.

She busies herself with something on one of the tables against the far wall, oblivious to my presence just behind her.

It's only a matter of time before she turns around and sees me crouching here, I think to myself frantically. *She'll tell Elias. I need to do something.*

My answer comes in the form of a small rock chip I spot resting on the rim of the furnace. Trying not to make any noise, I shift my body and pick up the stone. I pitch it down the hall and into the common room, where it clatters loudly onto the floorboards.

"James?" Mrs. Ellis calls out, pausing whatever it is she is doing. "Is that you?"

She turns and walks into the common room, her eyes sweeping over my position without seeing me. I don't even dare to breathe until she is out of the kitchen.

When she is gone, I emerge from my hiding place and make a break for the back door, but not before pausing to thumb out a few coins onto the counter to pay for the items I took.

I quietly open the door and step out into the field behind the inn without so much as a glance behind me.

The stable is on the side of the building, a squat wooden structure capable of housing half a dozen horses or so.

Luckily the Ellis' do not have a stable boy, so I don't run into any resistance as I enter and begin untying my chestnut brown mare. I pat her haunches as I load up my saddlebags, whispering calming words as I prepare her for departure. Then a thought strikes me.

Zara arrived with the other mages in those fancy carriages. She probably doesn't have a horse of her own.

I bite my lip and look around, trying to find a solution in the dim light of the setting sun. Taking food without asking is one thing, but I don't want to steal a horse if I can help it; especially, if anyone needs it to travel. When my eyes fall upon Elias' pack mule, I grin.

Elias probably won't be going on any hunts any time soon.

A few minutes later, I ride out of the stable on my mare, guiding the pack mule by her reins behind me.

There is only one road leading up to the top of the hill, but at this hour, it is undoubtedly bustling with activity. I instead decide to ride into the woods behind the inn to avoid being seen. The terrain is rough, but I know of at least one trail that will lead me up the bluff to the governor's mansion. My hope is to meet up with Zara there.

Glancing at the setting sun, I click my tongue and urge the horse and the mule to go a little faster. I'll have to hurry if I am going to make it to the top before sundown.

Every passing second brings me one step closer to the concealing darkness of night.

CHAPTER 14
ZARA

A breeze rustles leaves in the darkness, sounding like a thousand hissing snakes around me. I pull my robes tighter against the chill, knowing full well that I am not shivering from the cold. The thick gray fabric could hardly protect me from whatever menace may be lurking in the woods.

Night has already fallen, and I stand by a cluster of trees outside the governor's manor, clutching my bag tightly against my chest.

Light almighty, if Owyn does not come, I will feel like the world's biggest fool.

A twig snaps somewhere behind me, and I spin, quickly touching my crystal talisman and pulling in source energy. I drop my pack and am about to fill my palms with magefyre when the ranger's apprentice materializes out of the shadows, holding the reins of a pair of horses.

"Sorry," he whispers, a ghost of a smile on his lips. "I didn't mean to scare you."

I release the source energy and pick up my bag with a scowl. "You did *not* scare me," I say indignantly. "You only startled me a little. What took you so long, anyway? I've been waiting here for half an hour!"

"I had to make sure that there was no one watching before I rode up here." He hands me the reins to one of the horses. "The whole village is on edge with the recent attacks, and I did not want to leave until we were under the full cover of darkness."

"Oh," I reply, my annoyance somewhat melting away. "I suppose that makes sense."

I look warily from him to the horse, not really sure how I should proceed. The great beast is saddled, and it looks at me placidly with soft brown eyes reflecting the light of the moon. Even so, I can't help but feel a little hesitant about mounting the unfamiliar animal and riding it through the forest in the dark.

Owyn gives me a strange look. "You do know how to ride, don't you?"

I shrug, trying hard to feign nonchalance. "I've seen it done before. How hard can it be?"

His jaw drops open, incredulous. "You've never ridden a horse before?"

"Look, bumpkin," I hiss, annoyance creeping back into my voice. "I've spent the last five years living in Tarsys, training so that I could become a mage. There weren't a lot of opportunities to ride horses. So, how about instead of standing there, slack-jawed, you just tell me how to do it, okay?"

His expression darkens, and I feel a slight twinge of guilt for letting my temper get the best of me. *He deserved it,* I think defensively. Though, I realize that my frustration is due to my embarrassment more than anything. *Not that I'd admit that to him.*

He takes my pack and roughly attaches it behind the saddle with some ropes. "This isn't a horse, by the way," he says quietly, rolling his eyes at me. "It's a mule. But I'll show you how to ride it in any case."

"Whatever," I snap. "Just tell me the basics okay, farm boy?"

He glowers at me but proceeds with a quick lesson. "Pull on the reins to get her to stop. When you're riding, use your legs to guide her. You can also tug on the bit depending on which direction you want to go." He then points to the stirrups. "Use these to get her to go faster by kicking her with your heels. Don't worry, you're not going to hurt her. Other than that, follow me, and you should be okay." He steps back, folding his arms and glaring. "Happy?"

"Thank you," I say, smiling sweetly. "That was simple enough."

He grunts and walks over to his own horse. Pulling himself up with ease, he settles comfortably into his saddle.

He makes it look so simple.

Hiking up my skirts, I put one of my feet in the stirrups and clumsily pull myself onto the mule. "Okay," I mutter under my breath, "you can do this, Zara." I gently tap my heels against its belly, and it lurches forward, causing me to squeak in a most unflattering fashion.

Smirking at me, Owyn guides his mount effortlessly through the trees and begins riding down the hill without so much as a backward glance to see if I am following.

We take a winding, twisting path down the hill, avoiding most of the buildings and terraced farms built into its side. The game trails we follow are extremely narrow, and the path is often treacherous. I spend most of the trip holding my reins in a white knuckled grip and whispering softly to myself that everything is going to be all right.

Eventually, the hill levels out, and we make our way into the dense forest, the lights of the town fading into the distance behind us.

Despite the cloudless sky and the stars overhead, the woods remain perilously dark, and I have a difficult time seeing our surroundings. Luckily, Owyn seems to know where he is going, and I make certain to remain close on his horse's tail to avoid getting lost in the trees.

It is not long before we are completely alone in the wilderness with all signs of civilization left behind. When I first arrived in the Emberwood, I had thought the forest looked so beautiful. Now, the trees look more like menacing skeletons, reaching for me in the dark with their finger-like branches.

I hope that I am not making a colossal mistake, I think to myself, trying to ignore my overactive imagination. *But this could be one of the biggest discoveries in centuries! If there is a hole in the Arc and demons are getting through, I am obligated to go out and investigate. Elva will understand, won't she?*

Somehow, I doubt it. The Arch-Magister does not seem like the understanding or forgiving type.

It feels like hours before Owyn finally pulls his horse to a stop, though in truth, I have no idea how long we have been riding. Time is hard to discern without the guidance of the sun.

"We'll camp here for the night," he says, sliding out of his saddle and leading his horse into a small clearing. "We can start back out at first light."

"Why are we stopping? Shouldn't we put more distance between ourselves and Forest Hill?"

"No," he says, tethering his reins to a tree. "We've gone far enough. Riding in the dark is dangerous, and I don't want to do any more than is necessary. Besides, we are still a good distance from where I saw the demon, or darkhound, or whatever it is called. We'll need some rest in order to complete the journey."

The mention of the demon helps to put things in perspective. It also casts a pall over the both of us. Without saying another word of protest, I dismount and tether my animal, then begin untying my pack.

I watch out of the corner of my eye as Owyn clears away some of the woodland debris, picking up fallen branches and stones and tossing them to the side. I imagine he is doing this in order to make room for the tent.

Pulling my pack free from the saddle, I approach him and set it down in some ferns. "Do you need help lighting the fire?"

He shakes his head. "No fires."

"No fires?" I ask in disbelief. "How are we supposed to eat?"

"I have plenty of jerky," he says simply, still working on cleaning the forest floor. "And bread. Things that don't need to be cooked. If my master comes out looking for me, I don't want to lead him right to us."

I sigh. "Fine. At least we will be warm inside the tent."

He reaches for his pack and begins pulling out his bedroll. "No tents, either."

"No *tents?*" I repeat, unable to hide my incredulity. *I can't believe what I am hearing.* Does this rube actually expect for us to sleep *outside?*

"No tents," he reaffirms, unfurling his bedroll onto the ground. "We travel light. Tents are too cumbersome for rangers." He looks up at me, and I can see his white teeth as he grins at me in the darkness.

He seems to be enjoying this.

"I'm not a ranger," I say, stubbornly crossing my arms. "What about the elements? What about animals?"

I can practically feel him rolling his eyes. "We'll be all right. I promise."

Huffing, I open my pack and take out the bedroll I borrowed from the governor's manor. It is a plush thing, probably very expensive, and I cringe as I spread it out on the dirt.

Owyn hands me a hunk of bread and a water skin. "Here," he says. "Eat this and try to get some sleep. I'll take first watch, and then I'll wake you so that you can take lookout while I sleep. Fair?"

I take the food and reluctantly agree. "Fair."

"Good." He picks up his bow and draws an arrow. "I'm going to scout around a bit, but I won't be far. If you need an extra blanket, you can take one from my pack."

And with that, he disappears into the woods with hardly a sound.

Nibbling on the bread, I try to make myself as comfortable as possible in my makeshift bed. The ground is hard and lumpy beneath my mat, and my training exercises from the afternoon have left me physically drained. I take a final sip of water and lie down, staring up at the stars from my back.

The sounds of the forest wash over me, making it hard for me to fall asleep. I hear the leaves rustling in the wind, and now and then, the noise of a branch snapping or a twig popping reaches my ears, making me wonder what sort of creatures lie in wait just out of sight.

What are you doing, Zara? What have you gotten yourself into? It is not the first time I have asked myself that question. My heart tells me that I am making the right choice, but my mind is not shy about reminding me what this little stunt could cost me.

Becoming a mage is all I've ever wanted. Is it really worth throwing all of it away to follow my conscience?

Yes, I conclude after a long moment of reflection. *If demons really are coming through the Arc, then everything changes. I'm not certain about what will happen if I continue on, but I do know that I would be remiss if I did nothing.*

I turn my head and look through the darkness and see that Owyn has returned to our makeshift camp. He is standing a little way off with his back to me, looking out at the forest with his bow in hand.

Suddenly, I become keenly aware that this is the first time I have ever been by myself with a boy, let alone traveling and sleeping in the same place as one. The dormitories at the Academy are separated by sex, and boys and girls intermingling with each other is strongly discouraged by the Conclave. *Oh, how the rumors would fly if my classmates could see me now!*

Owyn is a handsome one, though not much of a conversationalist, and the way he clings to the old ways of doing things, to the ways of a woodsman, is maddening. He seems better suited to the life of a hermit than to life in civilized society.

Still, I think to myself, settling down onto my back as I close my eyes. *Being out here with him is better than being out here alone, I suppose.*

My thoughts are a jumbled mess, but at long last, I start to drift off. The last thing I picture before I fall asleep is the stern visage of Elva, shaking her head in disappointment.

CHAPTER 15
OWYN

It seems that I closed my eyes for only a few short minutes when Zara kicks me awake.

Hells, did she really just kick me?

I open my eyes and glare up at her, finding her smiling innocently at me beneath the hood of her robes. "Rise and shine," she says in an overly pleasant voice. "It's time to get up!"

Grunting, I pull myself out of my warm bedroll and attempt to rub the sleep from my eyes. I have a sinking feeling that this is going to be a *very* long day. Pulling my own cloak around me to ward off the morning chill, I look around while waiting for my head to clear.

The purple and pink hues of dawn brighten the sky, and I can hear birds chirping in the trees around us. We are several leagues away from Forest Hill, in a dense thicket far from any town, home, or farmstead. If we start riding soon, we should be able to reach the clearing with the herd of slaughtered deer before sundown. I can't remember exactly where it is, but I am familiar with the general area. Once we get close, it shouldn't be too difficult to find.

Clearing my throat, I begin rummaging through my pack, pulling out a wax-covered block of cheese, a heel of bread, and a pouch full of dried grapes. Dividing the food between us, I shove some of the bread into my mouth and hand the rest over to Zara, who glances at me distastefully like I am some kind of barbarian.

It's too early for me to even summon the will to care.

Why did it have to be a mage? I think to myself as I eat, the morning fog clearing from my head. *Why couldn't it have been anyone else in Tarsynium?*

She looks down at the meager portion as if uncertain about what to do with it. "Eat," I urge, taking another bite. "We have a long day of riding ahead of us, and judging by your riding abilities, you are going to need all the energy you can get." I resist the urge to chuckle at the withering look she gives me.

"I think I'll get along just fine, thank you."

She breaks off a piece of cheese and begins delicately nibbling on it, reminding me of a squirrel eating a nut.

I take a swig of water and decide to break the uncomfortable silence that has settled between us. "If we keep a good pace, we should arrive sometime this afternoon."

"Good," she replies simply, before popping a couple dried grapes into her mouth.

I swiftly finish my meal and begin packing up our things, stuffing my bedroll into my pack and securing it to the saddle of my mare. As I work, I speak without looking at her. "What do you expect to find out there, anyway? It seems like an awful lot of trouble sneaking away like this, looking for something that might not even be there at all."

"I can ask you the same question," she replies without missing a beat. "Why leave your master in the middle of the night to help some Conclave initiate you don't even know?"

I shrug, pulling the leather straps tight on my saddle. "You are the only one who believes my story. It wasn't like I had many options to choose from."

She is silent for a long moment before responding. "My colleagues' reactions astounded me. I've been studying demons for some time, and your description matched them perfectly. If the mages are not going to do anything about it, then it is up to me to investigate."

I glance over my shoulder at her. She sits upon a rock looking down at a piece of bread, brow furrowed as if trying to convince herself that she made the right choice in coming here.

Hells, I think to myself. *She looks as uncertain as I do about all of this. How did we get thrown into this together?*

"Let me help you with your things," I say gruffly, making my way to her neatly packed bags. I hoist them up and begin strapping them onto her mule.

"Thank you," she mumbles before taking another bite. I nod but do not reply.

In a matter of minutes, she finishes eating and we mount up. Leaving behind our little campsite, we make our way deeper into the Emberwood, riding down game trails and overgrown foot paths. I take the lead, keeping my mare at a decent pace so that we make good time. Every so often, I look behind me to make sure she hasn't fallen behind.

The weight of responsibility begins to press down on me. *Light, is this what Elias feels like every time we go out to make our rounds?* Without me, I know that Zara would be hopelessly lost in this forest. It is a sobering thought indeed, taking leadership over someone else's well-being.

We travel in silence for the better part of the morning, the sky growing brighter and the air growing warmer around us as we ride. The forest itself seems to come alive with the rising sun. I spot a doe and some fawns drinking water from a stream while birds sing and insects buzz in the leafy, green boughs. The sounds of the woodlands are soothing to me; they remind me of simpler times when the most pressing issue was learning how to properly trap a rabbit.

How quickly things have changed, I muse silently, turning my attention back to the path.

Around midday, we begin eating lunch in the saddle. Zara pulls her mule up next to mine and regards me with a curious look on her face. This section of the forest is less dense, so we can easily ride side by side without the fear of colliding with a tree.

"Why did you decide to join the rangers?" Her voice breaks the silence, her question coming out of the blue and catching me off-guard. I'm not exactly sure how to respond.

Taking my lack of an answer as a sign that I am upset, she tries to rephrase it. "I don't mean to offend you or anything. I'm genuinely curious. I mean, of all the things in the world to be, why be a ranger?"

I shrug my shoulders. "The rangers are the protectors of the realm," I find myself saying. "They guard the borders of the land so that everyone else can live comfortable and safe lives. I am honored to stand among them."

She rolls her eyes. "Yes, yes, and the mages safeguard the Heart of Light and all of that rubbish. I mean *really*, what made you want to join? And don't repeat all of that nonsense you're *supposed* to say."

I frown. "What, is my answer not good enough?"

"Your answer is all well and good, but it's not the truth of *why* you joined the rangers. For example, I didn't join the Conclave because I wanted to guard some giant crystal in the Pillar of Radiance. I joined because I wanted to become the greatest mage Tarsynium has ever seen."

I give her a sidelong glance. "That's quite the goal you have there. And how's that working out for you?"

She crinkles her nose at me. "It was going fine until you got me wrapped up in all of this talk about demons. But don't change the subject. Why did you want to join the rangers?" she repeats.

Sighing, I decide to give her just a fraction of the truth. "My father was a ranger, one of the best, or so I have been told. It has always been a dream of mine to follow in his footsteps. I wanted to live up to his example."

Zara's face softens. "You never knew your father?"

"Barely," I reply, shaking my head. "He died when I was very young. I was raised by my mother in a town called Edenshire, on the other side of the kingdom. After she passed away, I made for the Grand Lodge in the Ashwood as soon as I had the chance and joined up with the rangers."

"I'm so sorry, Owyn," she says softly, "I had no idea."

"It's nothing." I look away from her and study the path ahead of us. "Don't worry about it."

For a moment, there is only the sound of our horses' hooves clopping on the forest floor then Zara speaks up again.

"You know, my mother also passed away," she remarks. "Years ago, when I first entered the Academy. A fever took her in the night. New initiates are not allowed to leave the city, so I could not go and see my family. It was a... difficult time for me."

Again, a grim silence settles between us. Finally, I clear my throat and speak, hoping to bring up a less depressing subject. "So, are you a great magic user?"

"What do you mean?"

"Your quest. Are you on your way to becoming the greatest mage in Tarsynium?"

She laughs, and I find the corners of my mouth tugging up in a faint smile as well. "Well, considering I am not yet a full mage, no. But I am at the top of my class, so the future looks promising. That is why Arch-Magister Tyrande invited me to come along on this mission, to be her ward."

"What does a ward do?"

"It is similar to that of an apprentice," she explains while gazing out to the left of us at a meadow full of wildflowers. "I am here to learn and to aid the Arch-Magister with whatever she needs help with. Most of my duties are quite dull, I assure you."

"Being a mage doesn't look dull to me," I reply. "Though, I'll admit, I understand little about your kind."

"*Your kind?*" she repeats, raising an eyebrow at me. "Light, I'm not an animal. Have you ever even met a mage before we came here?"

I shake my head, slightly abashed. "Not personally."

"Well, consider this your introduction to magecraft." She turns toward me and pulls off a small chain from around her neck. On it hangs a blue crystal about the length of her forefinger. "Do you know what this is?"

I shake my head again.

"This is called a talisman. All mages have one, and it is required for using magic."

"What's it made out of?"

"Source crystal," she says matter-of-factly to me, though again, it's something I've never heard of before. She continues to explain. "It is a mineral that used to grow naturally on our world, before the Doom. Now the remaining shards are owned by the Conclave and loaned to initiates and mages for the duration of their life."

She closes her fingers around the crystal and shuts her eyes. Opening her other hand, a ball of blue flame appears, burning in the air a few inches above her skin.

"Impressive," I say, genuinely surprised. From what little I know about mages, even creating a small amount of fire is said to require a considerable amount of skill.

Zara opens her eyes and the ball of fire vanishes. "Source energy, drawn through the source crystal, is the basis for all radiant magic. With it, mages can do some pretty incredible things. They can cast spells that conjure magefyre, shields, missiles, and even artifices like the Arc of Radiance itself."

"I had no idea," I reply, as I try not to let the awe show on my face. In truth, my own skills seem a little pathetic compared to what she can do. I knew that mages could summon fire—I had witnessed it firsthand back at the inn. Though, I never fully comprehended the extent of what they were capable of until now. "How long have you been in training?"

"About five years. But don't let my little show fool you. Most of a mage's time is spent studying, practicing, and doing research. I've spent more time in the library poring over dusty old books than I have out in the field making fireballs."

I chuckle. "I can't remember the last time I read a book." My smile turns to an awkward frown. "Honestly, I can't really remember spending much time indoors."

She laughs as well, and we continue on our way, chatting off and on over the next several hours. She asks me about my life as a ranger's apprentice, and I try to learn more from her about mages. Overall, the conversation is quite pleasant, which is a surprise to both of us.

It is midafternoon by the time we finally reach the clearing.

Remarkably enough, I have little trouble finding it. It lies in a region called the Silver Vale in the eastern reaches of the Emberwood. This cursed place, so close to Haven, has been forever burned into my memory.

As we approach, I pull my horse to a stop and dismount, unslinging my bow, before tying the reins to a nearby tree. A quick look around reveals that Zara is doing the same, clutching her talisman firmly in her right hand.

"Up here," I say in a low voice, leading the way into the clearing.

The corpses of the deer have decomposed even more than they had a week ago, flesh wilting like dead moss into the ground only to be reabsorbed by nature. Unlike the day I found it, the place is buzzing with flies. Most of the bodies look picked clean by carrion eaters, and little white maggots can be seen worming their way through the remains.

The demon must be long gone by now, I think with relief.

Zara lets out a small gasp as she sees the carnage, but I do not pause to regard her. Instead, I scan the tree line for any signs of predators.

"It's so much worse than I imagined," she whispers as we make our way into the center of the clearing.

"Could it be the work of the darkhound?" I ask solemnly. She looks around but doesn't answer, the same question written on her face.

Fortunately, there does not seem to be any sign of the creature in the clearing. "Consider yourself lucky. When I was here before, the stench was much worse."

Still, she wrinkles her nose at the foul smell. "I can see why you and your master were concerned," she says. "What happened here was... brutal. Most of the meat was left behind to rot. It's as if whatever did this was only interested in killing, not in feeding."

We spend a few minutes walking around the clearing, but there really isn't much to see. After we take a second turn, I look at Zara and gesture to the horses. "Are you ready to go back now?"

She shakes her head. "Not quite yet. There is something I want to try." From out of the folds of her robes she produces a small notebook, which she flips through until she finds a certain page. "Remember that old book I told you about? The one on demonology? Well, there is an incantation that ancient mages used to track demons during the Great War." She looks around as if searching for something. "Where exactly did you see this demon standing?"

I point to a spot on the edge of the clearing.

Stepping gingerly over the mangled bodies of rotting deer, Zara makes her way to the position. "Here?" She asks.

I nod.

Holding her talisman in one hand and the notebook in the other, she begins speaking words in a language I can't understand. It sounds like she is casting some sort of spell. A few seconds later, a globe of white light appears in the air in front of her. Suspended at eye level, it glows with a soft, humming energy.

I approach her warily, bow held at the ready.

"Fascinating," she mutters, looking from the globe, back down to her notebook. "Give me just one more minute."

She crouches down and touches the point of the crystalline talisman into the dirt, holding it there for several seconds before standing back up and regarding the globe.

At first, nothing happens, and I hear her grunt in displeasure. Then, the globe begins to shimmer, the light changing from a pure white to an angry, deep red.

She takes a step back and puts a hand up to cover her mouth, then turns to look at me. Her face is as white as a sheet, her eyes wide with fear. "The spell worked," she says quietly. "And you were right all along, Owyn."

"Right?" I ask, confused. "Right about what?"

"Demons leave behind a latent energy wherever they go," she explains, waving a hand and causing the crimson globe to dissipate. "It's called infernae. It is invisible to our eyes, but it sticks to everything they touch. Radiant magic can reveal it."

The meaning behind her words dawns on me, and I feel the blood drain from my face.

"Owyn," she whispers, "there *was* a demon here. Recently."

Just then, we hear a shrill, bone-chilling howl coming from the woods nearby. It sounds like it is no more than a mile away. From experience, I know that it is not a wolf, cougar, or any other kind of animal native to the Emberwood.

It is something else entirely. *The demon.*

CHAPTER 16
ZARA

C'mon!" Owyn urges, grabbing me by my sleeve. "We need to leave here. Now!"

I do not argue. Whatever made that horrible sound is close.

And it sounds dangerous.

We sprint across the open clearing, jumping over the decomposing remains of the deer and making for our mounts, which are tethered just outside the wide ring of trees. When we arrive, both of them are pulling against their restraints, whinnying nervously and stamping their feet.

"Whoa, whoa," Owyn says soothingly as he spreads his arms wide and gently rubs his fingers on the nose of his horse. "Easy there, girl."

I flinch, attempting to do the same with my mule, who seems to be even more spooked than Owyn's horse. Its eyes roll back in its head, and it tugs hard against the reins, trying to break free. *Please don't step on me, please don't step on me.* I timidly touch its neck and try to speak comforting words, but it doesn't seem to do much good.

Having successfully calmed his own horse, Owyn intervenes. "Easy now, easy." His touch soothes the mule almost immediately, as if he has a special connection with the animal. *He seems to be rather good at this,* I think to myself, chagrined.

We quickly untie their reins and clamber into our saddles, pulling away from the clearing as fast as we can.

Another long howl echoes around us, reverberating off the wall of trees. The sound pierces my ears, igniting a very primal fear I have never felt before. It causes the hair on my arms to stand on end, and my hand begins to shake as I hold the reign in a white knuckled grip.

"Try and keep up," Owyn shouts over his shoulder, before kicking his horse in the flanks and tearing off through the underbrush.

Steeling myself, I do the same. The mule lurches forward, and it is everything I can do not to fall out of the saddle. Using my legs to guide the animal, I do my best to follow through the maze of trees, cringing as trunks and branches fly past me at terrifying speeds. The mule, frightened by the second howl, needs little urging to move swiftly, and we manage to stay close behind Owyn as we go.

Despite the circumstances, I find myself actually *smiling* as I ride. The exhilaration coursing through me from the raw fear is thrilling as it fills my stomach with butterflies and makes me feel alive. As Owyn looks back and sees the big grin on my face, his eyebrows go up in shock. He turns away, shaking his head in bewilderment.

A third howl rips through the air, and my smile vanishes. *That one sounded much closer.*

"It's gaining on us!" I call out, but I'm not sure that he can hear me. He merely continues to ride at the same reckless pace.

The beat of the horse's hooves sounds thunderous in my ears, and the wind tugs at my hair and robes, cooling my skin and making my eyes water. A low-hanging tree branch nearly strikes my head, and I have to drop low in the saddle to avoid decapitation. *That was a close one,* I think, blinking against the salty tears clouding my vision.

I wonder just how long we can maintain this speed before one of us, or one of our horses, gets hurt.

Out of the corner of my eye, I see something dark moving through the trees alongside us. It is massive in shape, and it begins to outpace our horses, but when I turn my head, I lose sight of it, thick bushes springing up to obscure my vision.

"I think I see something!" I shout.

Again, no response.

Owyn turns sharply, and I barely manage to follow him around the bend, my mount almost pitching to the side into some jagged rocks. He turns again, zig-zagging through the woods like a jackrabbit running from a pack of wolves.

There it is again! A hulking blur of black speeds through the trees to my left, racing ahead of us and onto a small hillock that stands directly in our path.

Just when I think things couldn't possibly get any worse, Owyn yanks on his reins and brings his horse to a grinding halt, giving me almost no time to stop myself. I pull back on the reins with all my strength, but my mount's hooves skid in the damp leaves of the forest floor and slide off the path.

We go down, careening into a gulley, and I can't help but scream as I lose control of the animal. I hear a loud *snap* as I am thrown violently from the saddle, but luckily, I manage to land on a relatively soft blanket of ferns. The wind blasts out of my lungs, and as I lie there on my back trying to regain my breath, I can hear my mule screaming somewhere nearby.

Dizzy and disoriented, I attempt to pull myself into a sitting position. Strong hands pull me to my feet, and Owyn frantically asks me if I am hurt, concern painted plainly on his face. Other than a painful ache in my side which will probably turn into a nasty bruise, I feel fine. No broken bones that I can identify.

I shake my head and look over at my mule, which is lying on its side beside a great oak. It paws at the air with its front legs and whinnies painfully; one of its hind legs is bent at an odd angle just below the knee.

Broken.

"The darkhound," Owyn whispers, nocking an arrow to his bow and pulling the fletching to his cheek.

I follow his gaze up the sloping hill where a large creature is stepping out from behind the trees. It looks like a mix between a wolf and a hunting cat, with powerful muscles rippling beneath its black fur. Its eyes glow with a feral red light, and it licks its razor teeth with a long dripping tongue.

It matches the picture in my book almost perfectly.

Lifting up one of its paws, which is adorned with three curving, hook-like talons, it lets out another howl so loud that it feels like my eardrums will burst.

Owyn looses his arrow, and it strikes the demon in the shoulder, burying itself deep into its flesh. Its howl is cut short by the shot, transforming it into an angry shriek. It turns its head to snap at the arrow sticking out of its body, teeth quickly breaking the wooden shaft in two.

He draws again and launches another arrow, this time sticking the monster in the leg.

The beast staggers and rears its ugly head at us, charging down the hill with a loping, otherworldly gait, moving unnaturally fast.

Throwing down his bow, Owyn pulls out the hatchet from his belt and steps to the side. "Do something!" he shouts, holding up his weapon to brace himself for impact.

His scream forces me to come to my senses, and I pull the talisman from around my neck, filling myself with source energy as quickly as I can. Horrified, I watch as the demon leaps the last dozen feet, its claws extended and its mouth wide open. Without thinking, I throw out my hand and shout the command word, "*Darian!*"

Just as the darkhound collides with him and knocks him to the ground, my radiant shield blossoms over Owyn's body, fitting around his form like a shimmering second skin.

The source energy leeches out of me in a burst, and for a moment, it leaves me in a daze, but I force myself to stay upright. Using the talisman, I begin pulling more energy into myself, silently praying to the Light for Owyn's safety.

The monster tears at the shield with its claws, but for now, my magic holds, its attacks bouncing harmlessly off its blue surface. I know that it will not last long, so I start preparing myself to cast another spell.

Roaring in frustration, the demon rakes at Owyn's skin but is unable to puncture the shield. Owyn struggles and tries to pull himself out from under the beast's immense weight, but he is completely pinned down, his hatchet lying on the ground just out of reach.

A ball of pulsing energy fills my open hand, and I raise it up, taking aim at the demon. "*Taflegryn golau!*" I shout, launching it forward with a *whoosh.*

The force of the blast is enough to knock it off of Owyn, who staggers to his feet as the demon tumbles into some bushes several yards away. "Thanks for that," he breathes, his eyes wide and his hair askew.

My magic missile evidently ignited some dead leaves on the forest floor, because a small blaze now burns between us and the darkhound. I watch curiously as the demon attempts to cross the fire, only to leap back with a squeal as it burns its forefoot.

A weakness.

Gripping my talisman, I begin to pull in more source energy than I ever have before. "Get ready," I bellow, keeping my eyes fixed upon the demon. My entire body begins to tingle with power, the source crystal in my palm radiating heat. *I'm going to be feeling this tonight,* I think to myself grimly, setting my jaw.

Owyn steps out in front of me protectively. "How are we going to kill this thing?"

"Leave that to me," I reply through gritted teeth. "You keep it distracted as long as you can."

"*Distract* it?" he asks incredulously, his voice going up an octave.

Fortunately, there is not enough time to argue. The darkhound uses its claw-like feet to kick dirt onto the fire, effectively putting it out. Its red eyes seem to glow even brighter as it looks up from the smoke and regards the two of us, growling deep within its throat.

Viciously, like a viper striking a mouse, it charges at Owyn again, teeth bared in a wicked snarl.

At the last moment, he ducks to the side, narrowly avoiding the monster's claws as it goes in for the kill. The darkhound stumbles but does not fall, turning ferociously around and searching for Owyn's whereabouts.

I continue filling myself with as much magic as I can possibly hold, letting my body soak it in the way a sponge soaks up water. I make sure to step off to the side, giving the battling apprentice enough space to fight our mutual foe.

This time, the shadowling approaches Owyn more carefully, weaving its way through the ferns as it backs him up against a tree. "Zara," he says uneasily, raising his hatchet to ward it off. "If you're going to do something, do it fast!" He chops at the creature's head, but it dodges with a frightening display of speed.

The demon raises one of its foreclaws in the air, and with a savage swipe, it strikes Owyn on the shoulder, knocking him back against the tree. Even from this distance, I can hear his head smack against the bark, and I watch as his body crumples to the ground, his weapon falling uselessly from his fingers.

Instead of going in for the kill, the darkhound turns its snarling visage toward me, jowls dripping with saliva. Its ruby eyes connect with mine, and I feel my blood run cold. My spell is still not quite ready to use. Swallowing, I face down my death and silently pray that the Light will aid me.

I begin moving backward, trying to put as much distance between myself and the demon as possible, but my progress doesn't amount for much. It begins prowling toward me, loping steps propelling it faster than I can move my feet. Its lips pull back in a rancorous sneer, and a low growl emits from the back of its throat, filling me with an even greater sense of dread.

As it closes the gap, I finally feel like I have gathered enough source energy to make a difference. Raising both my hands, I shout at the top of my lungs, "*Fos lasair!*"

The energy that fills every fiber of my being gets sucked out of me, gathering at my fingertips with a searing intensity. I begin to lose sight of the looming darkhound and its teeth, the blinding light of the magefyre filling my vision in a brilliant, shimmering display. A ringing fills my ears, and I realize that I am screaming, the sound coming involuntarily from my throat as the magic consumes me.

Just when it feels like I will be overwhelmed, the immense ball of magefyre blasts from my hands and knocks me backward several feet.

I land hard on the ground, momentarily stunned, and I think for sure that the shadowling will be on top of me at any minute. I close my eyes and wait for my death… but the moment never comes.

Blinking, I prop myself up on my elbow and peek over to where the beast was just seconds before. I see it lying in a twitching heap in the brush, fur and flesh utterly consumed by flickering blue flames.

Light almighty! It actually worked!

Pushing myself up, I stand on shaky legs and make my way over to where Owyn lies against the tree. For a brief, horrifying moment, I think he is dead. But as I approach, his eyelids flutter open, and he tries to focus on my face against the light of the sun.

"Did we win?" he asks weakly, lifting his head up from the ground.

I can't help but let out a small laugh. "Yes," I reply, smiling broadly despite my profound fatigue. "The demon is dead."

CHAPTER 17
OWYN

I pull myself up with a groan, my bruised ribs protesting at even the slightest movement.

"Are you alright?" Zara asks me, her smile fading when she notices my pained expression.

"I think so," I wince, looking down at my arm, which is throbbing painfully. My tunic is stained a deep red, and instantly, I know that some of my stitches have broken. *I'm going to have to fix that when I get back into town,* I think with annoyance.

A quick inspection of the rest of my body reveals that the darkhound's claws had not cut me. In fact, my cloak and tunic remain wholly intact.

"Incredible," she says, leaning in and examining my cloak. "It seems that my radiant shield lasted long enough to protect you from any permanent damage. *That* was lucky."

She looks into my eyes and grins, then quickly seems to realize how close she is standing to me, her hand still resting on my chest. Her cheeks grow red, and she takes a step back, clearing her throat.

I look past her to the smoldering body of the demon in the bushes. Its red eyes have grown dim in death. "*Eleven Hells*, Zara! What did you do?"

She shrugs her shoulders. "I cast a really powerful spell. It was my first time attempting it, so I'm glad that it actually worked."

"Worked?" My voice sounds disbelieving and, admittedly, more than a little impressed. "You incinerated the bloody thing!" She nods self-satisfactorily and places her talisman back around her neck.

Looking back over at her, I finally notice the bleariness of her gaze and the way she looks unsteady on her feet. When our eyes meet, I see a mixture of relief and exhaustion. For the first time, it's as if I am truly seeing *her*, and not the mage I had distrusted.

I suddenly feel a genuine concern for her well-being.

"Are *you* alright?" I ask, taking a step forward.

"Yes," she replies, though she sounds weak. "I'm just a little tired. That was more magic than I have ever used before... it certainly takes its toll."

We are interrupted by a whining sound coming from the woods off to the side. I look around the oak tree and see Zara's mule lying among some rocky terrain. Its leg is clearly broken.

"I forgot that I heard it's leg snap in the fall," Zara says behind me. Her tone shifts to one of worry. "Is there any way that we can fix it?"

I shake my head. "Not unless you know any spells that can mend bones."

Her already pale face grows even paler as I reach for my hatchet.

"You can't mean to kill it!"

"We must," I state firmly, putting on a stony mask that would have made Elias proud. Despite my calm exterior, however, I am awash with panic. Unbidden memories of the stag come rushing back, causing my stomach to churn. I ignore my growing sense of dread and look Zara directly in the eye. "Letting it live on like this would be cruel. There is nothing we can do."

I am surprised to see tears well up in her brown eyes. *I thought she wasn't fond of the old girl. Light, this is going to make things even worse.*

160

Doing my best to give her a sympathetic expression, I place a hand on her shoulder. "I'm sorry, Zara. It's probably best if you don't watch." With that, I turn and make my way to where the mule is lying, my heart heavy as a stone.

I place my hand on the animal's neck as I kneel beside it, gently stroking its hair, while whispering words of comfort. "Easy, girl. Easy. Everything is going to be alright." Its huffing breaths sound labored, and again I'm reminded of the stag that I all too recently had been forced to kill.

Elias' words come echoing back into my mind, *'It is part of being a ranger. Sometimes you will find an animal that needs to be put down. Better for it to die quickly rather than slowly. It would be a crime to let it go on living like this.'*

My pulse quickens, my heart pounding loudly in my chest. I just killed a man at the inn, but that was in self-defense. Somehow it felt... justified. I still felt sorrow, but it was nothing compared to this.

Why is this so hard for me?

I need to be stronger than I was before, I think to myself forcefully. *I need to be strong for Zara. Remember the oath, Owyn. Don't be a coward!*

Still whispering and stroking its mane, I locate the spot on its neck that Elias had shown me.

Sucking in a deep breath, I raise up my hatchet and bring it down as hard as I can. Once, twice, a third time. The mule jerks with every hit but I continue, forcing myself to finish the job. It gives one final spasm, but eventually, it lies perfectly still.

Breathing hard, I step back and watch its lifeblood get soaked up by the thirsty forest floor.

The whole ordeal probably lasted less than a minute, but to me it felt like an eternity. My stomach twists sourly, but in the back of my mind, I know I did the right thing.

Elias would approve.

I do my best to clean my axe blade on one of the nearby ferns, but without water, the crevices are still choked with blood. My hands and shirt sleeves look just as bad. When I return, I find that Zara is sniffling and trying to hide the fact that she is wiping away tears from her cheeks.

"We need to head back to town," I say quietly, breaking the silence. "We need to tell the others what we found."

"They likely won't believe us," she sniffs. Her voice is husky from crying. "Why would they?"

"You're right," I mumble to myself, frowning. I rack my brain, trying to come up with a solution. Then I have an idea.

"Follow me," I say, motioning with my hatchet and jogging over to the demon's side. Even though it is dead, getting close to the wretched creature fills me with trepidation. "If we can't bring them to the body, then we can bring the body to them. Or, a part of it, anyway." I crouch down beside the smoking corpse and glance up at Zara. "Evidence."

She raises an eyebrow. "It's a good thought, but there isn't much left."

True enough, the darkhound's body is mostly ruined. The blue flames of her spell have died down, revealing nothing but charred flesh and exposed bits of bone. Its red eyes have all but shriveled into its skull, and no fur remains anywhere to be seen. When my gaze falls on its feet, however, I note that the claws are all intact.

Grimacing, I bend down and use my hatchet to sever one of the claws from the bone. It does not come off easily, and when it finally does, I am careful not to nick myself on its jagged edge. For all I know, the thing could be poisonous.

I stand up and hold the claw for her to see, pinching it between my forefinger and thumb. "Think this'll work?"

She shrugs. "I'm no expert on animals. Do you know of any beasts that have claws that big?"

I shake my head. "None."

"Then I suppose it will do just fine." She makes a disgusted face at the still-smoking body beside us and shuffles a few steps away. "How are we going to get it back to Forest Hill? Your horse is gone and my mule… well, I don't think either of us will be able to ride back."

I slide the hatchet into my belt loop, then move to retrieve my bow and quiver. "My mare is around here somewhere," I reply, slinging them onto my shoulder and tucking the demon's claw carefully into my belt. "We'll find her, then you can ride with me."

Zara glances around at the trees skeptically. "And how do you expect to find her?"

I flash her a small smile. "I'm a ranger's apprentice, remember? Tracking things is what we do."

We set off through the brush, retracing our steps back to the path where I had been forced to dismount. The soil is hard and rocky in places, which makes finding her tracks difficult.

After a few minutes of circling around, I eventually pick up the trail and follow it through a dense thicket of bushes. I find my horse grazing in a small meadow a few hundred yards from our position, saddle and bags still safely secure. She is a little spooked, but I manage to soothe her enough to allow me to make room for Zara, shifting and retying my belongings.

As I work, I mentally memorize our location for future reference, visualizing a map of the Emberwood in my mind.

Elias is going to be so surprised when I show him the body of an actual demon. It is a relief to finally know that I am not going crazy after all.

Battered and exhausted from the day's events, we mount up and begin making our way back to the game trail, navigating our way through the trees toward Forest Hill. We agree to ride hard into the night in order to bring the news of the darkhound as quickly as possible to Elias and the Arch-Magister.

Taking one last look around, I kick my heels into the horse's flanks, and we are off, traveling eastward through the woods as fast as I dare to go.

Fortunately, it is still early enough in the day to give us several hours of sunlight. This will allow us to complete a large stretch of the journey before dark.

Zara's hands clasp my sides as we ride, and I am surprised to find her company rather pleasant. *She handled herself quite well back there*, I think to myself, feeling the warmth of her body pressed against mine. *In fact, I would probably be dead if she had not come along. Though, I probably wouldn't have been in this situation to begin with if she hadn't insisted that I take her out here.*

Still, she is the only person who believed my story, and because of her, we now know that demons are getting through the Arc. I only hope we are not too late to do something about it. With any luck, there will still be time for us to fix the problem before more people get hurt.

The adrenaline I felt from fighting the darkhound begins to quickly fade as we ride, leaving me feeling sore and drained. And I am sure Zara is feeling the same. As a result, we both fall into a brooding silence.

I am forced to slow our pace when the sun goes down, fearing that my own horse's leg will break on an unseen rock. Even so, we still manage to make excellent time and finally see the lights of Forest Hill a few hours after dusk.

"We're here," I announce to Zara as I guide my horse onto the hard-packed road. My poor mare is lathered and winded, but I push her onward. She'll be able to rest soon enough.

"Good," she replies wearily. "Because I don't know if I feel more sore from fighting the demon or from bouncing in this bloody saddle."

I can't help but agree.

We ride up the hill, our side road joining up with the main one, taking us through the heart of town. I don't know if Elias is at the inn or out running patrols around the outer farms, so I decide to head straight for the governor's manor, knowing that Zara's Arch-Magister will know what to do.

The town is mostly deserted, which is understandable due to the late hour. Nonetheless, I do notice a few townsfolk-turned-sentries wandering about, carrying old weapons and eyeing us suspiciously. *Apparently, the attack on the inn is being taken quite seriously,* I think, speeding past the makeshift guards. We make it to the top, where we are finally able to dismount and stretch our muscles, a cool night breeze buffeting us from the north.

"Good girl," I say to the exhausted horse, petting her nose. "You did well."

"C'mon," Zara says, gesturing to the front door of the mansion. "We've no time to lose."

I lead my mare to the stalls, making sure she has plenty of feed and water before following Zara up the wooden steps to the entrance. When we arrive, she opens the door without bothering to knock.

The inside of the large house is dark, but Zara seems to know exactly where she is going, so I follow her through the manor without a word.

We turn a corner and enter a hallway where I can see light pouring out of a partially opened door. Approaching it, Zara peeks inside and asks in a quiet voice, "Arch-Magister?"

"Enter," comes the terse reply, and both of us walk in a second later.

Arch-Magister Elva Tyrande is sitting behind a large wooden desk, looking over an assortment of maps, scrolls, and books spread all over its surface. She looks up at us with a stern expression, and her eyes narrow as she focuses on Zara.

"Initiate Dennel," she states formally. Something in the manner she says it makes Zara cringe. "I was starting to think that you had defected from the Conclave. I was about to issue a warrant to retrieve your talisman."

Zara blanches. "I'm sorry for leaving without saying anything, Arch-Magister. Please forgive me. I can assure you that I had the best interests of the Conclave at heart."

The icy-faced woman turns her stern gaze on me. "And you," she says flatly, "no doubt aided in my ward's disappearance. I had a feeling you would be trouble from the moment I first saw you."

That makes two of us, I think but keep my mouth shut.

"Please, Arch-Magister, you have to listen," Zara blurts out, not giving the elder mage a chance to begin lecturing. "I asked Apprentice Lund to escort me to the location where he claimed he saw the demon. Something about his story piqued my curiosity. When we were out there, I saw the deer, and it was just as he said it was. It was a horrible sight."

As she goes on, the words come out faster, Zara's tone becoming more urgent. "I used a tracing spell and discovered that the whole area was thick with infernae. We were just about to return to Forest Hill when we heard a howling sound, something terrible I had never heard before. That's when we saw it. A real, live demon here in the Emberwood! It was a darkhound, a sort of shadowling the R'Laar used to hunt with! Owyn was telling the truth!"

Taking a deep breath as if she had forgotten to breathe, she looks at the Arch-Magister expectantly, her brown eyes hopeful.

Elva regards us for a moment with a strange expression on her face, as if deep in thought. Almost reluctantly she asks, "Are you certain?"

Both of us nod emphatically.

"I was there, Magus," I say, trying hard to sound contrite. "Zara speaks truthfully. We fought and killed the demon, then returned as fast as we could to tell you." I reach for my belt and pull out the curved black claw, holding it up for her to see. "I took this from the demon's body as proof. We can take you there to see the rest of it, if you want."

Again, there is another pause. After a long moment, she finally turns and rings a silver bell that is sitting on the edge of her desk. "This is grave news indeed," she replies grimly, standing up from her chair and fixing us both with a deep frown. "The two of you are lucky to be alive."

The door opens behind us, and a pair of mages enter the room, holding their talismans in their fists.

"Unfortunately, your story is also a cleverly constructed lie."

Wait, what?

I look over at Zara, who is standing there with her mouth hanging open.

Elva continues. "You two are obviously in collusion with the Nightingales, spreading vile rumors to weaken the king's influence in the Emberwood. There are no demons on this side of the veil. The Arc is impenetrable, perfect in every way."

"But," I protest, my pulse starting to race, "what about the claw? This is proof!"

She snorts derisively. "A clever fabrication, nothing more. I've seen hundreds of trinkets like that for sale in the marketplaces of Tarsys. It's probably an eagle's talon, sold to you by some peddler."

"It is not an eagle's talon!" I reply angrily, slamming the thing down on her desk. "Look at it! It's bigger than my hand!" I look over to Zara for support, but she merely stands there, wide-eyed and stunned by the sudden turn of events.

Elva looks to the men standing behind us. "Seize them," she says coolly, clasping her hands behind her back.

Before I can react, blue shimmering bands of light constrain my limbs, squeezing me tightly so I cannot move my arms or even run away. A glance to the side reveals that the same thing is happening to Zara.

Magic.

"Zara Dennel. Owyn Lund. You are guilty of high treason against the crown. By my authority as Arch-Magister of the Circle of the Conclave of Tarsynium, I hereby place you under arrest and sentence you to *exile*. May the Light have mercy on your souls."

CHAPTER 18
ZARA

My life is over.

I sit sullenly on the hard, wooden bench of the prison cell, my head resting against the cool stone of the wall. Something drips incessantly from somewhere in the basement, but there is not enough light for me to know for sure where it is coming from. The cell is cold, dark, and small.

Just like my future, I think miserably.

I was shocked when Elva had ordered our arrest. The fact that she would accuse us without any evidence of working with the Nightingales makes me question her motives. However, when she sentenced us to *exile,* a fate reserved only for the vilest of criminals, I was completely floored. *How, in the name of the Light, could she turn from being my benefactor to becoming my executioner so quickly?*

None of it makes any sense.

Owyn stands in the cell next to mine, examining the bricks on the wall. I assume he is trying to search for a weak point, anything that could help us escape our fate.

"It's pointless," I say to him, my voice sounding unintentionally annoyed. "Even if we did manage to break out of here, the entire building is full of mages. We wouldn't be able to make it two steps without being burned to a crisp."

"It's worth a shot," he snaps back at me. "Anything is better than waiting here to die."

When the mages had bound us with radiant magic, Owyn had struggled and tried to fight back. But radiant lashings are stronger than steel, and the chances of an ordinary human breaking free are almost nonexistent. Knowing it was pointless, I did nothing. Elva ordered all of our things, including the darkhound claw, to be confiscated. Owyn fought and spat curses at our captors as we were led downstairs, but all his bluster came to no end.

Left here in this dank prison, we can only wait for our judgment to come.

"We're never going to get out," I mutter, closing my eyes in resignation. "You might as well accept it."

"Do you know what it means to be exiled?" Owyn asks, walking up to the thick iron bars separating our cells. Without waiting for my answer, he continues, "It means banishment to the wastes, to live out our days in the realm of the demons. It's a fate worse than death. I do not intend on letting them do that to us. Not when we're bloody innocent."

I, of course, have never seen an exile, but I have heard the stories. The offender is always escorted to the border by a contingent of mages tasked with carrying out the sentence. When they arrive, a priest reads the final rites and prayers offered to those before they die. Then, in a display of power, the mages open a doorway in the Arc, and the criminal is forced out into the Great Waste beyond the shield. Nobody knows what happens to those who are exiled, but their fate is easy to imagine. There is only starvation, disease, and death on the other side of the Arc—probably at the hands of some twisted demon.

Owyn goes back to inspecting his cell, and I continue sulking in silence, drowning in my own thoughts.

All of that effort, all those years of studying in the Academy, has been for nothing. I am going to die a disgrace to my family in the worst way possible, and there is nothing I can do to stop it.

Minutes pass into hours, and I lose track of how long we have been locked up down here.

"Hey!" one of the guards shouts. I jerk my head up to see what is going on. Owyn is picking at the lock with a small sliver of wood. "Get away from there, traitor!" He steps up to the prison door and shakes a fist clutching his talisman. I think his name is Rodrick. "If I see you try anything like that again, I'll burn the fingers right off your hand!"

Owyn glowers at him but does not respond. Instead, he backs away from the door and sits down on the bench.

"That's better," Rodrick sneers. He glances over at me then leaves, walking over to a side room just beyond our jail cells where he and the other mage are stationed.

For a time, we both sit in silence.

Why would Elva do this? I think to myself. *Why would her first reaction be to condemn me as a traitor? I thought that she was beginning to like me... at least as much as someone like her is capable of liking another person.*

As Arch-Magister, Elva is able to wield the full power of the Circle to do pretty much anything she wants. Aside from the High Magus, she is the most powerful woman alive. The crown and the Conclave are the ultimate authorities in Tarsynium. Until now, I believed their rule was right and just. The fact that one of their representatives could sentence Owyn and me to exile without so much as a trial, leads me to believe that there is a fundamental flaw in the system.

Maybe that's why the Nightingales are in rebellion.

Owyn abruptly gets up and moves toward me. His feet scuffing softly on the cold stone floor shakes me from my reverie. He crouches down, his head resting against the bars that are separating us. "There is one thing that bothers me more than anything else," he whispers, his tone no longer defiant. Surprisingly, he sounds sorrowful.

"What is that?" I reply, looking over at him in the low light.

"We risked our lives going out there to find that demon," he says. "We left town to investigate when no one else would, and we put both our futures on the line knowing that if we were wrong, we would probably be severely reprimanded." He looks up at me, and our eyes meet. "We didn't have to do that, Zara."

I shake my head sadly. "No, we didn't."

"Then why are we being punished for doing the right thing? Why does nobody believe us?"

I pause for a moment, considering. "I suppose that, deep down, people no longer consider the R'Laar to be a threat. That, or they don't want to believe that we're no longer safe." I let out frustrated sigh. "Perhaps they're too afraid to consider the thought that we may be right. Or maybe they honestly believe that we *are* in league with the Nightingales. I don't know."

Owyn hesitates before speaking again. "If you could go back, would you do anything different? Would you have stayed behind and ignored my crazy story about the demon?"

I pause, honestly considering the question. Then, after a moment, I answer, "No. I probably would have done the same thing again."

He nods resolutely. "Me too."

"Though, I probably would have gone to Elias instead. In fact, I would have stayed as far away from Elva Tyrande as humanly possible."

Despite our desperate situation, we exchange a light-hearted chuckle.

My mind wanders as I watch Owyn stealthily make his way back around his cell, renewing his search for any weak points that he can exploit. I'm not really sure what his plan is if he does manage to escape. We have nothing to fight with, his weapons and my talisman all confiscated. Not to mention the fact that we are surrounded by dozens of mages and a town full of angry people who are no doubt looking for someone to blame.

My mind continues to ask itself the same questions. *What could have caused Elva to react the way she did? It was almost as if she wanted to silence us, to prevent us from ever being able to tell our story. In fact, there was a troubling look on her face when I claimed to have killed the darkhound. Shock? Worry? Anger? Probably a mixture of all three.*

One thing becomes certain to me as I sit pondering in this depressing little cell: the Arch-Magister is hiding something, and it all relates to the demon, the Nightingales, and the Conclave itself.

And here Owyn and I are, getting swept up in the middle of it all.

Suddenly, Owyn stops moving and looks around, confused. "Zara," he hisses. "Do you hear that?"

I snap out of my thoughts and try to listen, but all I can hear is the sound of water dripping on stone. I shake my head.

He tenses. "Someone's coming."

Light almighty, does he have the ears of a bat? I still can't hear anything. I hold my breath, straining to hear something, anything, that seems out of the ordinary. After a few minutes, I catch an odd sound coming from somewhere on the other side of the basement. It sounds like someone choking.

"Rodrick?" a guard asks nervously in the other room. "Is that you?"

Abruptly, I catch a series of dull, thudding sounds, then a soft crash like a body hitting the ground.

More silence follows.

Owyn and I look at each other in alarm, the same question obvious on both of our faces. *What in the name of the Light is going on out there?*

The answer comes in the form of a hooded figure materializing out of the darkness in front of our prison doors. The figure is tall and broad-shouldered, with a bow slung on his shoulder and a long-bladed knife hanging from his belt. When he removes his hood, I recognize him immediately.

Elias Keen, the ranger.

"Master!" Owyn says excitedly. "You're here!"

Elias nods sternly and produces a ring of keys from his pocket. "Follow me. I'm getting you both the Hells out of here."

CHAPTER 19
OWYN

Elias unlocks my cell door, then goes to help Zara, moving with the cool efficiency I have come to expect from my master.

"How did you know that we were here?" I ask quietly, stepping out into the basement's main chamber.

He opens Zara's cell and places the keys in a pocket within his cloak. "I returned from scouting the perimeter of the town when one of the militiamen standing watch mentioned that he saw a horse carrying two riders up the hill." He turns his stony gaze on me. "After finding your note the other day, I assumed that it could only be you."

Something about the way he says that gives me pause, but I don't have the time to think too deeply on the matter.

"Thank you for rescuing us," Zara says, exiting her cell. "But how are we going to get out of here? This whole building is full of mages."

"This way," Elias replies gruffly, leading us into the little room where the guards had been sitting.

The two mages who had been watching us lie in crumpled heaps on the stone floor, though it is apparent from their shallow breathing that both of them are still alive. They've merely been knocked unconscious, fresh bruises marring their heads and necks.

Stepping over the bodies, Elias leads us to an open window in the upper wall of the storage closet, just large enough for a person to squeeze through.

As he begins to help Zara climb up to our exit, I stop and gesture at the stairs. "What about our weapons?"

"There's no time," Elias replies, using his hands as a foot step for the young mage to reach the window. "We can retrieve them later."

My heart sinks. *That blasted old mage has my father's hatchet.* I decide to say nothing; instead, I walk over to one of the knocked-out guards.

"What are you doing?" Zara whispers suspiciously, her head halfway through the window.

"Being useful," I snap back. Reaching around one of the mage's necks, I pull off a chain holding a small, bluish crystal.

A talisman.

"Here," I say, handing it up to Zara. "These things can be used by anyone, right?"

She nods in surprise and takes the chain before squeezing the rest of the way through the window. *Well, at least two of us are armed now.* I make a silent vow to return here and retrieve my father's hatchet as soon as I am able.

Once she is out, Elias turns to look at me. "Your turn," he says in a low voice.

I do not argue. Stepping on his cupped hands, I propel myself up to the window where the cool night air greets me like an old friend. Grasping the stone wall for support, I pull myself out, sliding through dirt and leaves from the garden on the northern side of the house.

Zara is up there waiting for me, crouching behind a shrub and holding her arms tightly around herself. I brush myself off and move to crouch right beside her.

"Are you alright?" I whisper.

She nods but makes no other reply. She glances around nervously as if she expects her former colleagues to bear down on us at any moment.

Now that I think about it, they just might.

The dark sky is covered with a smattering of clouds, so it is hard to judge the time, but I imagine that we are still a few hours away from dawn. Even after the exhausting day we've been through, including the fight with the darkhound, I find that my mind is razor sharp. My sore muscles and bruises are numbed by the anxiety of our escape and the fear of what will happen if we are captured.

Elias pries himself from the narrow window, somehow managing to remain almost completely silent despite his large frame and the gear he is carrying. I shake my head in wonder at how he managed to do that *twice* while carrying a longbow and a quiver full of arrows.

"What do we do now?" Zara asks, her voice sounding uncharacteristically timid.

My master points to the line of trees on the edge of the hill, perhaps a dozen paces away from the manor. "We make for the forest," comes his reply. "I have horses and supplies waiting for us in the woods."

"What if someone sees us?" Zara hisses.

He gives her one of his signature hard looks. "Stay low and move quickly. We'll be alright. Most of the house is still asleep."

Pausing only for a moment to look around, he takes off across the wide lawn, moving in a sort of half-run, half-crouch. He does not look back to see if we are following.

"Come on," I say to Zara, stepping out from behind the shrub. "It isn't that far."

I can hear her curse softly as we both start running, going as fast as we can across the grass. With the lights of the manor at our backs, I feel exposed out in the open, but we manage to make it more than halfway across without any incident.

Then we hear shouting.

The unconscious bodies in the cellar have been discovered, and the house begins to buzz with activity, reminding me of a disturbed hornet's nest. We practically dive into the bushes of the tree line as we make it to Elias' position, doing what we can to hide in the shadows. We glance back to see if we have been spotted.

More lights begin to turn on, and we can see figures moving frantically within the governor's mansion, shouting and gesturing wildly. I know that it is only a matter of time before they discover the open window and start sending search parties into the woods to come after us.

"Let's go," Elias grunts, disappearing into the trees like a ghost. If it wasn't for the months of training that he has been giving me, I doubt Zara and I would be able to follow him in this gloom.

He leads us down the hill to a shadowed clearing where three horses are tethered to a gnarled oak. My mare is not one of them, and I find myself hoping that wherever she is, she is okay. These horses are fresh, and the saddlebags hanging over their sides appear to be bulging with supplies.

We mount up in silence as the shouts of angry mages follow us deep into the woods. Zara looks like she is about to fall over from exhaustion, so I take her by the hand and help her onto one of the horses. She gives me an odd look as I place my hands on her waist, though I pay it little mind.

The situation is too tense for propriety.

Looking back, I can see that search parties are beginning to organize outside of the manor house, flickering torches held high to shine light in potential hiding places. We are quick to outpace them on our horses and soon lose all sight of civilization.

Yet Elias does not relent. Even when I feel like the danger has passed and we have escaped Forest Hill, he pushes onward, leading us deeper and deeper into the Emberwood. We take game trails and narrow paths through the undergrowth, twisting through the trees in dizzying pathways until even I am disoriented and confused.

Finally, after what seems like a full two hours of riding, we pull our horses to a stop near an outcropping of rocks.

My master dismounts and looks around, making sure that we are alone and secluded. Then, satisfied, he invites us to do the same.

I slide out of the saddle and take a deep breath of the cool night air, the tension leaving my shoulders now that I know we can finally rest. It feels good to be free after spending hours in that miserable cell, and I can't help but grin at our sudden change in fortune.

As I turn to regard Zara, Elias lunges at me, grabbing me roughly by the collar of my tunic.

"Hey!" I protest as he pushes me up against the trunk of a tree. My wounded arm, which I never had a chance to re-stitch, is pressed up hard against the rough bark, sending shockwaves of pain into my shoulder.

"What in the Eleven Hells were you thinking, Owyn?" he growls, his face not two inches from mine. For the first time since I have known him, he looks absolutely enraged. It is, perhaps, the first emotion I have ever seen him outwardly express.

At the moment, I'd much rather face another darkhound.

"I was only trying to help!" I answer weakly. My panicked voice cracks, but Elias does not release me.

His slate gray eyes glitter dangerously in the low light of the stars, and for a brief, terrifying instant, I think he might kill me. "Your recklessness has put us all in incredible danger. What could possibly be worth making enemies of the Conclave?"

"It was my doing," says Zara timidly. She stands behind Elias with her hands clasped in front of her. "I convinced Owyn to take me to the place where he saw the demon."

Elias glances over his shoulder at her, but he still does not release his grip on me. "Then you share the blame equally. Now, one of you start talking. Why did I risk my neck to break you two out of prison?"

Zara begins to tell our story.

"When your apprentice testified in front of the mages, something about his story caught my attention. I wondered how someone could fabricate a tale and yet still be able to tell it so convincingly in front of some of the most powerful mages in Tarsynium. So, I started to do some research. I have an ancient book on demonology in my possession, and it confirmed his description of the demon. It led me to believe that Owyn saw something called a darkhound."

Elias stares at her for a moment, then finally lets me go. I slump against the tree and rub at my chest where he held me.

"When I came by the inn the morning after it was attacked, it was to see him and to ask him a few questions. His story and the book seemed so similar that I concluded it could not have been mere coincidence. I managed to convince him to sneak away with me, just for a day or two, to show me where he had seen the demon."

Finally finding my voice, I speak up to finish the story. "We rode straight away and found the clearing with the deer, but nothing was there. She cast some sort of spell that revealed the demon had been there. That's when the darkhound showed up and attacked us."

An expression flashes across Elias' features—this time surprise. "Are you certain? Could it not have been a feral mountain lion or a wolf?"

"It was a darkhound. A subspecies of a demon called a shadowling," Zara says seriously. "It matched perfectly with the description in my book."

"We managed to fight it off, and Zara used her magic to kill it." I point west to emphasize my point. "Its body is still out there. If we can find it, it will prove our innocence."

Elias rubs his chin thoughtfully and begins to pace the small clearing beneath the stone outcropping. After a few minutes, he looks over at us, his expression perfectly neutral once again. "Did you tell the Arch-Magister everything you just told me?"

Zara nods, her brown eyes growing sad. "We tried. When we arrived back in town, we went straight to her. But for some reason, she would not believe us and wouldn't give us a chance to prove our innocence. She called us traitors and sentenced us to be exiled on the spot."

Elias seems to consider this for a moment. "Perhaps she is afraid that the presence of a demon within the Arc would make the Conclave appear weak. It is possible that she sees it as a threat to her power."

Zara and I remain silent. The gravity of our situation and the sheer exhaustion of the last day and a half finally seem to have caught up with us.

My master abruptly makes his way to the horses and begins to unload our things. "We'll camp here for the rest of the night. We should be far enough away that we will not be discovered. In the morning, you will take me to see the corpse of this demon." He tosses me my bedroll and begins rummaging through one of his packs. "I don't believe that you two are lying to me, but some things a man just has to see for himself."

I glance over at Zara, and she offers me a weary smile. *I suppose that's the best we can hope for, considering the circumstances.*

Elias continues. "If it is true and demons are finding their way into the kingdom, then we are facing the biggest threat humanity has seen since the Doom. That makes a little treason look like nothing in comparison."

He hands Zara a small parcel of food. "I will stand watch for the rest of the night. You both look in need of some rest."

Zara and I murmur in agreement.

As we begin unfolding our bedrolls, I wince at the pain in my arm. *The damn thing feels infected,* I think to myself as I touch it tenderly with my fingers.

"You're hurt," Elias observes, walking over to me with his hand on his belt knife.

I nod. "From the fight back at the inn. I must have burst some of the stitches when we fought the demon."

Zara looks over at me as she lays out her bed roll, her eyes concerned.

"Let me see it," Elias says gruffly, stepping next to me and helping me pull up my sleeve. After a minute, he makes his way over to his saddlebags without another word and begins rummaging through them.

When he returns, he carries a small pouch from which he produces a needle, a roll of gut, and a small vial. "You shouldn't have waited this long to take care of this, Owyn," he mutters with a scolding tone. "This will need antiseptic to kill the infection."

"Between the demon and being thrown in jail, I haven't had a lot of time," I grumble.

He ignores my remarks and begins working silently on my arm. Every stitch is extremely painful, but I endure it stoically so as not appear weak in front of Zara. She pretends to be asleep, but I can tell that she is still covertly watching us. When Elias applies the antiseptic, however, I can't help but grunt in pain. It stings like acid as it pours over my wound.

When it is finally over, Elias leaves to put away his supplies.

"Thank you, master," I say, gingerly going to prepare myself for bed.

He merely nods and picks up his bow, beginning his quiet watch so that we can rest.

I am so exhausted that I don't even bother eating or getting out of my cloak. The events of the last several days have taken a lot out of me. I slowly unroll my sleeping mat and climb under my blanket.

Blessedly, I fall into a light but dreamless sleep.

CHAPTER 20
ZARA

We manage to get a couple hours of sleep before Elias wakes us up, although it feels like I have barely closed my eyes. For a moment, I just lie there tired, hungry, and homeless, before I can summon enough energy to get up from my bedroll.

Elias and Owyn, *Light curse them*, are up and already packing away their things.

Blinking away the sleep from my eyes, I kneel down and wind up my bedroll, forcing my complaints down with considerable difficulty.

How quickly my life has fallen apart. What have I done to deserve this? I have literally gone from being the brightest star at the Academy to becoming an escaped convict in the middle of some conspiracy that will probably get me killed.

Owyn seems to notice my foul mood, so he offers me some bread and honey. "Here," he says gently, giving me the wrapped bundle of food. "You eat while I saddle your horse."

I begrudgingly take the bundle and hand him my pack. "Thanks," I mutter, and he nods stoically. The bread is fresh, and the honey is sweet, but it does little to lift my spirits. Too much has happened too quickly for me to even enjoy the taste of food.

What's going to become of me? Am I going to live like a vagrant the rest of my life?

Before long, my breakfast is gone, and the rangers are preparing their horses for departure. I follow suit, despair being replaced by apprehension as I approach my mount. The black and white mottled horse looks at me with a big, black eye, and memories of being thrown from the saddle start to flood my mind.

Owyn glances at Elias, whose back is to us, then takes a step toward me, offering a hand as he did last night.

I look from him to his hand and then back again, raising an eyebrow questioningly.

He clears his throat. "Need a hand?"

I shake my head. "If I'm ever going to get over this *perfectly rational* fear of horses, I'm going to have to face it head on."

He nods and backs away, dropping his hand to his side.

Swallowing my anxiety, I place my foot in the stirrup and pull myself up. My heart pounds as I ease into the saddle, but miraculously, nothing happens. The horse just stands there, placidly eating grass. I flash Owyn a triumphant smile which he returns, looking more than a little impressed.

He turns to his own horse and deftly jumps into the saddle, making the action look effortless.

I roll my eyes at him. *Show off.*

As the two rangers pull away, I nudge my horse forward, its hooves plodding along on the hard-packed dirt. We leave our little campsite by the rocks behind as we descend into the woods, the temperature of the early morning dropping considerably as the trees cut us off from the sunlight.

I settle into a groove as we ride, the nervousness of being back on a horse somewhat lessened as we navigate through the tangled woods. We are not going nearly as fast as we were when the demon was chasing us, and the current pace is slow enough to give me a small measure of confidence.

Unfortunately, the less I think about being on this four-legged beast, the more I dwell on the bleak outlook of my current situation. Considering that the Arch-Magister has labeled me an outlaw, my life's goal of becoming a mage is gone. To top it all off, there is a very real chance that demons are invading Tarsynium, and that the last kingdom on Byhalya is going to be completely destroyed or enslaved.

It could be worse, I suppose, I think to myself bitterly. *It could be raining.*

Contrary to that last dreary thought, the weather grows warmer, and the Emberwood seems to come alive as we continue our ride. I let myself watch idly as a squirrel scampers up a nearby tree, and I listen to the sounds of the birds chirping and singing in the boughs above our heads. *Nature doesn't care about the struggles we go through. People die, kingdoms fall, and still, life goes on.*

There is probably a lesson in there somewhere, but right now, I can't see it. Or perhaps I don't want to.

Sometime during the late morning, Owyn slows down his horse and begins riding right next to me. "Listen," he says. "I've been thinking..."

"That's a surprise," I reply, then flash him a slight, sarcastic smile to show him I am joking.

He gives me a flat look. "Very funny. Remember when you told me that the Nightingales who attacked us had been bewitched by a demon?"

I nod. "I remember. It is a process called mindflaying. The R'Laar used to do it to the people of old Byhalya during the Great War."

"Were darkhounds responsible for mindflaying?"

"Darkhounds? I'm not sure."

He hesitates, gathering his thoughts. "It's just that... I find it hard to believe that a darkhound would be capable of casting a spell. I mean, the creature we fought was fearsome, but I don't think it had the mental fortitude to control people's minds, do you?"

I take a moment to consider his observation. "No," I reply thoughtfully. "No, I don't think so."

"Exactly. That's my point... if the Nightingales were bewitched, wouldn't that mean that there is a more powerful demon out there right now, controlling them?"

"I suppose that it would." The thought of more powerful demons roaming the wilderness is a disturbing one.

A grim silence passes between us as the implications of this revelation sink in.

After a minute or two, Owyn speaks up again. "This leads me to another question. How are the Nightingales involved at all? What is their role in all of this?"

I actually do have an answer to this. "Perhaps this demon, whatever it is, saw the Nightingales as a possible scapegoat. Who better to frame their atrocities on, than the people rebelling against the king? It would be a good way to cover their tracks. Just maybe, we can use this as an excuse to unite with the rebels against a common enemy."

Unexpectedly, his face darkens. "The Nightingales are scum, Zara. Cutthroats and traitors, all of them. I would not ally myself with them if the kingdom itself were falling down around us."

"That is a rather narrow-minded viewpoint," I reply tersely.

His frown deepens to a glare, and he clicks his tongue, nudging his horse forward and pulling away from me.

Apparently, our conversation is over.

I quirk an eyebrow at his back. *Testy, aren't we? Though, I suppose, I would also harbor ill feelings against the Nightingales if they had attacked my comrades and me in the middle of the night.* Still, I can't help but wonder why my suggestion to work with the rebels would evoke such an emotional response from the normally sober apprentice.

Shrugging, I turn my gaze back out to the woodlands, watching the trees and letting the scenes of nature occupy my thoughts. I am no expert in navigation, but I imagine that we still have many hours to go before we arrive at the demon's body.

Despite my attempts to lose myself in the scenery, the question Owyn asked me the night before still nags at me. *If you could go back, would you change your decision?* My answer had been no, but that was just my gut reaction. As I sit here, riding uncomfortably in my saddle, I can't help but question my earlier reply.

It leaves me feeling uneasy for the duration of our journey.

By midafternoon, our surroundings start to become more familiar to me. Even my untrained eyes can spot landmarks I only just noticed the other day.

We are getting close now, I think to myself, hand straying up to my talisman, grateful to Owyn for taking it off of our mage guard.

Elias seems to notice the same thing, and it is not long before he pulls his horse to a stop, gesturing for us to gather around him.

"You mentioned that you fought the darkhound somewhere around the clearing," he says with the same gruffness that I have come to expect from him. "The deer are about two hundred paces in that direction. Owyn, you take the lead from here. Bring us to where you killed it."

Nodding, Owyn pulls ahead and begins guiding us through a dense thicket of trees and up a gently sloping hill. I start to feel tense as we draw nearer to the area where we had fought the demon, as if there is still danger lurking about. It becomes obvious to me that I am not alone in feeling this way. Both rangers have their bows out with arrows nocked, eyes warily scanning the woods around us.

I wrap my fingers reflexively around my talisman, though I do not attempt to pull in any source energy. It makes me feel better just to have the warm crystal up against my skin.

My eyes catch a glimpse of something lying in a gulley, a sight that sends a shiver down my spine.

Resting in the ferns is the still form of a dead mule.

We're here, I find myself thinking, my palms becoming slick with sweat. *The darkhound should be just on the other side of these trees.*

Owyn dismounts and begins tying up his horse, gesturing silently for us to do the same. Due to the uneven terrain, it is easier for us to continue on foot. After making sure that our mounts are secure, we begin hiking through the underbrush and toward the small clearing beyond.

As we walk, I begin to see signs of our battle with the demon. Gouged earth here, scratches on a tree there. I even see the scorch marks on the ground that had been left by my magefyre. There is only one problem.

The darkhound's body is gone.

Owyn sprints over to the bushes where we left it, bewilderment painted clearly on his face. "It was right here!" he exclaims, poking through the bushes with the bottom of his bow. "I swear, we left it here in the bushes."

Elias looks about, his brow furrowed. "It is clear to me that there was some sort of fight here, but I see no sign of a demon."

"It's true," I insist, joining Owyn in the search for the shadowling. "I shot it with my magefyre, and it landed in these bushes. It was clearly dead."

Elias folds his arms in front of him, frowning at Owyn. "What sort of game are you playing at, boy?" His voice is low and gravelly, reminding me of a growling wolf.

"I'm not playing a game!" Owyn's voice grows louder, his tone clearly indicating that he is upset. "That thing, the same one I saw a week ago, almost killed us! Zara burned it to a crisp, and we left straight for Forest Hill."

"There's a spell," I say, cutting in gently but firmly. "It can detect the foul energy left behind by demons. If you give me a moment, I can prove that we are not lying."

Elias stares at us both and raises a skeptical eyebrow. Then, abruptly, his skepticism replaced by a look of concern. He cocks his head to the side and appears to be listening for something, the way a dog might listen for some sound imperceptible to human ears. He curses.

Drawing his long-bladed knife, he casts his eyes about the thicket, searching for something that Owyn and I cannot see.

"What is it?" I ask, reaching my hand back up to touch my talisman. "Is something wrong?"

Owyn narrows his eyes and cocks his head as well. "I hear it, too. We're not alone." He nocks an arrow to his bow in one swift motion and draws, looking at the trees surrounding us, in search of an unseen threat.

I finally notice as well, but it's too late.

Hooded figures step out from behind the trees—a few at first, but then more, all carrying loaded crossbows pointed directly at us. Soon, we are completely surrounded, their black cloaks stark against the greenery of the forest. I count nearly two dozen of the rogues, but their numbers are not what trouble me. It is the bird-like emblem sewn across each of their cloaks.

Nightingales.

One of the men steps forward and removes his hood. He is a rugged-looking fellow with a bushy black beard and a puckered scar on his cheek. He fixes us with a dangerous glare. "Put down your weapons and nobody will get hurt. We have you surrounded, and we will not hesitate to kill you all."

CHAPTER 21
OWYN

I watch in mute horror as Elias drops his knife in the dirt and removes his bow, complying with the traitor's request.

How can he give up so easily? I think to myself, furious.

Two hooded men, crossbows still trained on his heart, approach Elias and pick up his weapons, proceeding to search him thoroughly.

As if by some hidden cue, the rest of the Nightingales surge forward, closing in on Zara and me. I stand there for a moment, staring down the shaft of my arrow at a gaunt man holding a crossbow, when the bearded one speaks up again, his voice sounding coarse and annoyed. "This is your final warning, boy. Put down your arms and submit. Your stubborn pride isn't worth losing your life over."

Finally, painfully, I lower my bow, fixing everyone around me with a hateful glare.

Anger boils in the pit of my stomach as the Nightingales pat me down and remove my weapons. They are comprehensive in their search of my person, and rough in the way they tie my hands in front of me, efficiently cinching the rope tight against my wrists.

Instinctually, I look over and see that Zara is receiving similar treatment. Apparently, they recognize the gray robes that she is wearing, because they make a point of removing her talisman.

Once we are defenseless and tied up, the bearded man, whom I assume is their leader, orders his men to blindfold us.

Great, I think bitterly. *Add insult to injury.*

Thick cloth is tied around my head so that my eyes are covered, the scratchy fabric stretching from my forehead to the tip of my nose. It is uncomfortable, but it is nothing compared to the rope digging into the flesh of my wrists.

Suddenly, I feel something sharp prod me in the back. "Move," a raspy voice orders in my ear. "And if you even think about running, I'll slip this knife right in between your ribs."

"Got it," I reply, though my voice is full of defiance.

We briskly start to walk.

Our captors lead us through the woods in a haphazard path that I'm sure even Elias cannot remember. My guard is kind enough to ensure that I keep up with the hurried pace of the group by jabbing me here and there with his blade. His pokes are not hard enough to injure me, but it is more than enough to keep me from slowing down.

The Nightingales mostly travel in silence, guiding us through the forest toward an undisclosed location. I pass the time by fantasizing about breaking free from my bonds and sticking my captor in the eye with his knife, but I make no effort to escape.

If anyone has a plan to get us out of this mess, it will be Elias.

It seems that we are walking for hours, and I eventually realize that we are moving uphill. I take a deep breath and notice the scent of pine in the air, trees that only grow in the Ironbacks. *Could we be heading toward the mountains?*

Every so often, I trip over a rock or a root, but rough hands make sure I do not fall and slow the group down.

I am able to glean little from the snippets of conversation I manage to overhear, but there are several words that stand out to me. *Kingsmen. Bad omens. Dagger's Point.* That last one sounds like a place. Perhaps that is where we are going?

When we stop for a short rest, we are given sips of water and bites of grainy bread, but they never allow us to remove our blindfolds. Evidently, the Nightingales don't want us to see where we are going; that way, we will not be able to disclose the location of their hideout in the future. *Smart move,* I think to myself. *Though, I bet Elias will be able to figure out where we are within a minute of getting his blindfold off.*

"Where are you taking us?" I ask to no one in particular during one of our infrequent breaks.

I hear a few people chuckle around me.

"You'll walk until we tell you to stop, little ranger," someone replies with a snicker, ignoring my question. This elicits more laughs from his fellows.

"You lot are traitors and cowards," I growl in return. Somewhere, I hear Zara quietly begging for me to stop. I ignore her warning, the words bubbling out of my throat like a pot of boiling water. *I don't care that Elias and Zara are listening. I don't even fear for my life.*

My anger against the Nightingales runs too deep.

"What," I continue with a sneer, "are we to become your prisoners? Forced to be bargaining chips so that you can get a little gold from the king? You're nothing more than bandits and cutthroats, too weak to mount any real sort of rebellion—"

The breath is blasted out of my lungs as somebody punches me in the gut. I double forward and fall hard on my knees. My ears fill with raucous laughter that makes my face flush with heat.

"We're taking you to our leader," says a familiar voice above the laughing. I recognize it as belonging to the bearded man with the scar. He sounds deadly serious. "These are troublesome times and to catch two rangers and a mage exposed in the wilderness is a rare find indeed. We will take you to William Pyke, and he will decide what to do with you."

I finally manage to suck in a ragged breath as he raises his voice and yells, "Move out!"

We begin our hurried march again, and this time, I decide to keep my mouth shut.

Hours pass and judging by the drop in temperature, it is getting close to nightfall. The skin on my wrists is raw and bloody from rubbing against the coarse rope, and every bouncing step is agony on my hands. When I feel like I cannot possibly go any further without passing out from the pain, I hear the grating sound of metal hinges and the creaking noise of a large door or gate being opened.

My senses tell me that we have once again come to civilization, though I wonder how civilized these Nightingales really are.

The scents of wood fires and cooking stew fills my nostrils and the pinging sound of a hammer on an anvil rings somewhere close by, along with the chatting voices of dozens of people whispering eagerly about the new prisoners.

We have finally arrived at the Nightingale camp.

I feel my feet step onto a wooden platform, and soon we are being ushered up some stairs, the buzz of the populace growing fainter behind me. It comes as something of a surprise, however, when I am forced to my knees, and the blindfold is torn unceremoniously from my face.

I blink for a moment against the sudden brightness.

When my vision clears, I see that Elias, Zara, and I are kneeling in a wide chamber of roughly hewn timbers in front of two iron braziers containing flickering orange flames. On either side of us stand our captors, still aiming their crossbows at our chests, facing forward with grim expressions on their faces. There are several black banners in the room depicting the silver image of a nightingale in flight.

In between the braziers stands a man behind a desk covered in maps, papers, and books. He is tall and well-muscled and is wearing a steel breastplate and a wolf pelt cloak around his broad shoulders. He looks at each of us with appraising eyes.

"What have you brought me, Barus?" His voice is powerful and strong.

The bearded man, apparently named Barus, steps forward and salutes the man in the breastplate. "General, we captured these prisoners near the border of the Arc of Radiance, not far from the village of Haven. These two are rangers, and the girl is a mage from Tarsys."

The general nods, but his face remains austere. "I see. And what business do two rangers and a mage have coming so close to the border?"

I want to stand up and yell at this man, tell him that rangers may go wherever they damn well please. But I wisely bite my tongue and remain silent.

After a few heartbeats, Elias speaks up with his head held high. "The Emberwood is our responsibility as rangers of the crown. There have been many disturbances in the forest lately, and we were attempting to investigate the matter when your men apprehended us."

He and Elias lock gazes, and momentarily, it feels like nobody breathes.

Then the general breaks the uncomfortable silence. "Disturbances, strange occurrences, abductions... these are indeed dangerous times." He reaches to his belt and pulls out a serrated knife from a leather sheath. "And often," he continues, looking down at the jagged blade, "dangerous times call for desperate measures."

He steps out from behind the table and approaches us, his studded boots thudding noisily on the wooden floor. Walking with a determined stride, he approaches my master with the knife gripped firmly in his gloved fist, a resolute look in his eyes.

Elias does not react at all but remains kneeling with his back straight and his jaw set.

I clench my teeth as the general stands in front of my master and raises the knife in front of his chest.

CHAPTER 22
ZARA

My stomach convulses as the Nightingale general lifts his knife. *This is it,* I think frantically. *He is going to execute us in front of his men. We're all going to die.*

Looking right into Elias' eyes, the big man brings it down and slices, not into the ranger's body, but into the ropes binding his wrists. He saws through the ties in short order, and soon, Elias is free.

I let out a breath that I did not know I had been holding.

The general steps over to Owyn next, then to me, using that wicked-looking knife to cut our bindings before returning it to his belt. He steps back and gestures for us to stand. "Forgive us for the rough way you were treated. It was not my intention to have you taken prisoner. But you must understand, we take the security of our people very seriously."

Owyn and I look at each other incredulously, but as usual, Elias is unfazed.

"Why have you brought us here?" he asks, his voice steady and cool.

The general regards us for a moment, then looks over to the other Nightingales in the room. "Barus, please give us some privacy."

The bearded warrior raises his bushy eyebrows and stares at us apprehensively. "But... general, are you certain?"

The general nods. "Yes. Now, leave us be." His commanding tone is final.

Warily, the cloaked men withdraw, leaving us alone with their leader. Before Barus shuts the door, he fixes the three of us with one final glare.

The door shuts, leaving us alone with the general standing in front of the crackling braziers.

The brute man lets out a sigh and walks back to the table, leaning heavily over the maps with his back to us. "My name is William Pyke," he says. "I am the leader of this expeditionary force and the lord of Dagger's Point."

"Dagger's Point?" Owyn blurts out.

I see Elias give him a sharp look.

"Yes," replies Pyke. "That is the name of this fort. Its purpose is to serve as a staging ground for the Emberwood and to keep a careful watch for King Aethelgar's agents." He turns around and looks at us, crossing his arms. "It would appear that we have found some."

"General Pyke," Elias interjects, taking a step forward. "Why have we been captured and brought here? You know as well as anyone that we are not mere soldiers."

It's a fair question, I find myself thinking as I rub the tender skin on my wrists. *Harming mages or rangers are capital offenses under the king's law. Though, I presume the Nightingales care little for the laws of the land.*

"I will answer your question," Pyke says coldly, "but not before you tell me why you were investigating the border."

Elias hesitates. "It is our duty as rangers."

"Then tell me, why is there a Conclave spy in your company?"

"Hey!" I find myself saying. "I'm not a spy!" All eyes turn to me, and I can feel my cheeks growing red. I silently berate myself for the outburst.

"As I said before," Elias continues, as if I'd said nothing. "We are looking into some recently reported disturbances and trying to uncover the truth of what has been going on in the Emberwood."

Pyke pauses for a moment, then asks more slowly, "And what has your investigation uncovered?"

Elias eyes the general, then matches his cold tone with one of confidence. "One of our villages, a small community called Haven, has been destroyed, its inhabitants brutally murdered. There have been reports of strange... animals roaming the wilderness. And your very men, or men wearing your colors, attacked the inn at Forest Hill and murdered several people under my protection. They were good, honest folk who did not deserve to die."

This seems to put Pyke on the defensive. For a second, he looks almost surprised. Then his hardened frown returns as if it had never left at all. "Those were not my men," he replies, turning his head to gaze into the coals of one of the large fires. "Not anymore, anyway."

We are all silent for a moment, letting his words sink in before the general begins to speak again.

"Those men had been turned," he says, looking back to regard Elias with a subtle hint of apprehension. He clearly feels uncomfortable sharing this information. "They ceased being human weeks ago when they disappeared while out on patrol."

"General Pyke," I say, drawing the big man's attention. "I have been aiding these rangers in their search for the truth, and I believe that we have uncovered something that could be a danger to both the Nightingales and the entire kingdom. Something that, until recently, has only been thought to be a legend."

"So," he says, looking at me intensely. "You've discovered the demons, then?"

Elias, Owyn, and I all share the same look of shock.

"Demons?" I reply. "Plural?"

He nods his head gravely. "It would seem that we share a common enemy, Magus. The demons have somehow managed to make it through the Arc."

"Then your men..." Owyn says, letting the words trail off.

"Turned," finishes the general bluntly. "They were bewitched by a powerful demon named Moloch."

"Moloch?" I ask, intrigued. "It has a name?"

"Yes," he says pained, gazing back into the flames. "A few weeks ago, one of our units stumbled upon something strange while on patrol near the border. They said that the Arc was *shimmering*. Rippling like a pond after you toss in a stone. During this odd occurrence, they witnessed a terrible creature step through the energy field and into our realm from the other side. Their report told us that it walked like a man, and yet it had horns, with skin and eyes as red as blood."

"A gorgon," I whisper, remembering an entry from the book.

He nods. "Behind it came a host of other creatures, over a hundred strong. My men tarried just long enough to overhear another demon refer to the horned one as Moloch. When they first returned, we did not believe their tale. How could we? Everyone knows that the Arc is indestructible. However, it was not long before we were forced to face these monsters on the field of battle. Many died in that fight..."

Owyn clears his throat in the ensuing silence, but his voice holds little sympathy as he recounts our own experience with the shadowling. "Zara and I fought one of these creatures near Haven. We managed to kill it, but it was a tough fight."

"It was a darkhound," I add, backing up his claim.

"Then you two are luckier than most," he replies gravely. "For they tore through our ranks like a scythe through wheat."

"I think that they have something of a weakness to magic," I say, reaching for my talisman out of habit. My stomach drops as my fingers find nothing but air.

"It doesn't surprise me. Regardless, I lost a whole unit of scouts to that red bastard, Moloch. He turned them all into mindless slaves."

"This shimmering portal in the Arc," Elias says, his eyebrows knitting together with concern. "Are more demons coming through every day?"

"That's the strangest part about all of this," Pyke replies, rubbing his chin. "My scouts told me that once the last of Moloch's host came through, it closed up like it had never even been there at all. It was as if they opened a door and closed it behind them."

"Eleven Hells," Owyn says, chewing his lip.

Eleven Hells is right.

"Look," Pyke grunts, his tone becoming commanding once again. "It is fortunate that you stand before me so that I can confirm that we had nothing to do with the recent attacks in Forest Hill. In fact, I believe that there is a way that we can help each other out."

Elias raises an eyebrow but does not respond.

"No matter our political differences, we all live under the radiant veil. That means the presence of demons threatens every one of us. I propose a truce between your people and mine, at least until we can defeat these demons and figure out how they are getting through."

Owyn looks completely floored by the general's suggestion, and I don't feel much different. *The Nightingales and crown are sworn enemies and have been at war for generations. Is it even possible for there to be peace between us?*

Even Elias looks skeptical. "Why would you want a truce with the king?"

"Because I have faced these creatures in battle, and I know what they are capable of." He takes a step forward, and for a moment, I see a flash of fear in his eyes. A recent memory, perhaps? "Apart, we have no hope of stopping the demons before they lay waste to this part of the country. But together, together we may just be able to defeat them."

Elias is silent for a few seconds. When he responds, his speech is slow and thoughtful. "Your words carry weight, General Pyke.

And your testimony, along with that of my apprentice and Zara, is enough to make me consider this threat to be real. Unfortunately, I am only a ranger. I cannot speak for the king or those living in the Emberwood. I would be happy to relay this information to Governor Prior as soon as possible, though."

The general heaves a sigh. "I suppose that is as much as I can hope for." He walks over to the door and pounds his fist on it three times. The man Barus and two of his soldiers stride through, his face drawn like a freshly loaded crossbow.

"You will be our guests tonight," Pyke says, gesturing at the door. "We will see that you are given proper lodgings, then tomorrow we will send you on your way, along with our message. Hopefully, we can then resolve this matter once and for all."

Elias bows his head in respect. "That is very kind of you, general."

I give him a slight curtsy.

Owyn does nothing.

After a brief explanation that we are to be escorted at all times by one of his men while we remain in Dagger's Point, he concludes our meeting and sends us on our way before turning back to pore over his maps.

We are brought out into the late evening air by Barus and our escorts and find that we are standing on a wooden platform overlooking a courtyard carved into the face of a large bluff. Walls made from sharpened spears of wood line the fortification and people mill around campfires in the central area, eating and talking amiably with one another.

There must be well over a hundred of them, I think to myself in amazement. *How could such a large group of people go unnoticed in the Emberwood?*

"This way," Barus says gruffly as he leads us from the platform to a walkway built into the stone of the bluff.

I look up and see a massive rock formation looming above our heads, a slab of granite worn by wind and weather to resemble the appearance of a large blade. *Well,* I think to myself, *at least now I know where Dagger's Point got its name.*

Our group of six makes its way across the walkway to a squat wooden building erected against one of the walls of spears. The roof is made of straw, and upon closer inspection, I see that mud has been used in place of mortar to keep the timbers and thatch together. A humble dwelling, to say the least.

"This will be your quarters while you stay at Dagger's Point," Barus explains, gesturing to the building with a gloved hand. "Dinner has already been served, so you will have to wait until sunrise to eat.

My heart sinks at this revelation, but I do not protest for fear of antagonizing them.

"If you need to make for the privy," he continues without missing a beat, "make sure that you bring one of us with you. You will have guards stationed outside your door all night." He gives me a meaningful look, and his companions snicker. My cheeks flush with heat, and at my side, I catch a glimpse of Owyn clenching his fists in anger.

Without another word, Barus opens the door and steps aside, motioning for us to enter.

We do so silently with the eyes of the entire courtyard on our backs.

The building, which I would probably compare to a cabin, is dimly lit by a fire pit dug into the center of the dirt floor. The ceiling is low, with a hole cut into the top to allow the smoke to escape, and the smell of soil and tree sap hangs heavily in the air. A few roughly hewn logs serve as the only furnishings in the main room. Three other rooms, which I assume are sleeping chambers, branch off from three of the four walls.

"Again," Barus says, a small grin splitting his bearded face, "if you must leave this area, let one of us know. Otherwise, you will be used for target practice." He taps the crossbow on his hip before closing the door and leaving us to our seclusion. We can hear their startlingly noisy laughter outside of our little hut.

For a minute, we stay there and look at each other, taking in our dismal surroundings as if none of us knows quite what to do.

Finally, Owyn coughs, breaking the silence. "I'm going to bed," he mutters and walks into one of the bedrooms. Closing the door behind him, he leaves Elias and me standing uncomfortably alone in the main room.

Looking around, I lower my voice to a whisper and ask bluntly, "What has Owyn so riled? He seems to hate the Nightingales more than most."

Elias regards me briefly before responding, his voice pitched low as well. "Owyn has some... history with the Nightingales that gives him some deeply held prejudices."

I raise an eyebrow. "Are you saying that he was once one of them?"

He shakes his head. "No, Zara. That's not what I mean." Letting out a sigh, he makes his way over to one of the logs and sits down next to the fire. "Owyn's father was a ranger."

I nod my head. "Yes, he mentioned that the other day."

"Well," Elias goes on, "he was a very renowned, very dedicated ranger... and he was also a close friend of mine."

Suddenly quite intrigued, I try to pull up a log next to where Elias is sitting. After a few feeble attempts, I sheepishly glance at him and shrug. He raises an eyebrow at me, then grudgingly rises to drag the log closer to his.

After a moment, he continues. "When Owyn was just a child, his father went on an expedition into the Ironback Mountains. This was during one of the largest Nightingale insurrections in recent years. His mission was to discover where their base was located, a hidden place called Dunmar City. While he was away, he and his partner were discovered and killed by the Nightingales.

That hatchet Owyn carries is all that he has left of his father, that and his legacy as a ranger."

"Light almighty," I whisper, genuinely saddened by his tragic story.

"I tell you this, not because you are a mage, but right now, the three of us are inseparably connected in this tangled web. I hope that now you can understand what he is going through and can be a friend to him while we make it through this mess."

"Of course," I reply simply.

He stands and steps away from the fire pit, his steel-gray eyes reflecting the light of the coals. "I think it would be best if all of us tried to get some rest tonight. I fear that there will be little sleep in the days ahead." He makes as if to enter one of the other bedrooms, then pauses and looks over his shoulder at me, his face a stony mask. "Zara, please keep this conversation quiet. Owyn does not like speaking about what happened to his father. Bringing it up will only cause strife between us."

I nod, and he disappears, leaving me alone in the common area. For a while, I just sit and watch the flickering flames dance upon the dying coals, my thoughts lingering on the enigmatic ranger's apprentice.

CHAPTER 23
OWYN

A cool breeze cuts through the early morning air like a knife and rustles the leaves of the Emberwood, the forest whispering its greeting with the dawn.

I open my eyes and find myself lying on my back in the middle of a clearing, staring up at the pinkish hue of the sky and watching the clouds being carried away on the wind. Taking a breath of fresh air, I sit up and look around, trying to figure out where I am. *How did I get to this clearing?* I think to myself curiously. *Why am I here?* My surroundings are unfamiliar, so I push myself up to my feet and begin to explore the area with no real sense of urgency.

Blades of grass and fallen leaves crunch softly beneath my bare feet, but my eyes are on the edge of the forest, looking for a pathway forward. No matter which direction I go, or how long I walk, the clearing never seems to end, and I'm never able to reach the trees.

Odd, I find myself thinking, *this clearing seems to stretch on forever.*

Something wet squishes between my toes. It is sticky and warm. I look down and realize that the ground and everything around me is completely soaked in blood.

My heart begins to race, eyes darting from my red-stained feet to a still shape resting on the ground close by. It is a stag with an arrow sticking out of its haunch, its throat opened wide as maggots pour out onto the ground.

I gag and take a step back, nearly stumbling over the rotting carcass of another deer. Horrified, I look around and realize that I am standing in the clearing Elias and I had discovered all those days ago, only the blood covering the grass is still fresh.

Slipping, I catch myself before I fall into one of the crumbling piles of flesh and bone. Looking up, I see eyes staring at me from the shadows of the trees.

Twin, red orbs glow in the darkness and gaze at me hungrily no more than twenty paces away. They are quickly joined by another pair of eyes, and another, until the entire forest around me resembles a sky full of crimson stars.

I hear a low growling sound that comes at me from all directions, and I gasp, covering my ears. The guttural noises still get through, filling my ears with the sound of a thousand starving wolves. The only thing that pierces the din is the sound of my own screaming, tearing painfully out of the depths of my throat.

Falling to my knees, I sink into the blood until I become stuck, and that is when the darkhounds emerge.

Hundreds, if not thousands of them, creep out of the forest, their slavering jaws stretching open to reveal wide mouths of curving ivory teeth. The growling sound intensifies as they approach.

Feebly, I reach for my hatchet to ward them off, but it is not there. My belt loop is empty.

They pounce, their scythe-like claws ripping my flesh to pieces, teeth snapping at me in a frenzy. I let out another scream, but it is drowned out by the gurgle of my own blood...

I sit bolt upright in my bed, heart thundering loudly in my chest. My eyes dart this way and that, searching for the darkhounds I know are still there.

It takes me several terrifying minutes to realize that I am alone.

My breath comes in great, heaving gasps as I try to calm myself down. My entire body is drenched in an icy cold sweat.

It's alright, I think to myself. *It was only a dream.*

Shifting on the lumpy mattress in the tiny closet of a room, I run a hand through my hair and force my eyes shut. *The Nightingale fort... I am here with Elias and Zara...*

It all starts coming back to me.

Shaking my head to push away the thoughts of demons, I reach over the side of the bed and begin pulling on my boots. I know that I will not be able to fall back to sleep, so I may as well get up and do something productive.

I throw on my cloak and step out of the bedroom, where I find an empty common area with ash-covered embers smoldering in the fire pit. *The other two must still be asleep*, I conclude. My stomach rumbles, and I decide to go outside to look for some food.

As I push the door open, I am confronted by two sleep deprived guards, who look at me with a mixture of surprise and annoyance. Stepping out into the brisk pre-dawn air, I return their frowns with one of my own. The sky is still dark, but my ranger senses tell me that the sun will be rising soon.

"I'm hungry," I declare simply as I wrap my cloak around myself to ward off the chill.

The two guards look at each other as if amused by my blunt attitude.

"Cook isn't up," one of them replies, his voice deep and scratchy. "Won't be food for another hour."

As if in response, my stomach protests angrily from lack of food, but I do my best to ignore it. "Fine," I say at length, taking a step away from the door. It closes shut behind me. "At any rate, I want to get out and stretch my legs."

I take a few more steps but stop when I hear a clicking sound behind me. Turning, I see that both of them are leveling their crossbows in my direction.

"I'm afraid we can't let you do that, mate," the other one says. "Captain's orders."

"I don't care about your captain," I respond with thinly veiled contempt. "Your bloody *general* said you were to be our escorts. Not our prison guards. That means you have to follow me."

I take another defiant step backward, and the first Nightingale, a portly man with a ponytail, raises his crossbow to take aim, his finger resting on the trigger.

"Go ahead," I say, working hard to keep my voice casual. "Shoot me. Then we shall see how your general reacts when he finds out you murdered his guest in cold blood." The man's confidence wavers, and I decide to push him even further by completely turning my back on him and walking away.

It is not long before I hear their hushed curses and the jingling of chainmail as one of them starts following me.

Not bothering to suppress a smirk, I continue forward, content to wander Dagger's Point with my lap dog in tow.

I take in my surroundings, examining the fortifications with a critical eye. Built into the side of a rocky bluff, probably somewhere in the foothills of the Ironback Mountains, it consists of sharp wooden walls and an inner courtyard, which is probably no more than fifty paces across. Across the courtyard sits the great hall, which was where William Pyke had met us last night. It is by far the largest building in the compound, followed by the wide barracks built just below. There are several squat little buildings like the one we are staying in, and I can only assume that those serve as supply stations or infirmaries.

My escort, the fellow with the ponytail, keeps silent as I wander about, and I make no move to speak with him. He is a traitor just like the rest of them, and his words are probably not worth hearing.

While walking, I spot what looks like a training area tucked into the side of the courtyard. Wooden dummies and targets are stationed against the wall, right next to an overhang housing several weapon racks, with a well-trod lane dedicated for archery.

Perfect.

As I make my way to the overhang, my escort makes a grunting sound, clearly uneasy about me approaching the weapon racks.

"I don't think that's a good idea, mate." He hefts his crossbow nervously. "Don't think General Pyke would appreciate you touching our weaponry."

"Let's say," I reply condescendingly, "for the sake of argument that I *do* try to use one of these weapons to kill you. What then? I'm still trapped in the middle of a fortress filled with your friends, and I'm separated from my allies. Even if I did manage to escape, do you really think I would make it very far without a horse?"

He knuckles the side of his head as he considers my logic, and I use this opportunity to open a cabinet against the wall. To my delight, I see that it is filled with archery equipment. I pull out one of the bows, a recurve made from elm, and sling a quiver of arrows over my shoulder, taking two more quivers in my free hand. I confidently make my way over to the shooting lane, ignoring the fidgeting guard as I begin counting my steps, thirty paces away from the target.

Once I am in position, I draw an arrow from the quiver and fix it to the string. The sky is already starting to grow brighter as the sun begins to rise, painting the yard in deep violet hues. Taking a deep breath, I pull the fletching to my cheek and aim down the shaft, taking a bead on the center of the target.

I let out my breath and loose, the string launching the arrow with a satisfying *snap*. In the blink of an eye, it embeds itself in the target about a hand's width to the right of the center.

Making a mental calculation, I draw another arrow and pull, only waiting a heartbeat before I release.

Thunk. This time it's a little to the left.

As I draw my third arrow, I notice that the Nightingale guard is watching me, his crossbow all but forgotten at his side. His heavy brows are furrowed, not in concern, but in genuine curiosity as he seems to observe my technique.

Taking aim, I release the arrow and grin with satisfaction as it hits directly in the center of the target, the shaft sinking deep into the wood.

I take five steps back and continue this process, sighting down the arrow and loosing until I can get into a rhythm of hitting the center every time. When my first quiver is empty, I drop it to the ground and pick up another one, taking another five steps and loosing until I feel comfortable shooting from that distance as well. Eventually, I find myself with my back against the wall of a building, probably fifty paces from the training grounds, but I do not stop. I put arrows in every single one of the targets and practice dummies, delivering kill shots almost every single time.

For a while, I get lost in the motions.

Draw. Pull. Sight. Loose. Repeat.

I've always found archery soothing, becoming one with the bow. In the back of my mind, I recite the ranger's oath, finding solace in the vow that holds me grounded to my purpose as a ranger. I keep up at this pace, my arms and back starting to become sore as my arrows quickly begin to run out.

The sky grows gradually brighter, and soon I notice that something of an audience has gathered around me. Men and more than a few women, all in Nightingale cloaks, watch me in awed silence as I shoot arrow after arrow into the targets.

I pick up the final arrow from the third quiver. Arrow number ninety.

Sucking in a breath, I pull it to my cheek and quickly release, landing a shot on the head of one of the dummies and breaking another arrow in two.

Standing there, I look with everyone else at the dozens of feathered shafts sticking out of the targets in tight clusters. *I'm getting pretty good at this*, I think to myself in satisfaction. My muscles feel worn out, but my mind feels much clearer than before. Every time I lose myself in the bow and arrow, I find peace.

Finally, I break out of my trance and walk up to my stunned escort, handing him the bow and breaking the silence. "Is the cook up yet?"

He nods, eyeing me warily, and escorts me to the cooking fires, a dozen whispered conversations following us as we go.

CHAPTER 24
ZARA

I wake up to thin rays of light filtering in through the cracks in my bedroom walls, painting the bare trappings of the hovel in a faint golden glow.

My jaw pops as I let out a yawn and stretch, recovering from a long and restless night of tossing and turning. I sit up in my bed and pull off the scratchy blanket the Nightingales had supplied us with, wiggling my toes to work the blood back into them. Last night had been cold and filled with bad dreams, and to make matters worse, my back aches from lying on this sorry excuse for a mattress. *What is this thing made out of, anyway?* I think to myself in annoyance. *Rocks?*

A hollow ache in my stomach reminds me that I haven't eaten since early yesterday, and the smell of wood smoke from a campfire reaches my nose as I tiredly rub the sleep away from my eyes.

Swinging my legs over the side of the bed, I slip my feet into my shoes and stand up, silently wishing I had worn thicker stockings. I shiver as I pull on my robes, the chill in the cold hut pebbling my skin.

I try vainly to tame my tangled hair with my fingers, combing it with my hands and hoping it will look presentable. *Light, what I wouldn't give for a brush right now.* Pulling out a small looking glass from my robe pocket, I look at my reflection and grimace. I can barely recognize the dirty, messy-haired girl gazing back at me.

Finally, after several long minutes of attempted grooming, I heave a disgruntled sigh. *It will have to do for now.*

Letting out another yawn, I step out of my bedroom and into the common room, where the small fire has all but burned out. Both Owyn and Elias' doors stand open, so I assume they are both out getting food. *Those rangers are not human. How on Byhalya can they function on so little sleep?* Stepping past the ash-filled fire pit, I push open the front door and step out into the courtyard of Dagger's Point.

By the position of the sun, I can tell that it is already several hours past dawn. The fort, which looks much less impressive in the light of the day, is already bustling with activity. Lines of soldiers stand in front of the cooking pots, waiting to receive their first meal of the day, their dark cloaks marking them all as Nightingale insurgents. People scurry every which way, busying themselves with various chores, and the sounds of industry rise up above the chatter of voices, hammers ringing out the songs of metalworking.

As I close the door, a guard walks silently up next to me, crossbow resting lazily on one shoulder. He begins dutifully following me but otherwise says nothing, his bored expression indicating that he perceives me to be of little threat. I choose to ignore him, making for the nearest cook pot to wait in line. I can feel the eyes of almost everyone around watching me curiously, but I try not to let it bother me.

Even so, time passes *very* slowly.

Lost in my own thoughts, I find myself looking around the jagged fortifications, inspecting Dagger's Point from the inside. High walls of sharpened timbers line the perimeter, and low, hastily-constructed buildings fill the inside. On the nearby gate, I can see strange objects adorning the tops of the spear-like walls. At first, I cannot make them out, but after a minute of squinting, it dawns on me.

Those are heads, I realize in revulsion. *Hairy darkhound heads!*

My stomach lurches, and I quickly look away.

Eventually, I make it to the front of the line, and a fat man in an apron ladles some gray porridge into a bowl. He hands it to me roughly, slopping some of it over the side, then waves for me to get out of the way so he can serve the next man in line.

I take the bowl and step aside, muttering an insincere, "Thank you," as I suspiciously eye the slop. Between the demon heads and the colorless food, my appetite is suddenly less severe.

As I spoon the first tasteless bite into my mouth, I am approached by a dour-looking Owyn and his escort, who appears just as disinterested in his duty as my own guard.

"Good morning," Owyn says, his smile looking forced.

I nod at him and swallow, grimacing as I do so. "Good morning," I reply, trying to force a weak smile as well.

"How did you sleep?" he asks, nodding at our little hut.

"Well enough," I answer, looking down at my bowl and trying to conjure the will to take another bite. "Where is Elias?"

Owyn points to the great hall above the courtyard. "Speaking with *the general*," he says, stating the title with a thick layer of sarcasm. "He's trying to convince him to let us return to Forest Hill without an escort of guards. He thinks they will only slow us down."

"I see. Then I assume we shall be heading out shortly?"

He nods. "Hopefully."

Disregarding my bowl of gruel, I notice that many of the Nightingales in the courtyard are giving Owyn a wide berth. They stare at him with a mixture of respect and hostility, as if he had done something to frighten them.

Strange, I think, giving them a curious look.

After a moment, I turn to my guard. "Here," I say tersely, handing him my bowl. "I'm no longer hungry." *I'd rather eat sticks and berries in the forest than try to stomach this stuff.*

Surprised, he takes the bowl, and I motion for Owyn to follow me.

"Let's prepare ourselves so that we are ready to move as soon as Elias gets out. I'm ready to leave this place far behind."

A real smile cracks his hard mask of stoicism, and he follows me. Together, we walk back toward our group's hovel on the far side of the courtyard.

Before we can reach the door, we stop, our attention drawn to a commotion near the front entrance of Dagger's Point. "Open the gates!" a man atop the wall shouts. "Scouts returning!" Many of the soldiers in the fort begin heading excitedly in that direction.

Owyn and I look at each other and silently agree to go investigate. We jog to the front of the fort just as the great wooden doors begin to swing inward, their hinges grinding noisily as they open.

A man on a horse, wearing the same dark cloak and armor everyone else has on, rides into the encampment at breakneck speed. Before he can trample any of his comrades, he reins in his mount, hooves kicking up large clumps of dirt. The horse is lathered and breathing heavily from a hard run, and the rider slumps exhaustedly in his saddle.

"What news?" someone in the crowd asks as the mob grows quiet, eagerly waiting for the response.

The rider looks up, and for the first time, I get a good look at his face. He appears as if he has not slept in days, dark circles ringing his tired eyes and an extremely harried expression on his face. "The demons are on the move," he declares, causing the crowd to murmur. "Moloch is gathering his troops."

"Make way!" a familiar voice shouts, and the crowd parts to reveal General William Pyke and Elias running up to where the rider sits on his horse. "You saw him?" Pyke asks when he arrives. "You saw Moloch with your own eyes?"

"Yes, general," the rider replies, nodding his head vigorously. "I'd not soon forget a face like that. Or those blood-red eyes..." His voice trails off as he shivers visibly.

"Then you're lucky to be alive, soldier." Pyke says, resting a hand on the hilt of a longsword strapped to his belt. "Tell me everything."

"I saw them while making my rounds near the Heart of the Forest," he states. "It was only a handful, sir, not the entire horde. They seemed to be hiding out, holding some sort of secret meeting. There were beasts of shadow that walked on all fours and ones that walked like men."

Darkhounds and gorgons, I think to myself, remembering my book. *Some of the most common fighters in the R'Laar armies.*

"They were gathering in a canyon, like they were trying to avoid being seen. Moloch, the big red-skinned one, was addressing them. I couldn't hear much, but it sounded like he was planning an attack on Forest Hill." The rider suddenly blanches, then lowers his voice. Everyone leans in to try and catch his words. "General, some of our brothers were there with him. They knelt in the grass before him like slaves."

A troubled look crosses Pyke's face. "How many were there?"

"Fewer than a dozen," he replies. "But we know from reports that there are *a lot* more of them. I have no idea where the rest are camped."

Pyke curses under his breath.

Barus pushes his way through the crowd and steps up to Pyke. Owyn and I inch closer to overhear what they are saying.

"General, this could be our chance to cut the head off of the snake. If Moloch is away from the rest of his troops, then we could find him and eliminate him without risking the rest of our army. We may not get another chance like this to strike."

Surprisingly, Elias speaks up, shaking his head as he does so. "It sounds like a risky move," he interjects, a frown cutting deep furrows on his forehead. "The demons have every advantage here. I know those canyons. They are a poor place to do battle."

"This, coming from a kingsman," Barus sneers. "Your words mean little here."

"Enough," Pyke barks, rubbing his temples as if he has a headache. He squeezes his eyes shut like he is trying to think, but after a moment, he opens them again. Having come to some sort of conclusion, he continues. "Excellent work soldier. Get yourself some food and rest. You've more than earned it."

The weary scout thanks the general and urges his horse forward, making his way for the barracks as the crowd parts before him.

"Ranger Keen," the general says once the scout is gone. "Your advice is appreciated. But Barus is right. This opportunity is far too precious for us to squander. Even though our position is less than ideal, the chance to kill Moloch once and for all is well worth the risk."

He turns to address the rest of the crowd, who are all looking expectantly toward him.

"Soldiers," he shouts, raising his voice high so that he can be heard. "The Nightingales are an organization built on freedom. Freedom from the king and the Conclave and freedom from tyranny. But right now, our freedom is threatened by these demons who have already taken so many of our brothers and sisters from us."

Almost all of the Nightingales around us bob their heads at his words, looking at their general with rapt attention. *I've never seen somebody command such respect,* I realize, impressed. *These people would follow him to their deaths.*

Pyke continues. "The day has come for us to put an end to this madness. I will be sending a unit of our best soldiers to find and kill this demon who has brought so much sorrow to our cause. We will fight back this threat like the legendary Legion of Light and cast those Hells-cursed monsters out of these lands!"

Pulling his sword from his scabbard, he thrusts it into the air and lets out a shout that is echoed by the cries of his fellow Nightingales, who draw weapons of their own. "For Dunmar City!"

Owyn, Elias, and I stand amidst the jubilant throng looking awkward and uncertain among the cheering soldiers. For the most part, I agree with Elias' assessment. This whole thing feels wrong for some reason. But I keep silent and instead choose to follow my companions out of the throng to an uncrowded location in the courtyard.

"What does this mean?" Owyn asks as soon as we are out of earshot. "Are we still going to go back to Forest Hill?"

Elias shakes his head. "No. We'll need proof of our claims, or else nobody is going to believe us that there are demons inside the Arc." He looks first at Owyn and then at me. "I don't like this, but we have no other choice. The Nightingales are capable warriors, and we have the element of surprise on our side." After a moment, he adds, "We are going to go with them and end this fight before it even begins."

Within the hour, Dagger's Point is abuzz with movement as the Nightingales prepare to move out and engage the demon Moloch.

Horses are brought out en masse, weapons are sharpened, and soldiers are outfitted with armor, making it appear as though the entire fortification is preparing for war.

When Elias had approached General Pyke about us joining them in the fight, he had been met with some resistance. At first, the general seemed apprehensive about having us beside them in battle, but after Elias pointed out the fact that having two more competent fighters and a mage would be a huge advantage, he relented and welcomed our aid. It wasn't long afterward that Barus begrudgingly relinquished our weapons to us.

Owyn was also unhappy about the arrangement. He had argued that the Nightingales are enemies of the king and that they cannot be trusted, but Elias would hear none of it.

"The demons are the *true* enemies," the ranger had said before he had departed to ready the horses. "We're all on the same side, now."

Owyn had not argued further. He had merely grown stone-faced and muttered something about following an oath before he strode away to prepare himself for departure.

Even now, his sour attitude continues to linger over him like a rain cloud.

I clutch my talisman in my hand as I watch the fully armored Nightingales, two dozen fighters who have been chosen to carry out this mission, prepare themselves to leave. Words come unbidden to my mind as I do, text from the dusty tome I brought with me from Tarsys:

> *Gorgons, far and away the most common type of demon in the R'Laar horde, represent the bulk of the foot soldiers. They are more intelligent than shadowlings and in many instances, hold high-ranking positions, leading raiding parties and overseeing mind slaves turned by the evil warlocks.*

I cannot help but shiver at the thought.

We are about to attempt to find and kill an actual gorgon, I think to myself, the scholar within me marveling. *Light, I'm not sure if I should be excited or terrified by the prospect.*

Owyn approaches me from the side and hands me the reins to a monstrously large horse. I stare at the white and black mottled creature with trepidation. "Are you looking forward to another long ride?" he asks with a faint smile.

"About as much as I am looking forward to fighting another demon," I reply curtly, forcing myself to reach up and pat the beast's neck.

"Something feels wrong here," he says after a moment, looking out at the open gate and the forest beyond.

I follow his gaze and reply, "I feel it, too."

An unspoken fear settles over us as we stand there, Nightingale rebels hurrying past in our periphery. *Are we on our way to liberate the Emberwood from the demonic presence plaguing it, or are we merely delivering ourselves into their hands?*

Only time will tell.

Elias leads his horse to our position, armed to the teeth and wearing a grim mask that puts his usual stoicism to shame. In that look, I know that he can sense it, too. "Are you prepared to depart?"

We both nod.

"Good," he replies, "Pyke has informed me that we will be leaving any minute."

Taking a breath, I begin the painful process of mounting my horse and situating myself for the journey. This animal seems more spirited than my last horse, and I find myself quietly praying that it will not throw me while we are on the road. Owyn does the same as I do, though he swings himself up into the saddle with an easy grace that continues to give me a twinge of petty jealousy.

It is not long before we are joined by the other Nightingales. Their horses paw the ground with their hooves, mirroring the eagerness of their riders.

General Pyke, resplendent in his plate armor and wolf's head cloak, trots his mount to the front of our group with Barus in tow. Both of them carry the same somber expression on their faces.

"Brothers and sisters," he calls, raising his voice high. "My fellow Nightingales. We ride now for the Heart of the Forest to put an end to the tyranny of the demons. Hold fast these fortifications until we return. Soldiers, ride out!"

He leads us through the open gate and into the trees beyond. Owyn, Elias, and I urge our horses forward to follow them. Glancing over my shoulder, I watch as the gates of the fort close shut behind us, as if sealing us to our fate.

CHAPTER 25
OWYN

It can't get much worse than this, I think to myself glumly as I follow the rebels through the woods.

Never straying far from Elias and Zara, I keep to the rear of the column, riding through the thick forest growth and avoiding contact with anyone else. The usual suspects, my saddle and horse, are not the current cause of my discomfort.

Rather, it is the present company.

My show with the arrows this morning had done more than make my arms and back sore. It had the unintended consequence of painting a target on my back. Rumors have spread through the Nightingale ranks like a disease making its way through a village, marking me as a threat as well as an agent of the king. Several of the soldiers steal glances at me as we travel, leveling glares and hostile looks in my direction. In addition to wariness, I detect a hint of respect in their expressions, but to me it is all the same.

I am surrounded by a pack of rabid wolves.

Zara and I make small talk as we ride, but it does little to calm my nerves. I can tell that both of us are afraid of what lies ahead.

"Even with the element of surprise, do we have enough people to defeat him?" she asks quietly. "You and I both know what these things are capable of."

"I know," I reply uneasily. Our fight with the darkhound is forever seared in my memory.

After a brief pause, she continues. "I only hope Pyke and the others have a plan. This demon, Moloch, sounds incredibly powerful. I mean, they have warlocks that can literally invade people's minds! How can we possibly hope to fight against that?"

Her question goes unanswered as a grim silence settles between us, the sound of our horses' hooves beating loudly in my ears. I cast my eyes around the dense forest, on alert for threats around us. For some reason, it suddenly feels like we are being watched.

The trees become thicker and more gnarled as we go, the foliage around us rising from the earth like a mass of green hands, clawing their way to the sky and blotting out the sun. I have been to this area several times with Elias in the past. We are entering a place known by the locals as the Heart of the Forest, a wild and largely uninhabited part of the Emberwood.

Several of the others appear to sense the unease I am feeling and keep their weapons at the ready, though the pace of our horses does not slow. I unsling my bow and nock an arrow, using my legs to guide my horse. Looking over, I see Elias do the same.

The forest grows denser and darker the further we ride, with rugged hills breaking up the landscape and causing snaking twists in the trail. Soon, we find ourselves approaching the entrance to a giant canyon with sheer walls of uneven stone rising up on either side of us.

Our column stops in the clearing just before the entrance, and Pyke motions for a few scouts to enter first. They dismount and run ahead while the general turns his horse to address us, his sword in hand. "This is the canyon our scout mentioned. According to his report, Moloch is hiding inside. We will dismount and proceed on foot with caution. Be ready to attack at a moment's notice, but do not strike unless I give the command. Clear?"

The men nod and mumble, "Yes, sir."

We proceed to dismount and tie our horses up to the trees and gnarled roots around us. We do so in silence, and it is not long before the scouts return, gesturing to us that the way is clear.

With a nod from Pyke, we begin to move forward, cautiously entering the canyon at the Heart of the Forest.

The cliff-like walls of stone are far enough apart for ten men to fit comfortably abreast, but I still feel uncomfortable, like a small animal entering a cage. Even with the dense trees in the woods, they offer a freedom of movement and seclusion that makes me feel at ease. Not so here. The mossy, lichen-covered walls of the crag feel like they are closing in the deeper we go, forcing us to bunch together.

Looking to my left, I see that Zara is clutching her talisman, eyes darting about in a way that perfectly complements how I am feeling. I try to bite back my fear and give her a warm smile, hoping that it doesn't look too much like a grimace, but she returns it with one of her own, apparently grateful to see a friendly face.

As we reach the center of the Heart, the canyon subtly begins opening up, revealing a small valley of sorts that is filled with a carpet of moss-covered stones. Moisture drips down the walls into a little basin, and scrawny ferns sprout up from the rocky soil, reaching eagerly for the little bit of sunlight that manages to filter down through the craggy boulders.

Our column stops dead as it enters the more open area, and for a moment, I am unable to see what has caused us to halt. Fifteen armored Nightingales block my vision, but after maneuvering myself between the crammed bodies, I am finally able to see what's in the middle of the valley.

My breath catches in my throat.

A tall bipedal creature, in the rough approximation of a man, stands proudly erect amid the stones, watching us calmly with a pair of glowing red eyes. His body is broad and muscular, covered in spikey black armor that glitters like polished obsidian. The flesh of his muscled arms is exposed, his skin color a bright crimson, the hue of freshly drawn blood. Twin horns, curved and sharp, protrude from his forehead, wreathing his red skull like a twisted, black crown. A great ebony sword is driven tip-first into the ground in front of him, and his hands rest easily on the pommel.

The demon smiles at us with a mouthful of jagged teeth, and I instantly know that I am looking at a gorgon. The creature perfectly matches the description Zara had given me this morning.

Eleven Hells… this must be Moloch.

"Greetings, humans," the demon intones, his deep voice echoing off the walls of the canyon. I am surprised to hear him speaking in the common tongue. "Have you come here to join me?"

General Pyke raises his sword, and the sound of rasping metal being pulled from sheaths fills the air as the rest of his men ready their weapons. "We have come to kill you, demon, and expel your kind from the face of this land."

Moloch lets out a laugh, a grating, guttural cackle that causes my hair to stand on end. "Strong words from such a little man," he says after his laughter subsides. "Are you certain you have enough men?"

I am struck by a thought, and it makes my insides turn to ice. *Why is he so confident? Something is not right here. How is it that he was already waiting for us to arrive?*

The soft sound of rocks crumbling forces me to tear my eyes away from the monster in front of me and look up at the canyon walls above. There, I see a pack of darkhounds looking down at us from a perch and baring their fangs in a quiet snarl. I glance at my two companions and see that Elias has noticed them as well. He stands at the ready like a taut bowstring, ready to snap into action at a moment's notice.

Hissing to get Zara's attention, I gesture up at the darkhounds with my bow. When she sees them, her face instantly blanches.

"Enough of your words, demon," Pyke declares, his voice reverberating through the canyon. "This ends now. Men, on me!"

Moloch draws his sword up from the ground and hefts it with a sneering roar. "Good! More meat for my army!"

I watch in horror as hooded figures emerge from the rocks above as well, coming out from hiding places and aiming crossbows down at us. *Eleven Hells, those are the mindflayed Nightingales!* I cannot keep it in any longer.

I scream just as the general runs forward, leading the charge. "Pyke, it's a trap!"

Swiftly, I hear the snapping sound of crossbows being fired.

I instinctively duck as a hail of crossbow bolts descends upon us, thudding into men and filling the chasm with screams. Several of the Nightingales stumble and fall, dead before they even hit the ground, while others are grievously wounded on their arms, shoulders, and legs. Somehow, perhaps by a miracle, Elias, Zara, and I avoid being hit by the deadly bolts.

But we have little time to rejoice. With a roar, the darkhounds begin leaping down from their perches above our heads.

I twist and launch an arrow at one of the beasts before it can land on me, striking it in between the eyes and practically knocking it out of the air. I draw again and shoot without missing a beat, hitting another in the chest.

Something hot roars past my head, and I watch as one of the darkhounds is engulfed in blue flame, its black fur smoking like wet kindling. I look behind me and see Zara wearing a look of concentration, her hand alight with flickering magefyre.

Unfortunately, some of the other Nightingales are not so lucky. One man is brought screaming to the ground by a pair of darkhounds. Another staggers with his throat ripped out, his blood cascading down the front of his breastplate.

In a matter of seconds, the entire canyon descends into chaos.

"Owyn!" Elias shouts. "Behind us!"

Zara and I both look to see a group of bewitched Nightingales with spears cutting off our escape. They are accompanied by another gorgon, this one smaller than Moloch with green skin and a different horn pattern.

Cursing under my breath, I loose another arrow at a darkhound and turn to face the blocked-off exit. "We have to get out of here!" I shout over the sounds of battle and dying men.

Elias nods and shoots his bow. One of the Nightingales holding a spear falls to the ground with an arrow in his heart. "The only hope we have is to rally everyone and make a break for the gap. We'll have to fight our way out of here, and if we act fast, there is still a chance."

Another volley of crossbow bolts is launched with a series of clicks. I wince, fully expecting to be shot in the back, but nothing happens. I look to see a shimmering blue shield of radiant magic surrounding us, emanating from Zara's talisman, which she holds aloft. Beads of sweat roll down the sides of her face as she releases the shield, dropping half a dozen bolts harmlessly to the ground.

"Thanks!" I say, nocking another arrow.

"Don't mention it," she replies, clearly fatigued. The use of magic seems to be taking its toll on her.

"Nightingales," Elias yells, waving his bow in the air like a white flag. "Follow me! Retreat!"

A handful of cowering soldiers, who have somehow managed to survive the carnage, pivot and begin making their way toward us, panic evident in their eyes. I look past them to see General Pyke engaging Moloch in combat. He looks like a child compared to the gorgon. The demon's black sword alone measures as long as his entire body, but he fights with an unexpected fury and appears to be holding his own. Barus tries to help him in the fight, but his left arm hangs limply at his side, a dark stain spreading across his cloak.

Our small band, now fewer than fifteen, starts to make its way back to the mouth of the canyon, but the gorgon guarding it advances toward us with his mindflayed spearman, a wicked grin on its face.

Hells, I find myself thinking, panic welling up inside me. *This isn't going to end well.*

With spears in front of us, darkhounds behind us, and archers above us, we begin making a desperate attempt to break through the line of enemies. Elias and I shoot arrows, and Zara throws fireballs as our Nightingale allies charge and engage with their mindflayed brothers.

They manage to fell more than a few of the mind slaves, but the enemy spears bring down a good number of our soldiers. I watch in horror as the green gorgon crushes a man's head with a savage swipe of his mace. Even from ten paces, I can hear his skull crunching with the impact.

Roaring, Elias charges the demon, throwing down his bow and pulling out his belt knife in one smooth motion. The gorgon turns to regard him with a toothy grin, red eyes blazing. They begin to fight, and it quickly becomes an epic struggle between two equally-matched foes.

Zara lets out a gasp, and I turn to see that she is holding up another giant blue shield. Many crossbow bolts hang in midair and the handful of remaining darkhounds stand snarling on the other side.

"Keep holding it, Zara!" I call out, trying my best to sound encouraging. "You're doing great! Just a little bit longer!"

She squeezes her eyes shut and nods, clearly straining under the stress of channeling so much radiant magic.

Through the blue energy, I can see Moloch ram his massive black sword through General Pyke's body, the black metal rending his armor as if it is nothing more than paper. The demon seems to savor the act of killing him, his face a rictus of perverse glee. Then something else catches my eye.

Barus flees toward our position, fear showing plainly on his pale, bearded face.

In that moment, I forget the way he treated us and the fact that he is a Nightingale. I forget that people like him were responsible for my father's death. I see only a man running for his life—a fellow human, a brother.

I know, here and now, that I cannot leave him to die.

Cursing myself under my breath, I aim at one of the darkhounds and shout for Zara to drop the shield. She gasps and does so, giving me a chance to shoot the growling shadowling directly in its open mouth.

You're a bloody fool Owyn, I think, sprinting forward. *I can't believe I'm actually doing this.*

For a moment, my enemies seem stunned by my mad rush into the fray, and I see hope glimmering in Barus' eyes as I approach. I slash and kick, trying to fend off the darkhounds long enough for Barus to get behind Zara. They snap their jaws at me and attack with their claws, and it is everything I can do to not be torn to shreds.

Just as I am about to be overwhelmed, Barus reaches our position, and both of us flee toward the mouth of the canyon as Zara covers our escape, spraying magefyre from her hands. Barus stumbles, and I help him up, grabbing his arm and throwing it around my shoulders. He is completely drenched in blood.

"Cut them off!" Moloch screams furiously, stepping over General Pyke's corpse and waving his sword above his head. "Don't let them get away!"

Barus yells frantically in my ear, "Run!"

The three of us barely manage to escape, the darkhounds hot on our heels.

Another one of the monsters leaps from a ledge above and jumps in front of us, its eyes glowing hatefully, and its razor claws lifted for an attack. With my arm still supporting Barus, there is little I can do to defend against it. Bracing myself for pain, I put my head down and continue running.

Luckily, a ball of magefyre engulfs the shadowling just before it is about to strike, causing it to shy away, shrieking in pain. I manage to run past it and join our forces locked in combat with the spearmen.

Light almighty, I think in astonishment, glancing over at Zara. *How many times has she saved my life?*

At the forefront, Elias dodges out of the way as the gorgon tries unsuccessfully to bash in his brains. The angry demon lets out a roar of frustration, twisting his head to try and see where the ranger went. I watch as my master cuts around the monster's flank and jabs his knife into its side, where I assume there is a weak point in the armor.

The gorgon screams and whips around, but Elias is too fast. He stabs again and again with his belt knife, piercing the demon in different places all over its body with pinpoint accuracy. Then, with the skill of a trained acrobat, Elias jumps backward and rolls, springing to his feet and throwing the knife directly into the demon's neck. The blade sinks deep, and the gorgon clutches at its throat, dropping the mace and emitting a panicked gurgling sound.

It falls to its knees and collapses in a heap, dark blood leaking onto the rocky floor of the canyon.

The very next instant, the Nightingales on our side manage to break through the line of spearmen, creating a small gap that is just large enough for us to escape.

Pulling his belt knife out of the gorgon, Elias runs through the gap and yells, "Now is our chance! Flee into the forest! Run now!"

Exhausted, Zara jumps into action, and I am right behind her, racing for the clearing and away from the roaring monsters. We barely manage to untie our horses and mount up, before the mind slaves are on top of us, trying to harry us as we depart.

More men fall as they bear down upon us, and we are forced to pull away rather than defend the fallen.

We spur our horses forward, galloping at top speed through the trees and into the Emberwood beyond. I look over my shoulder and see that Elias has managed to escape with the last two haggard-looking Nightingales, riding away from the spearmen as if the Hells themselves are right on their heels.

Crossbow bolts and mind slaves give us chase into the brush, but somehow, we manage to lose them in the dense forest.

The last thing I hear before we are out of earshot is Moloch's furious shouts, berating his troops and commanding them to pursue us.

CHAPTER 26
ZARA

Keep your eyes open, I think to myself forcefully. *Passing out now will surely mean death.*

Never in my life have I felt such a strong mixture of anxiety, fear, and fatigue. The very thought of channeling any more source energy makes me want to faint, and all adrenaline from the fight has completely faded, replaced with numbing exhaustion from using too much magic. It makes me want to curl up into a ball and cry… then perhaps fall asleep.

By sheer force of will, I manage to stay atop my horse as we race through the woods back to Dagger's Point.

We knew it was a bloody trap, and yet we went anyway, I think to myself in bewilderment. *How stupid can we get? We're lucky that any of us survived at all.*

Still, the scholar in me is amazed that I had seen not only one gorgon, but *two*, in a single day. I now know for a fact that the R'Laar have begun an invasion of Tarsynium, and the presence of the darkhound near Haven was not some sort of fluke.

Additionally, the fact that the Nightingale mind slaves were there, attacking their own brothers in arms, seems to corroborate the story General Pyke had told us.

My stomach twists into a knot when I think of the proud general. *He's dead now,* I think sadly. *A consequence of his own hubris.*

Our group is depressingly small as we flee the Heart of the Forest and head toward the mountains. Pushing our horses as hard as we can, we ride mostly in silence. I doubt we will even stop to rest before we reach Dagger's Point—not that I would want to.

None of us are safe in the vast reaches of the Emberwood.

About an hour into our flight, I look over at Owyn, who is riding with a pale-looking Barus sitting behind him.

In a stroke of heroism, Owyn risked his own life to go back to rescue the surly Nightingale, pulling him out of the canyon and away from certain death. His actions surprised me, since he has every reason to hate the Nightingales for what they did to his father, and I can't help but feel a small sense of admiration when I glance over at him.

Despite our speed, time passes slowly as we race through the forest. Every time I look over my shoulder, I half-expect to see a pack of darkhounds on our tail, ready to devour us if we show even a hint of slowing down. Every time I look, though, I see only trees.

The day grows late, and the sun begins to set when we finally enter the hinterlands of the Ironback Mountains. Only then, do I start to recognize our surroundings.

We are getting close, I think, furiously blinking my burning eyes.

Soon, the narrow path we are on converges into a wider dirt road, and we begin to climb out of the great forest basin. Within the hour, we finally start to see the large stone pillar that gives Dagger's Point its name.

By the time we pull up to the fortifications, I feel like I am on the verge of collapse.

"Open the gates!" somebody shouts from atop the walls. "Riders approaching!"

The large wooden doors swing inward, and we enter the courtyard of the fort, horses lathered and breathing heavily.

Our weary band of six finally comes to a stop, and we shakily dismount, a flock of Nightingales rushing up to meet us. They throw inquiries at us in an unintelligible deluge, their faces painted with concern. Through the jumble of words, I am able to gather questions such as, "What news from the battle?" and "Where is General Pyke?"

A few of the soldiers help the wounded Barus from his place behind Owyn, but he is in no place to confront the crowd. That responsibility falls, strangely, on Elias' shoulders.

The grizzled ranger dismounts and faces the eager onlookers with a grim expression, and I find myself annoyed by how kept together and unperturbed he appears. *How is it that nothing in the world ever seems to bother him?* I shake my head and force my sore limbs to get me out of the saddle and walk over to where he stands.

After seeing to Barus, Owyn immediately comes to join me.

Raising his arms to quiet the crowd, Elias begins to speak. "Please. Please! One question at a time."

Someone shouts above the din, and the gathered Nightingales finally begin to quiet down. "What happened out there?"

"It was a slaughter," Elias replies stoically. "We're all that's left."

People begin to murmur to one another. Someone else raises a hand. "What about General Pyke?"

Elias shakes his head. "I'm afraid he is dead. He was killed fighting Moloch in single combat. He died bravely."

More murmuring.

Elias continues. "They were waiting for us in the canyon. We were lured into a trap and ambushed by both demons and turned Nightingales. It was probably just a fraction of Moloch's army, and yet it was all they needed to completely wipe us out."

Somebody steps forward. I recognize him as one of the men charged with 'escorting' us on our first night here. "That means Barus is now our commanding officer. We need to defer to his judgment on how we should proceed."

"Barus is in no condition to command anyone," Elias declares, staring the man down with his iron gaze. "He needs rest and time to heal. In the meantime, Dagger's Point should double the guard and prepare for war."

"Who are you to make demands of us?" a bald Nightingale shouts angrily. There are more than a few nods and muttered words of agreement. "You're nothing but a kingsman. We don't take orders from you!"

Elias does not back down. "I'm the man who rescued your men and pulled us out of that Light-forsaken canyon," he snaps. His intensity is enough to make the firebrand take a step back. "If it weren't for us, everyone would have been massacred by the demons, and you would be left here wondering what happened. Then it would be too late to do anything of consequence."

Most everybody tries to avoid his gaze, the mood of the crowd growing sober in the failing light.

"The only hope we have," the ranger continues without missing a beat, "is for us to stand together. Moloch does not see Nightingale and kingsman. He sees humans of Tarsynium, all whom he seeks to conquer and turn into slaves. Our petty quarrels mean nothing if this kingdom falls to their might."

With that, he turns on his heel and begins making his way to the great hall on the far side of the courtyard. Owyn and I glance at each other, then race to follow him up the stairs.

"That was a good speech," Owyn comments when we reach him. "Do you think they'll listen?"

"They'd better," Elias replies gruffly.

"Why is that?" I ask.

"Because if they don't, every single one of us will be dead before the winter sets in."

Pushing open the double doors, we step into the main hall of the wooden lodge, looking more like ragged refugees than conquering heroes. A pair of guards hurriedly steps up to us from their place by the braziers, spears held nervously in their hands.

"Where is Barus?" Elias demands, approaching them without even slowing his stride. "We need to speak with him immediately."

"The captain," one of them replies, before grimacing and correcting himself, "I mean, the general, is not to be disturbed."

"The fate of the Emberwood hangs in the balance," Elias growls, looming over both of them as he stops just before the tips of their spears. "It is imperative that we speak with him. Now."

They look nervously at each other, but after a moment, they lower their spears and step aside. "In the back," one of them replies, casting his eyes downward. "The surgeons are seeing to his wounds." As if to emphasize his point, a muffled scream comes from a room behind the braziers.

We proceed forward without another word.

Elias opens the door, and I can see Barus laying on a bed, his shirt off and a rolled-up piece of leather clenched in his teeth. A woman with a white apron and bloodstained hands is pulling something out of his upper arm with a pair of forceps. Tears spring into his eyes from the pain she is causing him.

With a mighty tug, the surgeon finally manages to pull something out of the ghastly cut on Barus' arm: the broken head of a crossbow bolt. The bearded man leans back on the pillows, and the leather falls from his lips with a sigh.

The surgeon places the forceps and the metal shard into a small bowl and begins to stitch up the wound.

Wincing, Barus looks up at us with glassy eyes. "Ah, the rangers and the mage." His voice is husky, whether from exhaustion or emotion, I cannot tell. "What can I do for you?"

"How are you feeling?" Elias asks, his voice carrying little compassion.

Despite everything, Barus smiles weakly. "Considering the fact that I've lost my general and half my body weight in blood, I'd say I'm doing well." Then his smile turns to a snarl as the surgeon tugs one of the stitches tight. It's been hours since our battle in the canyon, and the flesh surrounding his wound has grown an angry red.

"You are now the general of Dagger's Point," Elias states matter-of-factly. "We need your advice. And your help."

"My help," Barus breathes, resting his head back against the headboard. "I cannot even help myself. It's my fault that we rode headlong into that trap. I persuaded General Pyke to go. His death... all of their deaths are on my hands."

"We can still make this right," Elias insists, stepping closer to the wounded man and taking a knee at the side of his bed. "I need your help if we are going to prevent any more deaths in the future. We still have a chance to save the Emberwood, maybe even Tarsynium itself."

Barus looks at each of us and grimaces as the surgeon pulls the final stitch tight, looping the gut to form a knot. "You all saved my life back there," he says thoughtfully, "even though you had every reason to leave me behind. I captured you. I mistreated you. And you repaid me by giving my life back to me." Shifting in his bed, he tries to sit up but falls back on the pillows with a grunt. He says the next words through gritted teeth. "If there is anything I can do to repay that debt, consider it done."

Elias looks back at us, and I see the barest hint of a smile on his weathered face. Turning back to regard the new general, he speaks with a careful tone. "You remember as well as I do what the scout told us. Moloch plans to march on Forest Hill and consume the entire Emberwood. We cannot let this happen."

Barus raises a bushy eyebrow. "So, what do you propose?"

"We need the rest of your troops to defend Forest Hill, to stand and fight so that we can put a stop to this once and for all. Only by standing together can we hope to defeat Moloch."

The bearded general lets out a wheezy chuckle. "Even if I could convince my Nightingales to march to your defense, what makes you think that your governor would even want our help?"

"We can convince him," Owyn says, speaking up. "I'm sure that we can."

"And I can speak with the mages," I add, squaring my shoulders and lifting my head high. "There *has* to be a way to get them to listen to us."

Elias nods in approval.

Barus actually appears to be considering our proposal. "It will be extremely difficult getting our two sides to work together. And even if we do succeed, we all know what the demons are capable of. We will be hard pressed to stop them before they destroy the entire town."

"So, we can count on your help then?" Elias asks, extending a hand for him to shake.

After another moment's consideration, Barus takes his hand. "You have my word," he replies.

I feel a wash of relief spread through my entire body. *Perhaps we do have a chance of winning after all.*

"I will spread the word to my people," he continues. "They will be ready to depart by dawn. You'll have fifty archers and a hundred swords at your disposal. Make those demons pay for every single one of my men they butchered."

CHAPTER 27
OWYN

"**I** never thanked you for saving my life back there," I say awkwardly, pulling my horse up to Zara's on the ride back to Forest Hill. "I would have been a goner if you hadn't used your shield to stop the crossbows in that canyon."

She glances over at me, one of her eyebrows arching up. "You are quite welcome; though, you seem to have forgotten about the darkhounds."

"The darkhounds?" I frown, momentarily confused. Then, I remember the demons she had burned in order to protect me and Barus. "Oh yeah," I reply lamely. "How could I forget about them?"

"It's nothing," she says, shrugging nonchalantly. "Though, I also recall shielding you from that darkhound several days ago." Her lips turn up into a self-satisfied smile as she glances at me out of the corner of her eye. "If I hadn't been there, you would be in that demon's stomach right now."

"Going there was *your* idea in the first place, remember?" I counter, growing annoyed. "But yes, you've saved me many times over. Thank you, oh gracious Magus, for your help."

"Of course," she replies, nodding smugly. "All in a day's work. You're making something of a habit out of this, you know. You may want to consider keeping a mage around you all the time to pull you out of sticky situations."

I give her a flat look. "I'd sooner keep a gorgon as a companion."

She turns toward me in her saddle and gasps in mock outrage. "Now *that* wasn't very nice! I expected more from a ranger's apprentice. Aren't you lot supposed to be honorable, or something?"

"We *are* honorable!" I throw my hands up in exasperation. "Eleven Hells... I'm trying to thank you! Are you always this difficult?"

She stares at me for a moment, expression neutral, then her face inexplicably breaks into a grin. "I don't try to be, but it can be quite fun."

"You... what?"

She laughs, a musical sound that completely disarms me. For an instant, I'm too confused to even speak.

"You need to lighten up, Owyn Lund," she says at length, her tone both friendly and chiding. "We have enough to worry about with demons and the looming threat of annihilation. Sometimes, you simply need to smile."

I open my mouth to respond, then close it again, not sure what I should say.

"And don't worry about me saving you," she goes on, turning her attention back to the road ahead of us. "I'm sure you'll have lots of opportunities in the future to make it up to me."

Finally, I find my tongue. "Well, I'd say I'm looking forward to it, but I think that would come off as a bit... morbid."

She laughs again, and I find myself smiling as well, despite my best efforts.

"Is that a smile?" she asks rhetorically, pointing at my face. "Careful, Owyn, you wouldn't want your master to see—he might reprimand you for actually enjoying a pleasant conversation."

This time, she actually manages to get a laugh out of me, which only makes her grin widen.

"I really do owe you," I reply when her laughter subsides. "You just wait. The next time there is a battle, I will be there to pull you out of danger."

"We'll see about that," she says, still grinning that mischievous grin of hers.

An amiable silence settles between us as we follow the winding path, making our way south with a long column of Nightingale soldiers. We have already been on the road for several hours, the midmorning sun filtering through the tree branches above us and offering spots of light amidst the forest shadows. I can see hints of the coming autumn in the woods around us, the faint scent of decay mingling with the late summer air.

By the time I look back at Zara, the momentary humor we had felt vanishes like smoke in the wind. "Do you really believe you can convince the mages to help?" I ask, breaking the silence.

She considers this for a moment, before finally nodding. "Yes," she replies, though I can see that her confidence is more feigned than real. "I have to. What other option is there? The only alternative is failure... that, and the inevitable destruction of all we hold dear."

"You won't fail," I say sincerely, looking directly into her brown eyes. "What are a few pompous old mages compared to a demon slayer like yourself?"

Her smile returns, and for a moment, a feeling of warmth settles between us, an almost-tangible energy that reminds me of the sun. It banishes the darkness of our current situation, radiating around us as we ride, and suddenly, I know what it is like to have a peer.

I know what it is like to have a friend.

For the next several hours, we talk of small things, enjoying each other's company as we make our way to Forest Hill. All of Dagger's Point has emptied, the Nightingales marching beside us down the leafy forest road. Elias and Barus ride at the head of the column, each carrying a large white flag on our journey southward.

Barus had insisted that even with his injuries he would be able to fight, but Elias told him on multiple occasions that he would need his leadership in the coming conflict, not his sword.

By the time we reach the outskirts of town, the sun is already on its final descent through the eastern sky.

Farmers and townsfolk look up in alarm as we pass their homesteads, clearly surprised at seeing the battle-ready Nightingales marching through their land. Luckily, nobody engages in fights, and no insults are thrown. The locals merely watch us uneasily from their fields as we pass by and then warily return to tending their crops.

Elias commands us to halt on the main road as soon as the hill is in sight. He says that he does not want any militiamen or mages to think this is some sort of attack. He sends a rider ahead to inform the governor of our arrival.

We wait for a time in uncomfortable silence, soldiers shifting uneasily on the road with hands on the pommels of their weapons.

Finally, perhaps an hour later, a delegation rides from the top of the hill down to our position. By the looks of it, it is mostly mages, but at the head of the group I see Governor Prior and Arch Magister Elva Tyrande, the former looking nervous and the latter looking displeased to say the least.

They pull up in front of us, and every mage holds their talisman at the ready.

When Elva speaks, all eyes immediately go to her, a silence washing over the crowd. "Subtle, Ranger Keen, bringing an army of rebels to our very doorstep. A simple admission of your treason would have sufficed."

"I am no traitor," Elias replies evenly. "And neither is my apprentice, nor your ward. We are here to help you."

"Ah, yes," she says, turning her icy gaze on Zara, who practically shivers beneath the Arch-Magister's stare. "My ward. Come back to betray me one final time before we destroy you?"

"Elva, please," Zara begs, her posture wilting somewhat under the hostile looks of her former colleagues. "Listen to him. We are not traitors. The Nightingales have agreed to help us in our fight against the demons."

Several of the mages scoff at her words as Elva continues to stare her down with cold fury.

"She's telling the truth," I interject, leveling a glare at each of the scornful mages.

"There *are* no demons, child," Elva states coldly, ignoring my words. "The only threat here is the one that rides with you. The Nightingales threaten the peace and prosperity of Tarsynium, and all that it stands for."

I can practically feel the soldiers around me bristling at her comments, but General Barus raises a gauntleted hand, gesturing for them to stand down. "We are opposed to King Aethelgar, it is true," he states in his deep voice, "but today, we carry an offer of truce, at least until the demon threat has been dealt with."

Governor Prior perks up, wiping his bald forehead with a handkerchief. "A truce? *You* believe that there are demons as well?"

Barus nods solemnly. "There is an army of them hiding in the Emberwood, and they plan on marching on Forest Hill next. Many of my men have already died fighting them."

"The Nightingales captured us after I rescued Zara and Owyn from their false imprisonment," Elias says in his typical gruff fashion. He looks pointedly at Elva as he says this. "We quickly found out that they, too, had encountered run-ins with the demons."

The Governor turns to look at the Arch-Magister, aghast. "You imprisoned them?"

Elva does not reply.

"They are led by a gorgon named Moloch," Zara says, gaining a bit of her courage back as the rest of us support her claims. "He has used an ancient magic called 'mindflaying' to control the actions of the people he captures. That's why those Nightingales attacked the inn that night."

Suddenly, the mages in the delegation do not look so certain. They eye one another and mutter quietly amongst themselves. Shaking her head, Elva appears unfazed. "If your claims are true, then why have we seen little evidence of demons on this side of the Arc? The word of a traitor is precious little for us to go by, even in such dire circumstances."

Seeing my opportunity, I speak up.

"You want evidence?" I ask, brazenly meeting her gaze. I reach into a sack hanging next to my saddlebags and grab what I had hidden there. A foul smell like rotting meat wafts up and threatens to overwhelm me, but I proceed to pull out a hairy, decomposing head of a darkhound I had taken from one of the spikes at Dagger's Point. I throw it unceremoniously on the ground in front of the mages' horses. "Here's your evidence. That is what we are up against," I declare, wiping my hands on my pant leg.

Several of the horses rear up in fright, and more than a few of the mages spit curses at the sight of the demon's head.

Zara trots her horse forward, her face a mask of confidence. "My fellow mages," she says, pointing, "*that* is the head of a shadowling known as a darkhound. The gorgon, Moloch, has scores of these at his disposal, as well as mindflayed Nightingales, and they are headed for Forest Hill as we speak."

Governor Prior pales considerably, and for a moment, it looks like he is going to faint. Even Elva looks like she is at a loss for words.

"Let us put our past differences behind us," Elias says, raising his voice for all in the company to hear. "Let us unite against the oldest threat humanity has ever faced. As you can plainly see, these are not fairy tales we are fighting. They are quite real."

Panicked, the governor nods his head vigorously. He averts his gaze from the rotting head in front of his horse and looks over at General Barus. "Nightingales, consider yourselves welcome at Forest Hill. You'll receive no trouble from me or my people."

Zara and I grin at each other, and I can even see a hint of a smile on my master's face.

"What?" Elva asks incredulously, turning her intense gaze on the sweaty governor. "You cannot seriously be considering working with these traitors."

Prior nods gravely, his eyes fixed on the darkhound's severed head. "I still have authority in this province, Arch-Magister. It appears that these monsters are actually real, and if what these people say is true, they threaten us *all*."

For a second, Elva looks like she might argue further. But after her gaze sweeps over the faces of all those opposing her, she bites back her words, her upper lip curling in disgust. Furious, she kicks her horse and rides back up the hill. Several of the mages move to follow her.

When they are gone, Elias begins speaking again. "Governor, we do not have long before Moloch and his horde arrives. We need to immediately begin working on fortifying Forest Hill's defenses."

Prior nods, though his face remains stark white. "Anything you need, I will ensure that you have it, ranger."

"Good," Elias replies. "We will start by informing the outlying farms that they must abandon their homes. We need to gather as many of the people together here in town if we hope to survive this."

At a look from Elias, Barus raises his fist into the air. "Nightingales," he yells in a commanding voice, "let's get this place ready for battle. Move out!"

The column begins to make its way unhindered into the town.

Zara lets out a relieved sigh. "That went about as well as we could have hoped." She looks over at me and beams. "That was good thinking, bringing that darkhound head."

Nodding, I look over at the wretched thing laying in the road. The marching Nightingales take care to go around it, giving it a wide berth.

"There still is much work to do," Elias reminds us grimly, urging his horse forward. "I fear that time is not on our side."

Zara and I both follow suit, guiding our mounts up the road and into town.

"First thing's first," I say after a moment, looking determinedly up at the governor's mansion.

"What's that?" Zara asks.

"I'm going to go back to that horrible Arch-Magister of yours and get my hatchet back!"

Out of the corner of my eye, I can see her rolling her eyes at me. Under her breath, I hear her mutter as I ride away, "What is it with rangers and their weapons?"

CHAPTER 28
ZARA

The rhythmic pounding of hammers fills the air in Forest Hill, accompanied by the steady sounds of sawing wood and the shouts of laboring men.

The sleepy frontier town has seemingly come alive with the threat of invasion on the horizon, the humble townspeople transforming their homes and shops into rough-hewn fortifications.

I watch curiously as makeshift walls are erected out of any materials that can be gathered, including doors and fence posts. The local blacksmiths, undoubtedly more accustomed to forging horseshoes, are hard at work producing spears and arrows for the townsfolk to use to defend themselves. The scholarly part of me wants to document the unusual transformation, but my more practical side forces me to pitch in and help where I can.

Carrying a bucket of water to one of the forges, I notice a pair of youths warily eyeing a Nightingale soldier digging a trench. They whisper to each other, dark expressions on their faces.

Unfortunately, the integration of the Nightingales into the general population of Forest Hill has not been the smoothest of transitions. Fist fights are a somewhat common occurrence, and an air of distrust hangs over all of us like a storm cloud, making everyone feel uneasy.

Still, I think to myself, depositing the bucket beside the blacksmith's anvil. *At least everyone is working toward a common goal. Mutual destruction is apparently enough to keep the two groups from constantly tearing at each other's throats.*

A mage nods to me in respect as he walks past. I believe his name is Roth. I wave to him pleasantly, pleased that many of the mages have welcomed me back with open arms. They seem profoundly interested in learning everything they can about the R'Laar and have spent the last day and a half questioning me thoroughly on the subject.

As my eyes wander up to the governor's manor, however, my heart sinks.

Unlike the other mages, Arch-Magister Tyrande has yet to see my side of things.

Elva and her closest advisors have locked themselves at the top of the hill, refusing to help with the defense in any way. Apparently, they don't want to be seen fraternizing with the enemy, and they plan on leaving us for Tarsys first thing in the morning.

How can they be so blind? I think, wiping a bead of sweat from my forehead with the back of my hand. *Can't they see that this battle is going to affect us all?*

Shaking my head in wonder, I begin making my way up the hill toward a pavilion that has been erected on the lawn just outside of the governor's home. It is a large tent that has a complete a view of the town and the forest beyond, a staging point of sorts. This is where the decisions are being made on how we should defend ourselves against Moloch.

I push open the flap, stepping inside and approaching a wide table where Governor Prior, Elias, Owyn, Barus, and a mage named Willus sit. The round-faced man is the de-facto leader of the mages who have chosen to stay and help. A map of the town has been laid out before them, wooden figurines representing the strategic placement of troops.

All eyes turn toward me as I enter the tent.

"How fairs the construction?" Barus asks me without preamble. Considering the fact that his troops are providing the bulk of the labor, it is a fair question.

"Well enough, I suppose," I reply, pulling up a seat at the table. "All of the roads leading up the hill have been barricaded except for the main one, and it looks like the wall will be up before the sun goes down."

"Excellent," Barus replies. He points to a spot on the map with the tip of his dagger. "My scouts indicate that Moloch's army is indeed on the move. They should be arriving on the outskirts of town an hour or two after sundown."

"The darkness favors their troops," Elias muses, more to himself than anyone else. He stares intently at the map, his brow furrowed as if deep in thought. "Governor, have all the outlying farms been evacuated?"

"Yes," Prior answers tiredly, dabbing his upper lip with a handkerchief. "Everyone knows to gather here within the hour with all the provisions that they can carry. The women and children will take shelter within my home, and every able-bodied man will be on the front line."

Somehow, I doubt that will include you, I think, examining his rotund frame.

"We have a hundred trained swords, fifty archers, and at least that many local militiamen at our disposal," Barus growls while eyeing the map. Then, almost as an afterthought, he adds, "And seven mages, of course."

"A sizable defense," Elias observes, his eyes still studying the map. "Better than I thought we would be able to muster, anyway. We've already sent runners to Omkirk and Green Harbor with a plea for aid. If we can hold out long enough, reinforcements should be able to arrive within a few days to support us."

"I don't mean to be a raincloud," Willus interjects, his fingers steepled in front of him in thought, "but by all accounts, Moloch has us outnumbered two to one. I'm not as familiar with these demons as the rest of you, but from what I can gather, even one of them is more formidable than many of our soldiers. Scarcely with these defenses, how can we hope to survive the night, let alone a few days?"

His frank words seem to cast a pall over the tent. For a moment, everyone is silent.

"I agree with the Magus," Owyn says with a frown. "We'll need to figure out a way to level the playing field. Maybe even divide his troops."

A thought suddenly strikes me. "What about fire?"

All eyes turn to look at me.

Summoning my courage, I explain. "Both times I faced these demons, I noticed that magefyre seems to be an effective weapon against them. They appear to be afraid of it and all other forms of radiant magic."

"The math still doesn't add up," Willus interjects. "Even at our full strength, we wouldn't be able to conjure enough magefyre to burn even half of his army."

"It's a good idea, Zara," Elias says more gently, "but the Magus has a point. I don't think that seven mages will be enough to significantly damage Moloch's forces."

"Magefyre works," I insist, "but I am fairly certain that they don't like regular fire, either."

Willus' eyebrows knit together, making his doubt plain. "Elaborate."

Taking a deep breath, I delve into the story of how I used radiant magic to fight the darkhound in the woods by Haven. I explain that the shadowling seemed afraid of the leaves I had ignited and how I had used magefyre to finally kill it.

"Interesting," Willus says after I finish, stroking his chin thoughtfully.

"If we can find some sort of ignition source, we can use magefyre to set it ablaze and keep Moloch's troops from advancing to the top of the hill." My voice becomes more excited as the plan starts to form in my head.

"Thomlin, the thatcher, uses pitch when working on roofs," Governor Prior offers. "From what I understand, it is extremely flammable."

Owyn chimes in. "By chance, does he have enough to cover one of the roads in town?"

Prior shrugs. "I'll have to check, but I'd wager he does."

Those of us around the table exchange meaningful glances.

"Allow me to lend my services to help you, Initiate Dennel," Willus says, clearly intrigued by the idea. "If we can strategically place our mages near barrels of pitch, we could inflict maximum damage upon this army of demons, potentially crippling them."

"Then it is settled," Elias states with a tone of finality. "Zara, Owyn, and the mages will work on a way to divide and destroy Moloch's troops, while the rest of our soldiers, led by General Barus and myself, defend the barricades. Hopefully, Light willing, we will be able to hold out until reinforcements can arrive from the neighboring towns."

Barus gestures at the map again with his knife. "My men will be able to hold the main road for a time, but I worry about the rest of our defenses. The very nature of a hill means that there are several paths up to the top."

"The bottom half of the town will have to be abandoned," Elias remarks, leaning forward and moving figures around the map. "The lower homes and farms are indefensible, and our people would be spread too thin."

"With the paths all barricaded and the wall being built near the top, it should not be a problem keeping the demons away," Owyn adds. "Parts of the hill are too steep for anyone to climb, even demons. The idea is to bottleneck them so that there is only one way for them to go."

Barus frowns at the map, but for the moment, he appears placated.

After a bit more discussion, everyone stands up and begins departing the command tent. "We still have a lot more work to do before this day is over," Elias says as we leave. "Our troops have to be ready before the enemy is within sight of Forest Hill. We have a long night ahead of us."

We exit the tent, all going our separate ways. Willus offers to go with me to track down the thatcher, Thomlin. I gladly agree, grateful to have the company of a fellow mage.

"I'm going to go speak with the builders about where we should place our fire trap," Owyn says, squinting as a cool breeze gusts across the top of the hill. "I'll meet you at the barricade once you've secured the pitch."

I nod and begin making my way toward the thatcher's with Willus. As I go, Owyn calls my name, making me pause.

"Yes?" I reply, looking back over my shoulder at him.

He hesitates. "We may not get another chance to talk before tonight. Working on the pitch will probably take the rest of our time before the demons arrive. I just… I wanted to say that I'm glad you came to talk to me after the attack on the inn."

Glancing at the two of us, Willus smiles slyly and continues down the hill, muttering, "Catch up with me when you are done."

I turn to regard the ranger's apprentice with a raised eyebrow. "What do you mean?"

He takes a step closer, looking deeply into my eyes. "You were the only one who believed my story, Zara. Even Elias didn't believe me in the beginning. And because of you, we now have a chance at defeating Moloch and making Tarsynium safe again."

Light, those eyes! Do they always look so intense?

"It was nothing," I reply, silently cursing myself for my lame response.

"Zara, it was everything!" he exclaims, his eyes wide and his expression earnest. He reaches out and places a hand on my arm. "If you hadn't convinced me to show you that clearing with the deer, we would still be here, thinking the Nightingales were to blame for the recent attacks. The last few days have been difficult, but I'm glad that now, at the end, I have a friend that I can trust."

I smile demurely at him, suddenly feeling a little lightheaded. "I think that's the nicest thing you've ever said to me, Owyn Lund."

He smiles back, then seems to notice his hand lingering on my arm. He quickly withdraws, face reddening as he clears his throat and adopts a more stoic expression. "We should probably get going," he says, hastily stepping away. "Good luck to you."

I watch as he makes his departure, taking a roundabout path down the hill separate from the one we are currently on. *He's certainly an odd one*, I think to myself, taking a deep breath of the fresh woodland air. *But I'm also glad that I spoke to him. If I hadn't, then I would have been deprived of something I never knew I needed.*

A friend.

Despite everything with the battle looming just a few hours away, I can't help but grin foolishly as I walk away to join Willus on the road.

CHAPTER 29
OWYN

The air is deadly quiet as the demon host approaches the newly-built walls of Forest Hill.

Standing atop a rickety parapet with Zara and Elias, I peer past the flickering torches lining the abandoned town at the enemies marching toward us, their dark figures like shadows in the night.

Among our own ranks, nobody dares to utter a single word.

It had taken up until sunset for our ramshackle defenses to finally come together, the barricades sealed shut and the gates locked with heavy chains. Scouts frantically alerted us of the demons' arrival soon after, waving their arms wildly and blowing their horns.

From there, we could only wait for the dreaded attack.

We watch in mute terror as dozens of snarling darkhounds prowl before rows of mindflayed Nightingales, their blank expressions staring up at our fortifications like statues, utterly devoid of emotion. Behind them, leering gorgons carry spears and swords, their horned heads bristling like a wall of thorns.

There are so many of them, I think to myself, a cold knot of dread settling in my stomach. *There's got to be hundreds, at least. How did so many get through the Arc?*

Somewhere out in the sea of glowing red eyes, I know that Moloch is commanding them, formulating a plan to exploit our weaknesses and slaughter us all like the villagers of Haven.

Light willing, we will prevent that awful fate from happening.

Our own army, about two hundred and fifty strong, stands silently in position, weapons held at the ready. Archers carrying a mixture of longbows and crossbows stand atop the wall behind any cover they can find, arrows and bolts set to fire at the ready. Behind the barricades, Nightingales and militiamen carry shields and weapons ranging from swords and axes, to pitchforks and shovels, clutching them tightly in white-knuckled hands. More than a few mutter prayers under their breath to the Light.

The wall itself is a construction of scraps—lumber and metal taken from anywhere we could find. Wooden fence posts are nailed to oak doors, braced by tabletops and wreathed with nails and sharp bits of metal. It probably won't stop a sizable battering ram, but it may be enough to hold back a charge of foot soldiers.

Just outside of bowshot, the demons come to a halt, hanging back like predators just beyond the light of the torches.

Eleven Hells, I think, tightening my grip on my bow. *What are they waiting for?*

Elias' stone-faced expression gives no indication that he feels any fear at all. He merely raises his hand in the air, motioning for everyone on the wall to prepare to fire. The creaking sound of bowstrings being pulled fills the air.

One of the demons steps forward from out of the ranks, and I immediately recognize it as Moloch bedecked in midnight armor. He is carrying his massive black sword, the one he had used to slay General Pyke. The blade rests easily on his metal-clad shoulder, and he looks up at us with confidence, a feral grin splitting his crimson face.

When he speaks, his voice booms throughout the entire town, reverberating off the walls of all the abandoned homes. "I see that you've been expecting us," he says, red eyes scanning our fortifications. "That is well. I haven't had a proper fight in centuries. Tell me, who is your leader? I would speak to him before the bloodletting begins."

All eyes turn to Elias, who frowns. "Say what you must, demon," he shouts, his voice projecting confidence. "We're all listening."

Moloch chuckles, a harsh and grating sound. "Humans," he says at length, his tone disparaging, "always so rebellious, even when death is imminent. I was there, you know, when the Prince of Darkness first led our glorious campaign to destroy this pathetic world. I helped bring your wretched civilization to its knees! Your people are weak, and I enjoyed killing your ancestors, every last one of them." He pauses, as if considering for a brief instant before going on. "Still, it does not need to be so tonight. Our horde finds itself in need of good slaves. Throw down your arms and surrender, and I vow to spare your females and younglings. Otherwise, every single one of you will die."

Silence follows, and many behind the barricade shift uncomfortably. Elias appears unperturbed. His face is a cold mask, his gaze as hard as iron.

"There will be no surrender, demon," he declares firmly. "We will oppose you here and now with everything we have. Archers," he shouts, once more raising his hand, "prepare to loose on my mark!"

Abruptly, Moloch lets out an ear-splitting laugh, and the rest of his army joins him, with the exception of the bewitched Nightingales, who continue to stand and stare blankly ahead. The chorus of shrieking laughter causes the hair on the back of my neck to rise.

When the cackling subsides, the demon hefts his sword and gives it a few practice swings. "You choose fire and blood, then. So be it. That is what my kind was made for." Even from here, I can see his toothy sneer glittering in the low light of the torches.

Turning to regard his own troops, he thrusts his black sword into the air. "The age of men is at an end. This petty kingdom will soon fall to the R'Laar, and the remainder of humanity will be ground to dust. The time has come at last. Destroy them all!"

Moloch spins and points his blade at the wall as the first line of darkhounds begins to charge, clawed feet bounding at top speed toward our position.

"Loose!" Elias commands a second later, bringing his hand down in a chopping motion. Everybody, including myself, releases their arrows, launching a volley across the divide that rains down upon the charging demons.

Many of the missiles miss, falling harmlessly to the ground, but there are more than a few direct hits, arrows sinking deep into darkhound flesh. Several of the beasts yelp, pausing their charge to nip at the fletchings protruding from their hides. Though, as far as I can tell, none of the wounds are fatal.

"Prepare to fire again!" Elias roars, pulling two arrows from his quiver and nocking them at the same time. After a few seconds, he shouts again, "Loose!"

Another volley arcs through the night sky, peppering the darkhounds like a razor-sharp rain. More arrows and bolts find purchase on the red-eyed demons, but it is not enough to stop them. They collide with our thin wooden wall and begin snapping at those standing on top of it, jumping on their hind legs and gnashing with their teeth.

Using my father's hatchet, I cleave into a darkhound's skull as it jumps up to bite me. I hear a sickening crack, and its eyes go dim. It falls to the ground in a heap and does not get back up.

Others are not so lucky.

A gut-wrenching scream rips the air as a militiaman off to my right is yanked off the side of the wall, one of the shadowlings managing to sink its teeth into his leg. He falls into the waiting darkhounds and is torn to shreds, his screams becoming lost in a feeding frenzy.

Elias shoots a darkhound point-blank in the face before drawing another arrow and shouting, "Fire at will! Send these creatures back to the Eleven Hells!"

I take a step back from the wall and almost bump into Zara. She hasn't used any magic yet, but that is according to plan. The mages have to conserve their energy. Elias had ordered her to be up here on the wall in case a quick shield is necessary.

Mumbling an apology, I slip my hatchet back into my belt and pick my bow back up. I begin shooting as fast as I can at the monsters, trying desperately to drive them back.

As I draw yet another arrow, something in the darkness catches my eye. The mind slaves begin moving forward as one, using the darkhounds as a distraction so that they can get closer. I notice that even as they are running, many of them have raised their crossbows and take aim at us up on top of the wall.

"Take cover!" I shout, but it is too late. They launch their crossbows and bolts begin thudding into our defenses.

Shrieks of pain fill the air as more men fall off the wall and into the waiting jaws of the darkhounds. Elias, Zara, and I manage to duck behind a wooden barrier made from a table, just as the bolts reach our position. We wait for several seconds before emerging from our cover, peeking back out to engage the enemy.

The wall is still heavily defended, but the crossbows have taken their toll. Several of our Nightingales and militiamen have been killed or wounded by the deadly bolts, while others continue to be harried by the demons. With every second that passes, more holes open up in the line.

"Ignore the darkhounds," Elias shouts, drawing another arrow and firing in one swift motion. One of the bewitched Nightingales pitches backward with an arrow in the eye. "They are a distraction! Concentrate on the mind slaves!"

Our side begins attacking with renewed focus.

Just like the night the inn was attacked, the mindflayed Nightingales show no fear of death. They do not try to dodge our arrows or retreat. Many of them die while reloading their crossbows, and by the time they are ready to return fire, more than a quarter of them are down.

"Take cover!" I shout again as they repeatedly fire on us. This time, fewer of our men die from their most recent volley.

While crouching behind the cover, something grabs my foot and nearly pulls me over the side of the wall. I look down and see the snarling muzzle of a darkhound digging its teeth into my boot. I cry out, grabbing the wall for support, but the creature's weight is incredible. I feel my fingers begin to slip as it pulls me off our perch.

Strong arms grab my shoulders as Elias struggles to pull me back, but even his strength is not enough to keep me from falling over the side.

Light almighty! I pray, panicking. I struggle and kick at the maw but to no avail. *Please, help me!*

Something abruptly slams into the side of the beast's head, spraying my face with dark blood. I instantly feel the pressure on my boot release, and I am able to scramble back up from the edge. Blinking furiously, I look up to see Zara holding my hatchet, looking as stunned as I feel. The blade drips with darkhound blood, its handle clutched tightly in both of her hands.

She must have pulled it from my belt while I was hanging from the ledge, I realize, shakily pushing myself back up to my feet.

She hands it back to me and lets out a nervous laugh. "Like I said, you're making a habit out of this, ranger."

I force a smile and put the hatchet away. "Thanks. I guess I owe you... again."

"Let's just concentrate on not getting killed tonight," she says, brushing a lock of hair out of her eyes. "We can focus on what's owed later." Despite her bravado, I can tell that she is quite shaken by the ordeal.

"You got it," I reply, once again retrieving my bow.

I resume shooting, trying to ensure that every arrow counts. With Elias by my side, and other defenders firing along the wall, the enemy Nightingales begin dropping like flies.

For a moment, it feels as if we might actually push the invaders back. They've thrown their might against us, and we've made them pay dearly for it. Our side is not without casualties, of course, but our losses are nothing compared to the sheer number of dead darkhounds and Nightingales on the road in front of us.

With a roar, our attention is suddenly drawn to the rest of Moloch's army.

As the darkhounds and mind slaves continue to pressure us, the ranks of gorgons begin to surge forward like an unstoppable tide of glowing eyes and bristling spears. Their collective battle cry fills the air and chills my blood, and their presence seems to strike fear into everyone defending the wall, causing many to shrink back in fright.

The gorgons push past their mindflayed servants and quickly close the gap between their line and our fortifications. Our archers begin concentrating fire on them, but a handful of gorgons in the front lift up their hands and produce barriers of garish green energy, which stop the arrows like Zara's radiant shields. Their magic seems different than the magic I have seen the mages use. The green light is harsher than the soft blue glow of source energy, and it crackles like lightning with dark tendrils rippling across its surface.

"Warlocks," Zara says, her face a mixture of horror and fascination as she stares down at the shields. "Light, what is that *power* they're using?"

Cursing, Elias turns and looks at her. "It doesn't matter. The time has come, Zara," he declares loudly enough for her to hear over the sounds of battle.

She blinks as if to clear away her thoughts and nods, then waves to get the attention of another mage standing on the wall to the far left of us. Clutching her talisman, she begins mumbling in some ancient language, and her entire body seems to glow with an otherworldly light. In a matter of seconds, azure magefyre leaps from her fingertips and lances through the air to the ground just in front of the gorgons. The other mage to our left does the same.

The pitch-soaked earth ignites with a great whoosh, engulfing a large portion of the road and several of the nearby houses, effectively cutting off Moloch and his gorgons from the wall. Several of the charging demons are caught up in the blaze, their battle cries switching to high-pitched wails of agony.

Those of us on the wall let out a cheer as we watch the monsters burn.

I look to my right and see Zara grow dimmer, the source energy all used up. She looks more fatigued than she did before, but with determination, her hand still clutches her talisman as she watches the twisting flames below.

Our cheers quickly turn into horrified gasps as a wave of infernal green light surges from beyond the wall of fire, snuffing out the flames, and creating a gap wide enough for a few of the demons to get through. They pull a strange device with them, a long metal tube on wheels, with its middle hollowed out and its sides carved with strange, alien runes.

"What in the Eleven Hells is *that*?" I hear somebody ask nearby. Several of his comrades voice similar concerns.

Whatever it is, I think, drawing another arrow, *it probably isn't good.*

My vision is obscured as I am forced to duck behind a covering to avoid being hit by a slew of crossbow bolts. When I look back up, my mouth drops open in disbelief.

Three gorgons now stand behind the great metal cylinder and appear to be channeling their green magic *into* it by placing their hands on its sides. Deep inside the device, I can see an emerald glow pulsing within, and I suddenly realize what they intend to do.

"Elias!" I shout. "I think they're going to shoot at us with that thing!"

Before he can respond, the strange weapon erupts, belching blinding green energy directly at the center of our fortifications. For an instant, time seems to stand still as everything is drowned out by the light and overpowering rush of wind. It is followed by an explosion unlike anything I have ever seen before.

The concussion knocks me back, and I feel a searing heat wash over me like boiling oil. The very earth seems to quake beneath me, and for a terrifying moment, I wonder if I am dead.

By the time I manage to pick myself back up, it is as if my ears have been stuffed with cotton. My eyes are partially blinded, and my brain is muddled and disoriented.

Blinking away the temporary blindness, I try to focus on the spot the gorgons had shot their terrible weapon. Where there was once a wall and a half-dozen defenders, now there is only a gaping, smoking hole.

My stomach sinks.

The wall has been breached.

CHAPTER 30
ZARA

I watch in shock as the enemy horde begins rushing toward the newly blasted hole in the wall.

That explosion, I think to myself, feeling numb. *I never read about* that *in any of my books!*

Shaking my head, I pull myself up and grab my talisman, blinking against the green afterimage of the demon fire. *Now is not the time for pondering*, I think to myself, gritting my teeth in determination. *It is the time for action.*

A group of darkhounds manages to jump through the smoking crater where the wall once stood. Gleefully, they tear into the stunned and confused defenders.

Clearing away all other thoughts, I fill myself with a large amount of source energy, pushing myself to my limits as I descend the makeshift stairs and step in front of the gaping hole. Speaking the words of power, I thrust my hands in front of me and begin channeling the source energy into threads of radiant magic, conjuring a shield.

Crystal blue energy blossoms in front of me, spreading out from a point in the open air and blooming outward like a flower, effectively plugging the gap and preventing any more demons from coming through. Deep down, I know that I won't be able to hold this forever, but it should give our defenders the time they need to prepare themselves for the next full-scale attack.

I only hope it doesn't take them too long to shake themselves off.

As the remaining demons and bewitched Nightingales reach my shield, they begin throwing themselves against it, trying to find a weak spot they can exploit in order to get through. This spell, however, is a smaller version of what was used to create the Arc of Radiance. Unless my strength gives out, there is no way they will be able to penetrate it.

Grunting with the exertion of keeping the shield up, I watch as the archers abandon their positions and begin to form up behind the wall, looking more than a little rattled at the demon's awesome display of power. Soldiers shout and clamor around me as they fight off the handful of darkhounds that had managed to get through, their ranks considerably thinner than when the battle had first begun.

Someone speaks words of encouragement in my ear, but I barely hear them. It is everything I can do to keep my radiant magic from faltering.

Finally, when I think I can't hold it any longer, someone tells me they are ready. They say that I can lower my shield. A part of me recognizes the speaker as Owyn, his voice thick with concern. Dropping the spell without hesitation, I nearly pass out as the source energy seeps out of me, draining from my body like water being squeezed from a sponge.

A strong arm wraps around my shoulders, and Owyn pulls me away from the crater just as the demons begin to pour through. Dazed from the effects of the spell, I feel like a leaf being blown on the winds of a tempest. I somehow manage to take a few faltering steps so we can make it to safety, despite the fact that the world feels like it's spinning around me. Even in my delirious state, I can hear the titanic clash as the two sides collide with one another, the clangor of steel on steel ringing in the cool night air.

"Are you alright?" I hear Owyn ask. He sounds like he is speaking from far away.

I nod groggily as everything slowly comes back into focus around me, realizing that I am now sitting on the ground.

"You did it," I rasp, looking up at him. *Light, why does my voice sound so funny?*

"What?" he asks, eyebrows knitting together in confusion.

I force a smile. "You finally managed to save my life."

He stares at me for a moment, looking completely baffled. Then, his face breaks into a wide grin. He chuckles and shakes his head, his expression a mix of relief and bewilderment. "I still have to save you a few more times before we're even," he replies, helping me get back up on my feet.

"The night isn't over yet." I stand with only a little difficulty and take a deep breath. My talisman is still clutched firmly in my hand, and I can feel the source energy pulsing within the crystal, waiting to be seized.

Together, we watch the carnage unfold in front of us, the area beside the smoking crater turning into a literal bloodbath before our very eyes. Farmers and rebels fight valiantly to hold back the advancing R'Laar, even as more and more of them pour in from the other side. Luckily, because of the bottleneck at the wall, the enemy army is only able to send in a small number at a time.

Even so, the might of the demons is a force to be reckoned with, and we watch as the defenders of Forest Hill die off one by one.

"This isn't working," Owyn growls, frustration creeping into his voice. He draws an arrow and aims but lowers it just as quickly. "I can't even get a clear shot."

"We're going to have to fall back," I reply, scanning the battle for any sign of Jarrius, the elderly mage who had helped me light the wall of fire.

He is nowhere to be seen.

Elias breaks away from the melee and staggers toward our position. He has a nasty gash on the side of his head, but otherwise, he looks unharmed. The short sword and the knife he wields are both slick with dark demon blood.

"Zara!" he shouts, eyes as hard and calculating as they've ever been. "Head up the hill to our fallback position. Alert the other mages. The outer wall is lost."

I nod and turn to run up the road. Owyn moves to follow me, but he is stopped by a harsh command from his master. "Owyn," he barks. "I need you down here. Find a spot on one of these rooftops and shoot as many of these creatures as you can. Take my arrows." He tosses his quiver at him. "Go, now!"

Without looking back at Owyn, I run as fast as I can.

The 'fallback position' is nothing more than a second barricade made from old wagons and furniture piled a little further up the road. General Barus is stationed there with several more of my colleagues and another contingent of Nightingale soldiers.

"What's going on down there?" Barus asks from atop his horse when I approach. Despite everyone's insistence that he stay out of the fight due to his wounds, he is outfitted in battle armor and holds a drawn sword in his good hand.

"The wall has fallen," I say, panting. "They have some sort of magical siege device they used to blow a hole right through it."

Barus curses bitterly, then leans over his horse and spits on the ground. The reserve defenders eye each other nervously. I can tell what they are all thinking. *The wall was not supposed to fall this quickly... how can we hope to hold them here?*

"Nothing can be done about that now," the general grunts, turning his horse around to regard his men. "In just a few minutes, our boys are going to be coming back up this hill. They're going to have an army of demons on their heels, so be prepared to fight. Remember, that bloody red bastard already stole many of our brothers. Make them pay!"

No cheers fill the night, only resolute nods and a few muttered prayers.

I cast my eyes about and locate the five remaining mages clustered off to the side of the barricade. I rush over to join them.

"Where is Jarrius?" Willus asks when I arrive.

I shake my head gravely, and he squeezes his eyes shut, muttering a curse under his breath.

The others glance at one another anxiously. Each one of them looks pale and frightened in the glow of the moonlight. These are scholars, not warriors. They've never had to use their magic to kill.

"We need to take up our positions," I find myself saying. Everyone looks at me, surprised to see an initiate taking charge. Not caring about the potential ramifications, I press on. "The R'Laar are through the wall, and our allies below cannot hold them forever. Any minute now, they are going to come charging up that hill. We need to be ready."

A couple of them nod at my words, but the rest of them look unconvinced.

"You are all mages of Tarsys," I continue urgently. "You are the best and brightest that this kingdom has to offer. Without your aid, the people here have no chance of surviving. We need to take a stand. We need to hold fast. We need to show everyone here the true power of the Conclave!"

Emboldened by my words, Willus finally speaks up. "You heard the initiate," he shouts, giving me an approving look out of the corner of his eye. "Get in position! Be ready to pull in source energy at a moment's notice. Move, now!"

The mages hurriedly disperse, leaving me alone with the elder magic-user. He turns toward me and his expression softens. "You are full of surprises, Zara Dennel. Your courage and bull-headedness continue to astound me."

"Thank you, Magus," I reply hesitantly. I cannot tell if it is a compliment or a criticism.

"The point is," he says gruffly, "without your tendency to act first and ask questions later, everyone in this Light-forsaken town would likely be dead already. You should be proud of what you accomplished."

The praise brings a faint smile to my lips. But when I look down the hill toward the battle, it quickly fades. "I'll be proud when we send these demons back to the abyss."

He snorts and nods his head. "That sounds like a plan. Let's get to it then."

With that, we part ways, each heading to our predetermined locations. My spot is near a tree off to the side of the road, a little way down from where Barus and the Nightingales are stationed behind the barricade. Down the hill, I can hear the sounds of fighting, steel ringing and men screaming in the darkness. It does not sound like things are going well for our side.

Clutching my talisman, I wait in nervous anticipation until I see haggard-looking militiamen running up the road, fleeing the losing fight at the outer wall. They filter up in gradually growing numbers, eventually becoming a flood of battered soldiers. Most of them look as though they have been through the Eleven Hells themselves, their clothing stained and their weapons slick with blood.

So few, I think to myself sorrowfully. *Far too few.*

It is not long before I spot Elias and Owyn running with darkhounds snapping close at their heels. They barely manage to make it behind the barricade, the shadowlings backing off as they are pelted with arrows.

The mages, including myself, remain hidden from the demons' view, dispersed along either side of the road among the trees and buildings. When the rest of Moloch's army begins making its way up the hill, they pass right in between us without noticing our presence. Even so, I cannot help but hold my breath as I watch the gorgons and mind slaves march by, weapons brandished.

My eyes flick upward as I wait for the signal. *It should be coming any second now...*

The demons stop just before the barricade and begin forming up ranks. The gorgons in front conjure large shields of strange green magic, blocking any attempt for the defenders to shoot arrows at them. I find myself once again curious about the source of their magic, but I force myself to keep my mind focused on the task at hand.

From a hidden location across the road, I catch a glimpse of brilliant white sparks shooting into the air. They erupt heavenward and arc over our two opposing armies like a meteor shower, winking out as they slowly descend toward the ground. Upon seeing them, I immediately begin filling myself with source energy.

The signal has been sent.

Along with the other mages, I channel the energy into magefyre, a compact ball of blue flames dancing in my palm. When it is ready, the fire shoots out of my hand like a storm, burning the demons and men in front of me and igniting the pitch beneath their feet.

In a matter of seconds, the entire road becomes a conflagration so bright that I fear I may go blind. The very air seems to shimmer from the heat of the inferno, bending around the screaming monsters as the fires consume them.

After a few seconds, I break my concentration, ending the spell and releasing the latent energy within me. I watch in sick satisfaction as the gorgons and shadowlings writhe in agony in the midst of the magical flames, their skin sizzling and sloughing off like wax melting from a candle. The bewitched Nightingales stand like statues as they burn, ignorant to the ability to feel any pain.

Forcing myself to look away, I disappear into a stand of trees behind me and begin creeping up the hill to join the others behind the barricade.

At least that plan worked, I think to myself wearily, trudging through the underbrush. *That should put a dent in Moloch's army.*

Halfway up the path, I stop dead in my tracks as a darkhound steps out from the shadows, its fangs bared and glistening in the light of the distant fires. My heart leaps into my throat, and for a moment, I just stand there, frozen and unable to move.

The darkhound growls, a guttural sound that cuts through the sounds of battle like a knife. Before I can begin pulling in source energy, it lunges toward me, jaws snapping hungrily.

Pitifully, I raise my hands as if I can stop the beast's advancement with willpower alone. But just before it reaches me, a glinting flash of metal spins from somewhere above and embeds itself in the shadowling's spine. The darkhound yelps and spins, looking for its attacker. An arrow whistles through the air a second later and plunges deep into its eye socket.

The creature falls twitching to the ground.

Owyn emerges from some bushes up the hill and pulls his hatchet from the monster's back. The blade emerges from its spine with a sickening *crunch*. Giving me a lopsided grin, he says, "That's twice I've saved your life, mage. We'll be even before this night is over."

CHAPTER 31
OWYN

Zara purses her lips and wags a finger at me. "If you think I'm going to let you save me again, you're going to be sorely disappointed."

This only makes me grin wider.

"Come on," I say, waving for her to follow me up the hill. "Let's get up there and join the others."

We pick our way up the narrow trail and find a small opening in the barricade, slipping inside and sealing it behind us with a wooden barrel full of stones. Passing through the weary defenders, we find Elias near the front of our gathered host watching grimly as the fires burn.

"You and your fellow mages did well," he remarks as we approach. "The rest of the demons have pulled back. I think your combined power was more than they had expected."

"Good," Zara replies, stifling a yawn. From the light of the flames, I can tell that she is exhausted, her face drawn and pale and dark circles forming beneath her eyes. Using so much magic appears to have worn on her, yet she remains upright without offering a word of complaint. "It's only a matter of time before they return. What's the plan?"

Barus, who has now dismounted from his horse, steps over to our little group and interjects. "This is it, Magus," he says, motioning vaguely with his sword. "We make our stand here. This is where we either hold out against them or fall."

I look up the hill to where the governor's mansion stands silently watching us before a canvas of stars. Reality sets in, reminding me that we are all that's left between the townsfolk hiding inside and an army of bloodthirsty demons. We have dealt them a blow, but the fight is far from over.

It is a sobering thought.

Eleven Hells... this is it, I realize, my heart sinking as I turn back toward the field. *Once those fires die out, they are going to throw everything they have at us. Will we be ready?*

Elias seems to recognize the discouraged looks Zara and I are both wearing. He clears his throat, then points. "We have positioned all of our archers in the buildings and trees around us. They will put pressure on the demons as they try to break through our barricades. Barus and the Nightingales will hold the line here while the remaining militia wait in reserve. They will rotate in shifts as the front-line tires out. They will also have shields to defend themselves against enemy crossbows."

"And what if they bring out that magic device again?" I ask, pointing out the obvious danger.

"That is where Willus and the other mages come in," Elias says. "When we see that thing prepare to fire, they will combine their strength and create a shield of radiant energy. Again, they will maintain it in shifts so that no one tires out."

I nod, but still feel skeptical. It is plain how tired Zara and the other mages are. *Can they really keep it up all night?*

"Prepare yourselves," Elias says as a runner hands him a fresh quiver filled with arrows. "The time is fast approaching."

Sure enough, I can see that the magefyre trap is starting to fizzle out, leaving behind a mass grave of twisted and blackened bodies. Through the haze, I make out the massive demonic host waiting beyond for their chance to converge on our location once again. Moloch stands at the front of his gorgon line, black sword piercing the ground before him like a gravestone. His glowing red eyes regard us with hatred beneath his crown of gnarled horns.

"Are you going to be alright?" I ask Zara in a low voice.

"I'll be fine," she replies coolly. She takes a long drink from a water skin then hands it over to me. "You just worry about yourself, alright?"

"Easy for you to say." I take the water skin but do not drink. "One of you mages is easily worth ten or twenty of us mere mortals."

Our conversation is interrupted as a blanket of green energy snakes out from the hands of several of the gorgons. The shimmering tendrils cover the low fires on the road and begin to snuff them out, making it safe for them to pass through once more. As they do so, Moloch lets out a battle cry that is echoed by the demons surrounding him.

The cacophony is so loud that I have to resist covering my ears.

With the fires finally out, the magic dissipates, and the horde surges forward in one big group. Elias gestures with his bow, and the archers stationed around us begin loosing their arrows at the charging army.

"Brace the barricade!" Barus shouts. "Don't let any of them through!"

Using shields and spears, the defenders support the makeshift barricade and prepare for impact, their bodies adding strength to the fortifications.

When the monsters reach them, the resulting crash is tremendous. The low wall, made from junk and furniture and anything else the townsfolk could scavenge from their homes, buckles under the pressure of the gorgons' charge. It is all our people can do to keep it from caving in altogether and letting in a flood of demons.

Arrows and crossbow bolts fly overhead like angry insects, killing fighters on both sides. Those on the front lines stab wildly with their swords and spears, trying desperately to score a lucky hit on enemies just feet away from them.

Amid the chaos and the bustle, I stand back and make use of my bow. I shoot arrows as fast as I can pull them out of my quiver, turning gorgons and shadowlings alike into pincushions. Despite my efforts and those of the other archers, the demons keep coming. Every one that falls is quickly replaced by another.

Zara unexpectedly calls to me over the sounds of battle. "Where is Willus?" Her voice sounds frantic, her eyes wide as saucers. "He's the one coordinating the mages. I can't find him anywhere!"

I cast my eyes about the battlefield but do not see the heavyset man. I shrug my shoulders and shout back, "I'm not sure."

She bites her lower lip, brows knitting together with concern, when a taunting laugh rips through the air, drawing our attention.

"So pitiful. Even your magic users are easy to kill!"

We look to see Moloch standing on a broken wagon behind his battling troops, his black sword held up in front of him with both hands. A figure of a man is impaled on the tip through the middle of his back, his body bent and bloodied.

Zara covers her mouth and gasps in horror. "Willus!"

I squint and see that the body is indeed wearing blue-colored robes, though most of the fabric is stained a deep red. *He must not have gotten through in time*, I think to myself, muttering a silent curse.

The remaining mages gather around Zara, each of them staring at their dead comrade with looks of consternation. They look small and frightened, a far cry from the intimidating figures who interrogated me all those days ago.

After a moment, Moloch lowers his sword and uses his foot to kick Willus' body to the ground. Leveling his glowing red eyes at us, he points and shouts something to his troops.

Almost immediately, we are assaulted by a barrage of crossbow bolts and green fireballs, forcing us to duck down behind the little cover that remains. One of the mages takes a crossbow bolt to the throat, while green fire splashes on the ground nearby, igniting another's robes.

"They're trying to pin us down," I shout at Zara, wincing as a bolt slams into the wooden beam a few inches from my face. "Eleven Hells. We need to do something!"

She opens her mouth to reply, then screams as demon fire ignites the overturned table she huddles behind, setting it ablaze. She scrambles away from the green flames, the hem of her robe smoldering from the heat yet the rest of her remains unharmed.

All around us, men struggle and die defending the barricade, valiantly holding back the assault. Though the demon advance has been halted, there is no doubt in my mind that they will eventually overpower us. Our side will need a miracle if it is going to survive.

Barus' deep voice carries over the sounds of fighting, his words thick with worry. "The machine!" he shouts, pointing with the tip of his sword. "Get ready! They're bringing forth the machine!"

A cold knot settles in the pit of my stomach. I peek out from behind my cover to see that the demons are indeed wheeling the metal tube to the front.

"Zara!" Elias calls out, getting as close to us as he can. "You need to cast your shield—*now!*"

She nods and grabs her talisman, but just as she and the other mages are about to stand up to begin their spell, another barrage of missiles pelts their position, forcing them back down.

I roll out from underneath the covering and spring to my feet several paces away, launching arrows at the attackers, but there are far too many. My shots become ineffectual.

As the device rolls to a stop, I can see green energy already glowing to life within. Everything seems to fade into black around me, and I can feel the blood draining from my face.

Light almighty, I think, numbly letting my bow drop from my hands. "Everybody," I begin, racing back over to Zara. "Take cov—"

An explosion rocks the battlefield, rippling through the very earth.

Like the sound of a thousand tree trunks breaking in half, the center of the barricade explodes, throwing debris and corpses back with a blinding flash of light. Zara and I are both knocked backward by the blast, an intense heat rushing past us in a violent, blistering gust of wind. Pain shoots up my back and shoulder as I land, ripping my stitches open and blasting the air out of my lungs. For a moment, I lay on the ground, too stunned to even move.

Grit and dirt rains down upon us, pelting us like hail, and in the silence that ensues, a high-pitched ringing fills my ears.

Somehow, I manage to prop myself up on an elbow and blink away my blindness, raggedly sucking in a breath of smoky air. Our forces, such as they were, have been blasted completely in half. A gaping hole now occupies the space where dozens of people had stood just moments before, fighting for their lives against the overwhelming odds. Bodies, soil, and shattered splinters of wood now litter the field, reminding me, oddly, of a child's toy chest that has been smashed to pieces, with ruined dolls scattered among the wreckage.

Moloch leads his demons through the hole in the barricade a second later, his leering visage twisted into a victorious grin. The reserve militia, those not still reeling from the effects of the explosion, scramble forward to intercept the demons, but it is a pitiful attempt at defense. As soon as they meet Moloch and his troops, they begin dying by the score.

A few of the Nightingales who also managed to survive the blast join the fight as well, but they are sorely pressed. The demons push them relentlessly up the hill, an unstoppable force making its way steadily toward the governor's house.

Words come unbidden to my mind as I lie there, too stunned to move. It is a mantra I have recited a thousand times before, one that has always given me comfort in times of need.

The ranger's oath.

> *I swear by my life and my hope for salvation that I will abide by the oath of the rangers until my dying breath.*
>
> *Our solemn duty is to protect the borders of the realms of men from those enemies who would seek our destruction. The wilderness shall be our homestead, the sun and stars our only hearth. We will sacrifice everything, even our very lives, for the defense of the kingdom, unto the death of those who would do us harm.*
>
> *We are the watchers in the woods, the arrows in the darkness.*
>
> *None shall pass by while we stand guard.*

Staggering to my feet, I watch as Moloch cleaves two men in half with one massive swing of his sword. I marvel at how powerful the red demon is, how mighty he is compared to ordinary men.

His fiery red eyes fall upon me, and his wicked grin widens. He hefts his blade and begins making his way toward my position.

Suddenly panicked, I reach for a weapon, for anything I can defend myself with. My hatchet lies several yards away, covered in a thin layer of dirt, but it is too far away for me to get to in time.

Not seeing any other option, I scramble forward, reaching desperately for the handle. Moloch delivers a kick to my side, forcing me to stop my crawl. I gasp, curling up in agony as it feels like several of my ribs have cracked. He lifts up his sword to impale me, time seeming to slow down as my life flashes before my eyes.

It's too late, I find myself thinking, gritting my teeth against the coming pain. *I'm done for.*

Just as he is about to plunge his black blade into my body, something collides into the tall demon's chest, knocking him off-balance and stopping him from making the killing stroke. Astounded, I look up and catch a glimpse of my savior.

Elias squares off against the great demon, wielding his belt knife and a short sword. "If you want my apprentice, you're going to have to go through me."

He immediately lashes out, blades flashing like lightning as he circumvents the demon's defenses and slices open his arm, drawing dark blood.

Moloch lets out a furious scream and turns his full attention on Elias, but my master is far too quick for his lumbering movements. He dodges out of the way of Moloch's attack and strikes out again, this time cutting his other arm.

Suddenly finding myself out of danger, I begin searching around for Zara. I call her name, wincing against the pain in my chest, but it comes out as little more than a croak. I finally spot her lying a little way up the hill from my position, her body in a crumpled heap. Crawling on my belly, I make my way over to her side to see if she is still alive.

"I'm sorry," she says softly, turning to look at me as I approach. Her lip is split, and it dribbles blood as she talks.

"For what?" I ask in reply, oblivious to the chaos unfolding around us.

"I wasn't... strong enough," she whispers. Her voice is so quiet, but I can read her lips amidst the raging sounds of battle.

I force a smile. "You were amazing," I say, trying my best to sound comforting. "The best mage I have ever known."

She lets out a small laugh, eyes glistening. "I'm the only mage you've ever known."

We both duck our heads as a bolt of green energy blasts a hole in the grass a few feet above us, showering us with dirt. I quickly glance about and see that the remaining militia have all but routed. Many of them have fallen, and those still fighting are being cut down one by one. In the middle of it all, demons and men alike give Elias and Moloch a wide berth, apparently not wanting any part in their fight.

I gaze back at Zara, who is still wincing in pain. *At least I won't die alone*, I find myself thinking. It's a gloomy thought, but it strangely gives me comfort. Reaching forward, I take her hand in mine and together, we wait for the end.

Abruptly, the demons pause in their relentless push forward. Everything stands still as the battle seems to pause.

Out of nowhere, a storm of magefyre rains down upon their heads, immolating dozens in an instant.

Like a whirlwind, Arch-Magister Elva Tyrande leads the remaining mages down from the governor's mansion, hurling magic missiles and balls of fire at the demons in a colossal display of power.

I watch in fascination as the very air around them appears to shimmer as they channel source energy. Their talismans glow brightly as they begin destroying every enemy that stands in front of them. Gorgons fall dead and darkhounds burst into flames, their pained screams drowning out all other noise as they burn.

The destruction so complete, that for a moment, I fear that I might be hallucinating. In a matter of seconds, the course of the battle begins to turn.

Zara and I watch in amazement, the lights so bright they sear our eyes. Even so, we cannot look away. Elva wields radiant magic like an artist, her movements precise and her effects both beautiful and devastating. Wherever she looks, demons die, and it appears there is no limit to the amount of source energy she can channel.

The scene is nothing short of spectacular.

Amidst the chaos, Elias begins to push Moloch even harder, and in the wavering blue light, I can see that the creature is covered in dozens of bleeding cuts.

The big demon roars in anger, screaming at his troops to press onward as he tries unsuccessfully to slay Elias. Despite his ranting, the demons begin to fall back, tripping over themselves in an effort to get away from the mages.

Ducking to avoid decapitation, Elias lunges forward with his blades held before him. He feints to the left, then spins right at the last second, driving his belt knife deep into the monster's neck. Red eyes bulge in surprise, and Elias follows this attack up by jabbing the tip of his short sword right into Moloch's belly. The blade plunges to the hilt, and Elias steps back, letting the demon lord fall to his knees. He lets out a death rattle in the form of an incomprehensible gurgle. When his body finally hits the ground, it lands with a heavy thud.

Upon seeing their master killed, the demons begin pulling back in earnest, the retreat devolving into a full-fledged rout. The mages, spearheaded by Elva Tyrande, blaze a path down the hill, leaving scores of charred demons in their wake. Upon seeing the mages' magical inferno, the defenders begin to take heart, pursuing the enemy until they have pushed them all the way back through barricade.

Within minutes, we are alone on the hillside.

Grunting, I haul myself to my feet and extend a hand to Zara, helping her up. She takes it and winces as I pull her to a standing position. Together, we gaze down at Forest Hill, the light of a dozen fires illuminating the retreating R'Laar.

"It's over," I breathe, relief mixing with emotion at having survived the battle. "I can't believe we won." Looking over at her, I see that Zara has tears in her eyes.

She blinks and shakes her head, the tears rolling down her grime-stained cheeks. "I don't think that it is over," she replies, glancing from me, to the corpse of Moloch, then back out into the night. "I think that this is just the beginning."

Sobered, I put my arm around her shoulders and follow her gaze down the hill. We stand there for a while, lost in our own dark thoughts as we watch the demons retreat into the woods, scattering like chaff in a warm summer breeze.

CHAPTER 32
ZARA

The sun rises to the east of Forest Hill, a red orb painting the sky in a soft orange hue that gradually brightens the darkened world. It illuminates a scene that is forever burned into my memory, a testament to the horrors and carnage of war.

The quiet border town, once so quaint and peaceful, has been reduced to little more than ash. Buildings lie in ruins with corpses littering the ground almost everywhere I look. Those who survived are left with the grim task of gathering their dead for burial and rebuilding all that was lost.

Walking amidst the desolate remnants of the town, I hurry down the path to where my colleagues are gathering near the bottom of the hill.

Although we have won a great victory here, there are no songs to be sung—actual war is much less glorious than it is portrayed in all the ballads. The bards always seem to gloss over the terrible sights, sounds, and smells that can only be understood by one who has experienced them firsthand. I watch numbly as the triumphant defenders weep over their destroyed homes and their fallen friends and family. Although the women and children of Forest Hill were saved from death and enslavement, they emerged from the governor's home to find a much different world than the one they had left. Many of them have lost fathers, brothers, and sons, left alone and haunted to pick up the remains of their lives.

Elias had, of course, led many of the remaining Nightingales into the Emberwood to hunt down the demons who fled. It is sure to be a long and arduous process rooting them all out of the woods, but I'm confident it is a challenge to which the ranger is well-suited.

Owyn went with his master, of course, not wanting to be left out of the action. I, however, decided to stay behind and help the townsfolk. The thought of participating in more bloodshed makes my stomach turn.

"I'm fine, you bloody vultures!" a voice shouts off to my right. General Barus berates several of his Nightingale soldiers while leaning heavily on a crutch, favoring a wounded leg. "I've weathered much worse than this. Go, make yourselves useful. Try to salvage this damnable contraption!"

The soldiers cringe under their general's harsh words, then turn to examine the molten metal gathered on the ground. The strange device the R'Laar had used to decimate our meager walls was destroyed, reduced to a pile of slag by the retreating gorgons. Apparently, they did not want us to have access to their superior technology, even if we do not yet have any idea how it works.

I sidestep the desiccated corpse of a darkhound and continue on my way, covering my mouth with my sleeve to block out the stench and smoky air around me.

It is not long before I approach the blue-robed mages gathered in a small semi-circle near a gutted farmhouse.

Of the ten mages who had accompanied Elva and me from Tarsys, only four remain, the rest having fallen in battle the previous night. Those left are among the most loyal to the Conclave, and two of them who had outright refused to fight during the siege. But it seems that once they were confronted with certain death, they were more than willing to change their minds.

The mages look up as I approach, stepping aside with worried expressions on their faces. Several of them even have tears in their eyes. As they part, they give me a view of what they are looking at. It looks like a human body covered in gore. As I walk up to the corpse, however, I see that it is no corpse at all.

It is Arch-Magister Tyrande.

Elva looks up at me from her back, eyes glazed and dried blood at the corner of her mouth. Her usually perfect hair is askew, and her pristine robes are ripped at the torso, revealing the broken shaft of a crossbow bolt protruding from her stomach. Judging by the sheer amount of blood pooled around her, it does not appear that she will survive.

For a moment, we simply stare at one another, and I am surprised to realize that I feel nothing as I look down at her pitiful form. This woman, once so powerful and intimidating to me, has been brought low, her life leaking away from a wound too terrible to be repaired.

Gazing down at her, I cannot help but feel that she got what she deserved.

"Zara," she wheezes, feebly raising a crusty, bloodstained hand to wave at me. "I am glad to see that you survived the night."

"No thanks to you," I reply acidly. The other mages gasp and give me angry looks. Even without a mortal wound, the Arch-Magister should not be spoken to in such a way.

Elva's mouth twitches up into a small, bemused smile. "Child… it was us who turned the tide of the battle. Without our intervention… the enemy would have won."

I resist the urge to sneer at her. Even now, on the brink of death, she cannot bring herself to call the demons what they truly are. "If you had intervened earlier, then many more would have survived. We could have beaten the demons before they even breached the first gate!"

"Perhaps," she says softly, before descending into a fit of wet coughing. When she gains control of herself again, she continues. "But I do not desire to argue with you, initiate. There is something you need to know."

With considerable effort, she manages to lift her head up and look me in the eye. "The Circle knows that the R'Laar have gotten through the Arc. We have known it all along."

The revelation feels like a slap in the face.

"You... *knew?*"

She closes her eyes and nods. "That is why we came here. To get the situation under control."

My shock is swiftly replaced with white hot anger. "You knew, and yet you decided to do nothing? We brought you evidence of their presence, and you chose to exile us! What... how—"

"Unfortunately, I cannot explain everything," she interrupts, still maintaining her air of command despite her grave situation. "My current... *predicament* has seen to that. But you must know that I only ever had the best intentions in mind."

"The best intentions?" I cannot keep the incredulity out of my voice.

"Yes," she replies simply. "We knew that the Arc had been compromised, but we did not know to what extent. I was tasked with keeping everything suppressed so that a full-fledged panic did not engulf the kingdom. The Nightingales provided the perfect scapegoat, someone I could blame for the attacks. That's why I was so adamant that it was them behind it all. If a few rebels should perish in the effort to destroy the demons... then all the better. I would let them destroy themselves, and afterward I would kill any survivors before returning to the Conclave. I had no idea so many had actually gotten through..."

Elva winces suddenly and goes rigid, as if in great pain. One of the mages jumps to her side immediately, but whatever it is passes quickly. She wearily waves him away.

"Zara Dennel, I need you to deliver a message to the High Magus for me. Tell her what has happened here, of the *real* threat we are dealing with." After a moment, she adds, "And tell her that I am sorry I failed."

My first reaction is to laugh in her face, to tell her that she can find someone else to be her damn messenger. But after a moment's consideration, I decide to nod my head, even though it pains me to do so. "I will deliver your message."

"Good," Elva rasps. "We do not fully understand why the Arc is failing, but if they know the extent of what we are facing, then perhaps the Conclave will divert more resources toward finding a solution." With a frail gesture she beckons me forward, and I reluctantly comply. When I am crouched by her side, she begins to speak again.

"In the name of the Light and with these four mages as my witnesses, I hereby recommend you to be raised to full mage within the Conclave. You've served the kingdom well, Zara Dennel. Your abilities will surely be needed in the days to come."

Nothing that has transpired over the last few days can compare to the shock I feel at hearing these words. I stand there, sputtering like a dimwit, unable to form a coherent response. This woman who had ordered my exile not three days ago, just gave me the greatest honor any initiate has ever received. *Has the entire world gone mad?*

"Congratulations, Magus," Elva says and for a second, she actually looks a little proud. "I always knew there was something special about you, and it appears I was right."

"I... don't know what to say," I manage to get out. I cast my eyes about and see that the other mages look to be as puzzled as myself.

"Say nothing," Elva replies, leaning her head back down against the ground. As I stare at her, I realize just how frail she looks lying there. "Inform the High Magus... protect the kingdom. You carry the hope of Tarsynium with you now, child. Do not fail in your quest as I did..."

It takes me a few moments to realize that she is dead. Her body, so pale compared to the blood staining her lower half, lies perfectly still in the morning light. Her expression gives the appearance that she has finally been able to find some small measure of peace.

Equally surprising, I find there are tears now streaking my own cheeks. *Why am I crying?* I think to myself. *This woman betrayed me!* And yet, despite my anger, I can't help but feel a twinge of sadness at her passing. The Arch-Magister saw something in me, led me on this Light-cursed adventure, and raised me to become a full mage. Even with her flaws, she was a talented magic user. Her loss is truly a blow to the Conclave itself.

After a moment, I stand up and regard the mages around me. They are weeping as well, and each of them wears a look of fear and apprehension that mirrors what I now feel in my heart. Sniffing and wiping my cheeks, I vow silently to myself that I will not fail in this quest. The High Magus will know of what happened here, and the R'Laar will be kept from snuffing out the last embers of humanity left on Byhalya.

I will gladly give my life for such a noble cause.

"Come," I say to the mages, who look in desperate need of someone to lead them. "There is still much work to be done." With that, I turn and begin searching the town for anyone in need of help.

Looking back, I am surprised again to see that they are following me.

CHAPTER 33
OWYN

We lower the final body into the ground, laying it to rest with the others in the shallow mass grave.

Straightening, I wipe the sweat from my forehead with the back of my hand, nodding solemnly to the other men I had assisted with the grisly task. At long last, the fallen are ready for their final burial.

Together, we grab our spades as a white-robed priest begins reading final rites, speaking in a low, reverent tone as he commends their spirits into the Light. The old man is a kindly fellow, and I used to enjoy listening to his sermons whenever I got the chance, but now, I barely register his words. My attention is drawn to the bodies lying in the dirt, my stomach turning at their pale skin and the wounds marring their still forms. My mind is recalled to another grave I had all too recently helped to dig—in the destroyed village of Haven.

The sermon is meant to be comforting, I'm sure. He speaks of the mercy of the Light and the great joy the souls of men will receive in the hereafter. But to me, the words are insufficient. There is still an enemy out there somewhere, and if it is not defeated, then many more souls will be sent to dwell with the Light.

He bows his head at length and says, "Amen," and then we begin filling in the pit, using our spades to cover the bodies with freshly-turned earth.

When it is finished, most leave the gravesite, moving on to work on the numerous other tasks required around town. I, however, linger for a few moments, offering a silent prayer and vow of my own.

I'll avenge you all, I think, somberly peering down at the dark soil. *I'll gladly give up my own life, if necessary, if it will mean stopping the R'Laar from doing this again. This I swear.*

A cool breeze blows from the north and ruffles my hair, and I look up to gaze around at the ruins of Forest Hill. Few buildings still stand after the battle; most having been burned to the ground. There are survivors, fortunately, but they each look like a piece of them has died—even the small children. Their innocence has been snatched away, replaced with an empty void beneath their now hardened, soot-covered exterior. I see it in too many of their faces as it mirrors my own grim expression.

The shadow of war has fallen over us all. The ugly truth of our fate has been uncovered and laid bare for all those who remain.

I had spent the better part of the day hunting with Elias and the Nightingales in the woods surrounding the town. We managed to catch and kill several of the demons who had fled the night before, but the rest eluded us. It will probably take weeks of hard tracking to find the remaining soldiers from Moloch's army.

Unable to relax after I returned from the hunt, I set out immediately to help those I could. I dug through the ashes to find belongings and gathered together as many of the salvageable weapons and armor that we could. After the bodies of all those who had fallen were taken to the green, I aided the townsfolk in burying their dead. Now, as the sun sets in the western sky, I find myself unable to do anything else. The exhaustion of the battle and the long day of labor finally seems to have caught up to me.

Blinking my bloodshot eyes, I take a deep breath and exhale, letting my shoulders slump. *Eleven Hells... I'm amazed I'm still standing. I haven't slept in days.*

I walk back to the main road and turn toward the inn. Surprisingly, it is one of the few buildings still left standing. It has become something of a hospital to treat the wounded, as well as a storehouse to provision supplies. Right now, I want nothing more than a long rest, a chance to forget about everything that has happened.

Light knows that all of us deserve one.

I pass townspeople and Nightingales alike on my way down the road, many of whom peer at me with haunted eyes or nod respectfully in silent greeting. A few of them carry on hushed conversations, but most remain quiet and reserved. It reminds me of a graveyard, the tone of the entire town mournful and subdued.

When I finally reach the inn, it feels like a physical weight has settled down upon my back.

The common room is filled with people. The majority lies upon makeshift litters on the floor as the rest scurry about trying to help in any way they can, carrying bandages and cups of water or medicine. The air is thick with the smell of blood, and intermittent groans break up the dreary silence.

I step inside and quickly close the door behind me, walking carefully past the prone figures of wounded men.

Mrs. Ellis spots me from across the room and immediately makes her way over to my side, wiping her bloodstained fingers on a towel. "Owyn! Is everything all right, lad? I was so worried about you! I haven't seen you since the fighting ended."

"I'm all right," I assure her, forcing a weary smile.

"That's good," she replies, grinning broadly. "And Elias? Is he still out hunting those horrible creatures?"

"Yes. I expect he won't rest until every last one of them has been found."

"Light bless that man," she says with a sigh. "We'd all be lost without him."

I nod. "Yes. Yes, we would."

She looks me over like a concerned mother, her lips pursing as if in dissatisfaction. "Just look at you. All unkempt and dirty. When is the last time you had a bath, dear boy?" Her expression softens as she looks into my eyes, and she seems on the verge of pulling me into a bone-crushing hug. "You look like you're about to fall over from exhaustion. Let me get you something to eat. A skinny lad like you, you're probably starving half to death."

"Don't worry about me," I reply, casting a meaningful glance at the wounded around the room. "Honestly. There are others in greater need of help."

Mrs. Ellis crosses her arms in front of her ample bosom and fixes me with a stern expression. "That may be so, but you should still eat. Even a ranger's apprentice needs to take care of himself every once in a while."

I hold up my hands in defeat. "Fair point. But I can fix my own meal—today, at least."

The big woman heaves a sigh and points to the kitchen. "We haven't had time to prepare anything, but you can take whatever you want from the pantry. You've certainly earned it. There may even be a little spiced wine left on the bottom shelf," she adds with a wink. "Now, when you're done eating, promise me that you'll get yourself cleaned up and have a good long sleep. I'll not have any of this nonsense about rangers not needing as much sleep as regular folk. Elias may be your master, but *I'm* the master of this inn."

I am unable to suppress a grin at her declaration. Though her husband, James, is technically the owner, Mrs. Ellis is known throughout Forest Hill as the undisputed matron of the inn, overseeing everything from the staff, to the cooking, to the changing of the linens. The homely building is her kingdom, and she rules over it with an iron fist.

Sheepishly, I nod my head and answer, "Yes. I promise."

With that, she takes her leave, bustling away to scold a serving maid for failing to properly change out a man's bandage.

I pick my way through the triage section and enter the kitchen, finding it empty except for a fat white cat sleeping on the windowsill. Smiling faintly, I make sure to keep quiet as I grab a plate and proceed to fill it with bread, cheese, and apple slices. Sure enough, I find a quarter-filled bottle of wine as well and take it with me.

With my supper in-hand, I make my way through the back door and out into the practice yard behind the inn, where the setting sun has bathed the grass in a warm glow. A gap in the trees provides a stunning view of the Emberwood, a sea of deep green trees dappled by the darkness of the coming dusk.

My eyes linger on the lengthening shadows, and for a minute, I consider heading back inside to eat by the light of the hearth. Eventually, my fatigue wins out and I sit down on the lawn, too weary to even walk back inside.

I quietly gaze out at the sprawling forest, my mind distant. Before I can begin eating my meal, I hear the sound of footsteps approaching from behind. I glance sharply over my shoulder and am surprised to see Zara, who smiles as she walks over to me.

"There you are," she says, sitting down on the grass beside me. "I heard that you came back. I was looking everywhere for you."

"Hey," I reply before peering back at the skyline.

She pauses. "Sorry—I didn't mean to interrupt you. You're clearly brooding about something. Would you like me to leave?"

"No," I reply, turning and offering her a half-smile. "Stay. I don't feel like being alone."

Together, we sit and quietly take in the scene before us, each of us lost in our own thoughts. I share my meal with her, and for a time, we simply rest and stare out at the beauty of the land before us, the last rays of the sun warming our faces and painting the world with deepening hues of red, orange, and violet.

After a while, Zara turns to me and asks, "What are you thinking about right now, Owyn?"

I glance at her. "Me? I'm wondering how many demons are still out there, how far they managed to get on foot. Did any more come through the Arc that we don't know about?" I shrug awkwardly. "And you? What are you thinking about?"

She takes a moment to think before responding. "I suppose you could say that I'm thinking about light."

I frown at her. "Light?"

"Yes," she replies wistfully. Turning, she points toward the setting sun. "It's beautiful, isn't it? I don't think I've ever seen a sunset so breathtaking. The colors are so vibrant the way they play on the trees, and the sky is like an enormous canvas painted with shades of light. In Tarsys, the towers and the Pillar of Radiance blot out the sun most days. They're all anyone seems to see. They're beautiful in their own way, of course, but they also distract from the beauty of the world around us." She sighs and turns back to regard me. "The more I think about it, the more I realize how important the light is—magical light *and* natural light. Without it, all of us would be lost in the darkness."

I quirk an eyebrow at her, a bemused look on my face. "You see all that in a sunset?"

She nods, her gaze drifting back out to the Emberwood. "I do, especially tonight."

Another silence settles between us, and for the moment, I am at a loss for words. I glance down at my hands, quietly contemplating Zara's words. Finally, I look back up, my expression troubled. "Can I ask you something, Zara?"

She turns, her brown eyes meeting mine. "Of course."

I hesitate before going on. "How can you focus on the light when nightfall is approaching? I've watched more sunsets here than I can count, and right now, all I can see is the coming darkness, the shadows..." I trail off, not sure how to adequately express what I feel.

Zara considers this, her appearance growing thoughtful. She brushes a stray lock of hair out of her face and tucks it behind her ear. "I know it can be difficult to focus on the good when we are surrounded by so much suffering. I don't pretend that the shadows don't exist." She looks at me meaningfully, her heartfelt gaze holding my attention like some kind of spell. "But I also know that even when the sun sets, we're never completely in the dark. We can make our own light, and help others become lights as well, and continue to do that until the sun rises again in the morning." She stares at me for a long moment before glancing away, her eyes looking back out at the view. Lowering her voice, she concludes, "The sun *will* rise again. That's what I try to remember, anyway."

I consider this for a moment, surveying the great forested basin in front of us as I mull over the things she said. *The sun will rise again. Such a hopeful phrase—poetic, even. But is it true when it comes to the R'Laar?*

As I ponder all of these things, my focus shifts from the encroaching darkness to the golden rays of light shooting over the trees. Squinting, I peer at the setting sun, marveling at the brilliance that illuminates the land. A warm sensation courses through me, a feeling of peace that seems to banish the gloom from my soul.

Suddenly, it is like I am seeing the sunset for the first time.

Looking over at Zara, I can't stop a smile from tugging at the corners of my mouth. She catches me staring at her and smiles as well. "What?" she asks, brows pinching together self-consciously.

"Nothing," I reply, scooting a little bit closer to her. "Nothing at all."

Together, the two of us watch the sun until it dips beneath the western horizon, veiling the world with the purple shroud of dusk. One by one, the stars wink into existence above, peering down at us through the translucence of the Arc of Radiance. The moon slowly rises, peeking over the Ironback Mountains and brightening a landscape covered in shadows.

After everything that has happened, it is hard to remember that beauty still exists in the world. Although the monsters of legend have returned, and the future of the kingdom seems bleak, there are still good people and peaceful places to be found.

There are still things worth fighting for.

EPILOGUE
ELIAS

Moonlight filters through the trees, casting the dark forest in a ghostly glow. A subtle chill settles over the Emberwood, a sign that summer is coming to an end and that winter is well on its way.

Elias Keen makes his way through the underbrush, his eyes well-adjusted to the low light and his feet familiar with the overgrown path. He moves as silently as a wraith on his excursion; no twigs break, nor does a single leaf crunch underfoot. Decades of living in the wilderness have given him a predator's stealth, the ability to travel silently, without being seen or heard.

Tonight, he takes every advantage of those skills.

He had crept out of Forest Hill under cover of darkness, making his way to the predetermined meeting spot without so much as his belt knife. He had promised not to bring any weapons with him, certain that his ability to sneak through the woods would serve him sufficiently enough to protect him should he fall upon an enemy.

Still, he thinks to himself, moving from one shadow to the next, *I'll need to be wary. These parts aren't as safe as they used to be.*

The Battle of Forest Hill is over, but the threat of danger still hangs like a black cloud over the Emberwood. Demons lurk in the deep places now, and there is no telling how many of them have gotten past the Arc since the fighting began. Things have changed drastically in Tarsynium, the world becoming a far more dangerous place than before.

He doubted things would ever return to normal. Allies would be important in the coming days, now more than ever.

Elias reaches the meeting place and finds that it is deserted. The small clearing is bathed in moonlight, revealing a single tree stump covered with a thick coat of moss in the middle of the open grass. He approaches the stump cautiously and looks around, making sure that he is alone. Then, satisfied there is no one watching, he hides himself in the gloom beneath a low-hanging tree, crouching down amid the ferns.

Waiting is nothing new to him. He has spent most of his life in waiting. The earthen scent of the woods smells good to him after the fire and blood of war, and the cool night air is refreshing after a long day in the sun.

Resting his back against the rough bark, Elias allows his mind to briefly wander, his senses focusing on his surroundings as his eyes repeatedly scan the clearing. *This could be the end of the world,* he muses silently to himself. *If Moloch and his horde could get through, then other demons can as well.*

With the kingdom so divided and the rangers spread so thin, it will be impossible to protect all the inhabitants of Tarsynium from being attacked. That means unity is the only chance to mount a real defense, the only chance for survival. There is no telling what is wrong with the Arc of Radiance or even if the mages can repair it. If they cannot, then it very well could mean the end of all things.

Several minutes pass by, and he hears someone walking through the forest to his left. The footfalls are heavy, heedless thuds in the distance, clomping through the undergrowth and doubtless alerting every animal and insect for a mile in each direction.

Narrowing his eyes, he watches as a large figure emerges from the darkness and enters the clearing, cursing and pulling twigs out of his black beard. "Bloody ranger," the man grumbles to himself, walking up to the stump and sitting down heavily. "What sort of crackpot man insists on meeting in the woods in the middle of the night?"

"The sort that prefers to be careful, Barus," Elias replies coolly, materializing from his hiding place.

Barus swears under his breath and spins around, raising a fist as if to strike. "Bah—don't do that! It's right unnatural, sneaking around like that."

Elias offers a simple shrug. "It's what we do. Fish swim, birds fly, and rangers sneak."

Barus gives him a flat look. "What do you want?"

"To talk," he replies, holding out both of his hands. "Nothing more."

"I gathered that much from the message you left me," Barus growls. "The fact that you told me not to bring any weapons was a dead giveaway. A part of me thought this might be an ambush. Though, you don't strike me as the kind of man who would kill someone while they're unarmed."

"I'm not," Elias confirms, meeting his gaze. "As I said. I only wish to talk."

Barus snorts. "All right, then. Talk."

Elias eyes him for a long moment before speaking. "The presence of the R'Laar changes things. We've beaten them once, but they'll be back—likely in greater numbers than before. It's more important now than ever that the Nightingales and the kingdom work together rather than against each other."

"Eleven Hells," Barus curses. "We just fought a bloody battle together! What do you call that, if not working together?"

"That was just one instance," Elias remarks calmly. "You and I both know that when we all part ways, we'll soon be back at each other's throats. We've been fighting each other for too long to so easily put aside our differences. That's why I need your help."

Barus frowns, his heavy brows forming a deep line across his forehead. "My help? With what?"

"Bringing the Nightingales into the fold."

The big man bursts into laughter. "You're a madman, you know that? The Nightingales will never agree to rejoin the kingdom. Not while that snake Aethelgar sits on the throne. You said it yourself—we've been fighting for far too long."

"I'm not suggesting the Nightingales rejoin the kingdom," Elias says. "I'm suggesting a truce."

Barus rolls his eyes. "Ah... a truce, you say? And what makes you think my Lord Protector will agree to that sort of thing?"

Elias pauses before replying quietly, "He will. I know it."

Shaking his head, Barus stands up and makes as if to depart. "You kingsmen are all the same. Think you know everything. I know the Lord Protector personally; he'd never agree to an alliance with Aethelgar."

Elias grabs him by the arm and stops him from leaving. "Wait," he says, dropping his voice low. "There's something you need to see."

Barus arches an eyebrow at him but says nothing. He crosses his arms and gives the ranger an expectant look.

Elias releases him and pulls up his own sleeve, letting the moonlight shine on his exposed skin. He turns, revealing a small tattoo on the inner part of his upper arm. It is a diminutive image, no larger than a coin, and depicts a black bird with its wings outstretched and three stars above its head.

As soon as Barus sees the tattoo, his eyes grow wide. "By the Light, you're—"

"Yes," Elias confirms, cutting him off. He immediately pulls down his sleeve. "And it's a closely guarded secret. I would appreciate your absolute discretion on the matter."

"Does the Lord Protector know?" he asks, still visibly stunned.

Elias nods. "He is one of the few."

"Hells," Barus curses, sitting back down on the stump and stroking his beard. "That's... not at all what I was expecting. I didn't know there was any of your kind left."

"Just me," Elias replies dryly. "Now—believe me when I say that peace is possible. It *can* be achieved if it is pursued in the right way. If we work together, I believe that we can make it a reality."

"And what makes you so damn sure? How do you know this *truce* of yours won't end up getting lots of folks killed?"

Elias looks the bearded man hard in the eye, his grim expression like that of a stone. "Because I know there are good people on both sides of this war, and if we don't unite ourselves to face our common enemy and the *true* threat here, then there's a high chance that all of us will die anyway."

Barus stares at him silently for a minute, his face contorted in a frown. He appears to be deep in thought, as if wrestling between two different decisions. Finally, he smiles ruefully and shakes his head, offering Elias a small, tired chuckle. "You're full of surprises, ranger. I'll give you that. Fine, let's hear it. What's your plan to save the world?"

The Story Will Continue In
DOOM BRINGERS
Fall of Radiance Book 2